THE HINTERLAND VEIL

THE HOUSE OF CRIMSON & CLOVER VOLUME IX

SARAH M. CRADIT

Cover Design by Sarah M. Cradit
Editing by Kathy Lapeyre

First Edition
SBN-10: 1530258995
ISBN-13: 978-1530258994

Publisher Contact:
sarah@sarahmcradit.com
www.sarahmcradit.com

ALSO BY SARAH M. CRADIT

KINGDOM OF THE WHITE SEA

Kingdom of the White Sea Trilogy

The Kingless Crown

The Broken Realm

The Hidden Kingdom

The Book of All Things

The Raven and the Rush

The Sylvan and the Sand

The Altruist and the Assassin

The Melody and the Master

The Claw and the Crowned

THE SAGA OF CRIMSON & CLOVER

The House of Crimson and Clover Series

The Storm and the Darkness

Shattered

The Illusions of Eventide

Bound

Midnight Dynasty

Asunder

Empire of Shadows

Myths of Midwinter

The Hinterland Veil

The Secrets Amongst the Cypress

Within the Garden of Twilight

House of Dusk, House of Dawn

Midnight Dynasty Series

A Tempest of Discovery

A Storm of Revelations

A Torrent of Deceit

The Seven Series

1970

1972

1973

1974

1975

1976

1980

Vampires of the Merovingi Series

The Island

and more

The Dusk Trilogy

St. Charles at Dusk: The Story of Oz and Adrienne

Flourish: The Story of Anne Fontaine

Banshee: The Story of Giselle Deschanel

Crimson & Clover Stories

Surrender: The Story of Oz and Ana

Shame: The Story of Jonathan St. Andrews

Fire & Ice: The Story of Remy & Fleur

Dark Blessing: The Landry Triplets

Pandora's Box: The Story of Jasper & Pandora

The Menagerie: Oriana's Den of Iniquities

A Band of Heather: The Story of Colleen and Noah

The Ephemeral: The Story of Autumn & Gabriel

Bayou's Edge: The Landry Triplets

For more information, and exciting bonus material, visit www. sarahmcradit.com

You can find a complete list of content warnings on my website: sarahmcradit.com

For my grandmother, Beverly Ann Cline
1932-2015

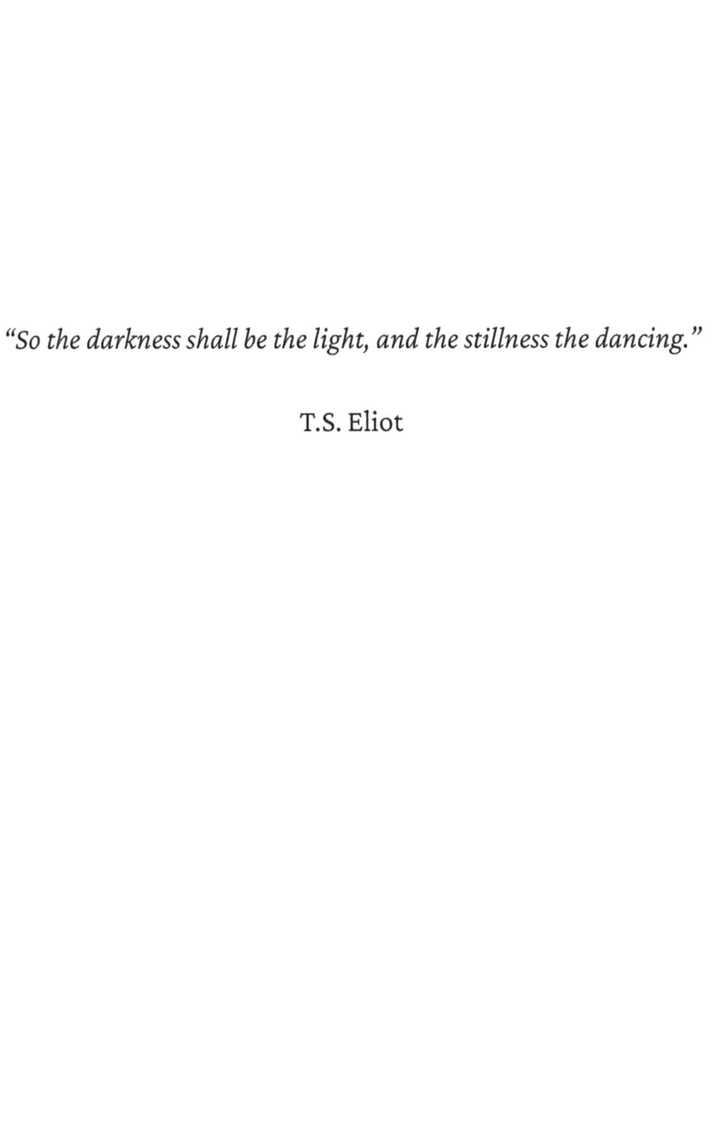

"So the darkness shall be the light, and the stillness the dancing."

T.S. Eliot

THE STAR

1
NICOLAS

Nicolas Deschanel negotiated the cavernous central hall at The Gardens, his footfalls echoing across a valley of ancient marble. The assuming rows of Corinthian columns, to his left and right, provided both vital supports to this generations-old manor, as well as serving a reminder of its colossal authority.

No matter the number of times he'd traversed the main connector of his aunt's home, Nicolas always paused, momentarily, questioning whether he was headed in the correct direction. Even among the looming Victorians and Greek Revivals of the Garden District, The Gardens felt excessive. Garish, and out of place. As if Zeus had thrust his palace on Mount Olympus down to earth, and it landed in the heart of Uptown New Orleans.

Of course, the Deschanels never did anything halfway. Not architecture, not love. Halfway-loving got Nicolas into this situation. All-the-way, soul-deep love is what brought him to The Gardens, desperate for answers, and as yet unsure if he would ever find them.

Aunt Colleen hadn't hesitated when he'd called, weeks ago, asking for help, a weakness until now he'd prided himself on rarely indulging. She had two rooms waiting for him when he showed up with a dazed Mercy on his arm. *Of course, darling, you're welcome to share a room as often as you'd like. I imagine you'll each want your privacy at times, though.*

As with all things that mattered, Colleen was strides ahead, thinking through logistics Nicolas couldn't comprehend because he was so rooted in the terrifying *present.* She'd been right, unsurprisingly. During their tenure at The Gardens, Nicolas and Mercy had slept apart far more than together, a statistic that caused him as much relief as distress.

Nicolas wasn't equipped for this. To love Mercy as he did had changed him. To ease her through an apparent mental breakdown, culminating in her soul-deep belief she carried the child of her god, Emyr, placed him so far from his element he sometimes longed for the easiness of his debaucherous youth.

Not enough for him to turn from Mercy. Adoration turned to affection, eventually to love, and despite his best efforts to fuck it up, he'd breached a critical precipice in his reasoning. He'd committed himself to her, to the bitter end, or the beautiful one... fate deciding.

His lover's delusions seemed a small consequence compared to the other events recently striking the family. The arrival of the necromancer, the starlight awakeners, and the near-fulfillment of the myths of midwinter had thrown every other priority into a tailspin. Three Deschanel Magi Collective Council meetings had been called since he and Mercy arrived. The immediate danger had been tempered, but their crazed ancestor, Margarethe, was still on the run, somewhere, and one of Katja's twins was also missing. Until both could be located, the family remained in peril again.

And when were they not? He couldn't recall a time where

talk of the Curse wasn't front and center at every family event. And now the problem had evolved to include another adversary.

Personally amazed at his willpower to even drag himself to attendance of the Council sessions, Colleen quickly brought him back to reality, finally chastising him for his daydreaming at the end of the massive oaken slab that passed for a table. He'd jokingly asked her once if they imported the thing from the mammoth dining hall at Windsor. She hadn't laughed, but she also hadn't denied it. *You are my eldest brother's only son, and in need of aid, but that does make all your behavior beyond reproach.*

Colleen found him gazing up the double staircase. "Most things, whether it be flora or people, thrive while visiting The Gardens. You've done nothing but wilt, dear nephew."

Nicolas stared down at his shuffling feet, unable to muster the smartass retort she'd always expected from him. "I can't go back to *Ophélie*."

Indeed, he'd done everything to avoid returning, even paying Oz's full attorney salary to reside there and replace him as master until he could sort himself out. His kind best friend had gone as far as pulling his children out of their school, enrolling them in a homeschool program.

He sighed, casting a glance toward the oiled portrait of his grandfather, August. Nicolas often wondered what his grandfather would think of him if he'd lived to see the family now; of all August's grandchildren, only one male had been born bearing the name Deschanel, and Nicolas had done everything in his power, sometimes intentionally, often not, to squander that honor. Bestowing the right of heirdom on Aleksandr had been the closest thing he could muster to a course correction. Hopefully, Ana's son would do better with the privilege than he had.

"A family full of goddamn healers, and not a one can help her."

Colleen rested a hand on his mid-back, and walked with him, steering him toward the rear of the house. "Nicolas, in all my travels and studies, I've met few who could heal a troubled mind. Understand, the ones I *have* met did so by transferring the pain to themselves. You can imagine the sacrifice in such an act."

"Anyone can be bought for the right price," Nicolas grumbled with a sneer he didn't feel. The harsh expression faded to a frown. "You know you can kick us out whenever you want."

His aunt stepped out onto the back porch, as broad as the dining room. "Don't be silly. If I had it my way, my children, my nieces, and nephews, would all be under one roof." She evidently caught his bewilderment in her peripheral. "You're the Deschanel anomaly, Nicolas, craving solitude and isolation. The rest of us feel greater in the presence of more of us. Even when gathering for wakes and funerals, which we've done far too often of late, I draw strength from our masses." Her smile was aimed away, almost separate of the two of them. "I digress. No, my words weren't meant to drive you away. Rather, I was hoping to motivate you. I know you came here seeking answers, but have you found any?"

With a brief hesitation, Nicolas shook his head. "I'm more and more convinced she's gone completely insane. And that, even knowing this, I love her more every day. Doesn't make a damn bit of sense."

"Her state of mind or your feelings for her?"

Nicolas sighed, then half-grinned. "Both."

Colleen nodded toward a plush chaise on the flagstone patio. He sat, and she took the one across from him, sheltered by palmetto and bird of paradise. Autumn was nearly upon them, but the heat hadn't dwindled with the changing season.

"Your ability to love another may be shocking to you, but I've watched you grow from boy to man. Your passions have always run deep, Nicolas. The variable has always been where you chose to swing them."

Nicolas took the glass of sweet tea from Aria, Colleen's head of household, who'd appeared as if on schedule and shrugged. Said nothing.

"As to Mercy's mind… we are still learning about who the Deschanels are, and where we originate," Colleen went on, drawing a sip from her own tumbler. "What it is to be Empyrean, or at least, to share their blood. By all accounts, Mercy's experience of being born Empyrean, dying as one, and being resurrected as human is wholly unique. We can't possibly know what she's going through, or what she's up against, intrinsically and otherwise. And without that knowledge, helping her becomes an exercise in intelligent guesswork and experimentation. Mostly the latter."

"She spends her days resting or praying. It never occurs to her the god who supposedly bestowed on her the next coming of Emyr was the same one who fucking abandoned her in her final moments," Nicolas rattled, not bothering to disguise his bitterness. "I could have expected her coming out of that an atheist, but this?"

"Faith is a powerful, eternal phenomenon," Colleen said. "One that sometimes rides the border of fanaticism and fantasy because throwing your control and life into the hands of something more omnipotent brings tremendous comfort in a world filled with chaos. That same abandonment you speak of, to Mercy, reads like a test from Emyr. She's passed this test and been rewarded. As she sees it."

"And how am I supposed to contend with her ridiculous, thousands-years-old dogma?"

"For starters, never use the word 'ridiculous' to describe another's beliefs."

Nicolas affected the start of an eye roll and stopped. "Fine. And I wouldn't, to her. I haven't. But, you know, a part of me wondered, even knowing it couldn't be possible, if what she believed really happened to her? Who am I to say Emyr didn't knock her up? That's why I brought her here. If anyone could put the sanity caboose on the crazy train, it's you."

Colleen nodded. The soft whir of the outdoor fan kicked in, followed by a fine, cool spray from the misters. They both closed their eyes, breathing in the relief. "While I can't speak to her faith, I've confirmed beyond a doubt she is not with child. Divine or otherwise."

"All right. So she's not pregnant. I'm wilting here, according to you, apparently, whatever that means. I haven't figured out yet how to fix her special variety of insanity. I'm hoping you have a Hail Mary suggestion because I'm at a loss." *Most of all, I can't return to* Ophélie. *My failings as a man, as an heir, start and end there. If I can't fix Mercy, I'm not worthy of the designation.*

"Have you considered stepping out of your comfort zone, and attempting to relate to Mercy on her level?"

"Sorry?"

Colleen set her glass down, crossing her legs. Her manicured hands fell over her knee as she watched him. "Consider the moments in your life when others have tried to convince you of the error of your ways. What was your natural inclination?"

"For them to fuck off."

"Of course, it was," she answered, unruffled by and entirely used to his colorful command of language. "Imagine, instead, if they'd gone along with your mischiefs? Tried to understand and even join you?"

"I can't picture you or any of my other aunts or uncles closing the bars down on Frenchmen with me, but okay. The point?"

"Instead of trying to convince Mercy of her error, why not instead try to see things through her eyes? Connect on her level. Suspend your disbelief, despite the hardship of such an endeavor. See her world."

"Aunt Colleen, she's *crazy*. And I've dated my share of crazies. This one chick I was with for a hot minute created her own ass-backward version of BDSM, but whenever I tried to use the safe word, she'd crack me across the face and scream at me to call her Xena—"

Long sigh. "Nicolas."

He held up his hands. "I'm just saying. I'm no stranger to crazy women, but this is the first one I've ever wanted to *fix*."

"Crazy is often a matter of perspective. To attack a problem, you must understand the source. And yes, that is my medical opinion as well." With a slight start, Colleen checked her watch and stood. "I must return to the hospital, but think about our conversation. You've already committed to the task. Now you need to define it."

MERCY HADN'T EMERGED FROM HER ROOM ONCE THAT DAY, A SIGN he'd come to recognize as her need to be alone in prayer. A rescinded invitation, if her silence was even an invite in the first place.

Nonetheless, Nicolas paused at her doorway. He slipped into the darkened room. The only sounds were an overhead fan and her light, even breaths.

To attack a problem, you must understand the source.

Mercy's face was a canvas of blissful peace, her silver hair, a gift of her resurrection, brushed off her face, cascading down the pillow. A band of it trailed over the bed's edge.

Walking away, as he always had before, whenever the pleasure of learning about another turned to the acceptance of baggage, no longer tempted him.

Yet staying terrified him.

Loving her frightened him.

Suspend your disbelief. See her world.

"I need your help, Mercy. I need you to show me."

2
CYLER

Cyler drew in a steadying breath and announced himself. He didn't dare venture beyond the strip dividing the doorway. "Aggie, I need you to listen."

Agripin, gazing at a sleeping Anasofiya, lost in thoughts Cyler was grateful not to be privy to, slowly rolled his neck toward the interruption. "You always talk. I always listen. Talk, talk, talk. Listen, listen, listen."

No. You pretend to listen while obsessing over a creature who bides her time to annihilate you. When she's done, she'll likely set her sights on the rest of us. "They're gone, or in the process of leaving. They're not coming back, and we need a plan."

"Who?"

"All of them."

"Define 'all.' You're here. I'm here. The empress is here. Who else matters?"

Cyler grunted, shifting. He prepared the same recitation he'd given his master a dozen times over. "Jorun and Yiva left before we departed Norway." *A fact you still have yet to notice or acknowledge.* "Thor and Trygve took off a couple weeks ago.

Maxima disappeared to investigate matters in Farjhem, for whatever they might be. Skadi turned south on the trip to Savonlinna." *I won't berate you about how Finland has never been friendly to the Farværdig. You already know this, and I suspect you're not keeping us here long. This is a stop, not a destination. I'd know for sure if you'd talk to me, but thus far you've chosen to live in oblivion with* her. "Most worrisome is Leif left this morning."

Agripin gently assembled his quilt over a sleeping Anasofiya and rose. His scarred abdomen beaded with sweat from the fire roaring in the nearby hearth, such heat overwhelming for one with the fiery blood of Emyr. Day and night, he kept the flames stoked for his empress, who, when not glaring her hatred at him through her magic binding, remained deep in soundless slumber.

Plotting, Cyler was certain. He didn't trust her quiet, not at all.

Agripin stretched, wearing a look frustratingly lacking in concern. "Leif is free to do as he wishes. As are all the drekar. Isn't that the *point*?" The last came out heavy with sarcasm.

Cyler clenched one fist at his side. The other blocked the doorway. Agripin had blown him off too many times since they escaped Farjhem. Their situation escalated closer to dire each day. "In case you've forgotten, Leif is the one responsible for Ana's magic bindings. You know, the only thing keeping her from ripping your beating heart from your chest and devouring it for elevenses."

Agripin scoffed. Tossed his eyes toward the ceiling. "So? They're adhered. And likely unnecessary, I might add. No one asked Leif to do so." He pulled his arms over his head in a casual yawn. "And you'll refer to her by her formal title. Even when it's only us."

Cyler bit the interior of his cheek. "*Grand Empress* Anasofiya might break free of her bindings. Then what?"

Agripin shrugged. "If she does, perhaps it's for the best. She's been tethered far too long. No way to treat the mate of the crowned prince of Farjhem."

"You're jesting, right? We're observing the same creature?"

"Cyler, you test me," Agripin said, growing visibly weary of him already. *I still recall when we could spend days together and it was never enough.* "And you speak with false authority on matters you know nothing about."

The emperor ducked under Cyler's arm with a disdainful groan and sauntered toward the stark, stainless steel kitchen. The entire cottage, though miles from other inhabitants and the city center of Savonlinna, was fitted with the sleekest modern accoutrements, reminding Cyler of their few weeks in the Upper East Side of New York. in the early days of his service to the crown. When this life came with a polished shine and the roses still tainted his view.

"She will be hungry when she wakes. The nights are colder now," Agripin muttered to himself or the furniture.

Cyler stormed in behind him. "Don't you want to know *why* they left?"

"No," Agripin replied, sorting through the cupboard as if reading a book in a foreign language. "But I venture you're going to tell me."

I should. I should tell you about how you've alienated every single one of our allies with your refusal to face reality. How dismissing their requests to send Ana—excuse me, grand empress *—back to her family, where she belongs, where she can heal and allow us to focus on our plans with a clear head, has caused them to see you as a poor decision-maker rather than an ally. Some were slower to leave than others, but you're about to drive even the most patient ones away. Dagr has been thirsty for war for centuries, and he hangs on, hoping once you snap out of it, he'll get the fight he craves. Birger and Astrid love you and believed in you. Stian goes* *where they go, and if you don't think they're next, you're even more deluded than you've been acting all these weeks.*

Both creatures pivoted toward the sounds coming from Anasofiya's room. "She's awake," Cyler said with a resigned sigh. Even had he said all he wished to convey to his master, the words would dissolve into the nether, clinging to the dwindling force of the great warrior Agripin had once been, before all *this.* "Go to her."

"Aye," Agripin replied, brushing past him. "See about supper. We shall talk later."

Cyler leaned into the marble counter, defeated.

He couldn't estimate how many empty promises he had left in him to receive, but it was not many.

Birger arrived at dawn. He'd been away seeking news of Farjhem. By the crestfallen expression on his face as he embraced his mate, Astrid, he'd returned with some, though perhaps not the news they'd hoped for.

"Oriana has taken over rule of Farjhem," he announced, dropping his traveling cloak over the sofa without waiting for the completion of pleasantries. The stark chill, steeped for weeks in the threads, passed through the room. "Already, she's designated a new Senetat. Hand-picked from the patrons of her Menagerie. Guards, sellswords, failed scholars. Hardly politicians and leaders." A dark cloud passed over his eyes. "They've kept busy."

Astrid sunk to her knees on the fur carpet. She fell forward in a sway, and her mate caught her. "So, it's true, what I've been sensing. They're murdering them, one by one."

"What the hell is going on?" Cyler demanded.

"The Senetat. They're activating marks across the globe. Killing off those who know no better, and who have served

Emyr under the rule of the Senetat. The devout," Birger answered, lifting Astrid to her feet and settling on the couch beside her. "Oriana is behind it. Trying to garner our attention. She's well aware we have those in our ranks, like Astrid, who can sense the deaths of our own. She seeks to goad us, but has no clear vision of the future and what it is she actually desires, other than her own freedom to practice her pleasures without restraint."

Cyler's hand instinctively traveled to his ass, where his own mark—a phoenix as brilliant as the day it was sealed in by magic—still burned hot against his skin. *Aggie, you motherfucker. You've made me keep this time bomb on my flesh far too long, for your own insecurities.* "Are you certain? How did you discover this?"

"Maxima has been *re-installed* to the Senetat." Birger's grin was humorless. Beside him, Astrid went pale, her eyes fixed on an unknown spot across the room. "She claims to have escaped Anasofiya's wrath by seeking refuge under a pile of corpses in Farsengel. So goes her official story to Oriana."

Cyler frowned. "So she played us all along?" He'd vetted her himself.

"No. She is ours, and I don't anticipate that changing. She remains our only view of what is happening under Oriana's new reign. I left her with a new set of instructions and misdirection, now that the landscape has changed. We can only pray it works as intended."

Astrid turned toward them, eyes bleary. "Birger, we cannot allow this genocide to continue. We cannot sit here while she brings the world down on our shoulders, unchecked. It isn't her right!"

"Of course not," Birger replied, drawing her closer. "But continue it will, until every last drekar on earth surrenders themselves to Oriana. The events in Farsengel, the destruction of the prior Senetat, no matter how malevolent, forced her hand. She cannot retire to her old life with such a threat in existence. And as long as we run free upon the earth, the threat will not disappear."

Blood and fury rushed to Cyler's head as he absorbed the full weight of Birger's discovery: Oriana would activate every mark on earth if she had to. Cyler's own life could be terminated in an instant. Without warning.

Surely Agripin was absorbing this from the other room. Certainly, he would insist Cyler remove the threat from his being.

Right?

"Emyr help us," Stian whispered from the doorway, lowering his head.

3
ALEKSANDR

Aleksandr decided he could live here forever.

The Quinlans existed as all Emyr's creatures should, in Aleksandr's opinion. Their world was an ongoing exercise in simplicity and compassion, taking only what they wished to give back in other ways. Though aware of, and affected by, the strife within the Empyrean world, a peacefulness rested in the afterthoughts of every word, every action. Each moment was sacred.

Aleksandr had not realized just how heavy his heart was until he was given leave to set his burdens at the base of the *crann bethadh*. Since that first time, he'd approached the massive oaken tree every morning and uttered private supplications. He stopped short of thinking of them as prayers, as he truly had no idea who was listening.

The Quinlans' minimalist, no-fuss households called to him on a deep, intrinsic level. While Uncle Jon and Anne lamented their lack of modern luxuries, Aleksandr kept to himself that he'd never known enough stability to appreciate perfumed shampoo or goose down pillows. His entry into this world had been tumultuous; every moment since had been no less so.

Home, for his youthful body and old soul, was wherever his loved ones rested.

Too much time had passed since he'd fallen asleep in his mora's arms, or heard her soft, husky tones promising him all would be right. Far promised they would find her, and Far never said words he didn't mean.

If Nora and the other Quinlans were to be believed, Aleksandr and his family's arrival here was anything but accidental. They promised to help Finn and the others recover Aleksandr's mother, and professed to have the means to do so.

Aleksandr sensed no lie in their words. This absence of deception was key for him; he'd recently discovered one of his natural abilities to be the talent of seeing through the veil of dishonesty. As of yet, he'd told no one about this budding ability, a deception of his own and an irony not lost on his young mind.

Far spent his days training with Padraig, something he took a begrudging, if sincere, interest in. Jon and Anne helped around the tribe, doing odd jobs.

Aleksandr was given only one basic instruction since arrival: unwind and absorb. The first would be impossible as long as his mora was in trouble. But if Aleksei had one gift above all others, it was his love of the world around him. Absorbing, he could do. *Would* do, without even trying.

Other than the place of his birth, in his great-grandfather's remote cabin nestled deep in the Scottish Highlands, he'd never set foot in a place he could say truly felt magical. Lying under the *crann bethadh*, legs dangling over the ancient roots, eyes hazy as he beheld the whistling wind passing through the changing leaves, he knew he'd entered a realm few had stepped through before. A casual traveler, wandering the woods, would find their path veering north, around the tribe boundary, without ever knowing what he'd missed.

Aleksandr closed his eyes and permitted the luminous magic to deliver him even further from his troubles.

"There you are," a soft voice interrupted. He smiled before opening his eyes.

Fiona.

"You caught me daydreaming when I was supposed to be collecting fennel for supper," Aleksandr confessed with a shy grin.

His friend—really, the only person in his short life he could truly bestow the moniker on—stood before him. Fiona's wavy russet hair wisped on the breeze. Her crystal blue eyes sparkled, delighted. "I *might* be persuaded to keep quiet."

Before she could react, Aleksandr snaked his leg behind her knee, catching her off guard. Fiona wobbled, falling forward, and he broke her fall, rolling amidst the leaves and moss as their giggles rose through the trees in tandem.

"That's what happens when you go from a baby to a man in a matter of months," she chided from beneath him. The copper and amber leaves snarled her hair, an effect resembling a swirled autumn crown ringing her head.

"Don't be jealous that you've forgotten how to play!"

"It's nearly Mabon. Plenty of time for playing then," Fiona answered, sitting. She brushed the vegetation from her wool sweater and pants, followed by a haphazard attempt to retrieve the rogue forest detritus from her hair. Aleksandr stifled a chuckle at her futile efforts.

"You think it's funny?" she inquired, straightening her posture. With a focused, double blink, she snatched two handfuls of leaves and smashed them into his short auburn hair. "There. Take that, King of the Forest."

"King." Aleksei puffed his chest out. "Sounds about right."

Fiona rolled her eyes and shoved him back into the pile.

She rose with a careful glance at his hands and feet to make sure he wasn't attempting further shenanigans. Confident she was safe, she backed away, this time making an earnest effort at cleaning herself. "Now you've gone and messed me up. I'm going to meet Declan tonight."

"You're going to tell him?"

"Goddess, no!"

Aleksandr frowned. "I don't see why not. Do you really plan to sneak around forever? He loves you. He'll understand."

"No, Aleksei," Fiona countered, dropping her voice with a purposeful shake of the head. "He comes from a different world. Way different. Trust me, he would *never* understand."

"My mora and far come from way different worlds."

Fiona opened her mouth, then dropped her eyes, deciding against whatever words rested on her tongue. She brushed her hair back off her face and forced a smile. "Anyway, if my mother comes looking for me, you know what to tell her."

Aleksandr, who had, over the course of the nearly three weeks he'd been with the tribe, come to see Fiona as more than simply a casual friend, felt it his duty to push forward. "Ona, you've been seeing Declan off and on for how many years?"

She sighed and shifted one foot to a protruding root. "Eight. You already know that. We've been over this, Aleks—"

"Well, he's put up with your stubborn head for almost a decade. You think he can't handle some magic?"

Fiona pretended to smack him again, but then laughed and leaned against the thick hide of the *crann bethadh*. "The world must seem so simple to you. I wish I could see it through your eyes."

"Don't confuse simplicity with being naïve," Aleksandr returned, tensing. The ribbing of their age difference was a satisfactory joke until it encroached on his perceived wisdom.

"My place is in the tribe. One day, I'll replace my mother. She expects me to lead. They all do."

"Your place is wherever you want it to be," Aleksei countered. "Do you want to lead the tribe?"

Fiona crossed her arms over her chest. "It isn't about what *I* want. You know that."

Aleksandr conjured the wisdom Aidrik often shared. "We're nothing without our free will."

She laughed. "Who did you hear *that* from? Those are lovely words that mean nothing. Especially coming from the heir of the prophecy! What will you do when the time comes, my dear, sweet Aleksei? Let the world burn so you can enjoy your so-called 'free will?'"

Immediately, Fiona's face fell. The color drained from her cheeks, and her breath hitched. "I shouldn't have said that."

Aleksandr stood, shaking off his debris. "I don't even know what you're talking about, but I'm tired as hell of people keeping secrets to *protect* me."

"I know, kid," Fiona said, stepping forward. When she pressed her forehead to his and released a long breath, the aroma of warm honey filled his head. "But it really isn't my place to tell you."

His heart surged though he didn't understand the cause. "Everyone else keeps things from me, Ona. Please, don't you do it, too."

A new breeze settled between them. Her damp breath tickled him; his own had ceased altogether. "Okay, Aleksei. Not now, though." She rested a kiss against his forehead. "Tonight, Declan awaits."

Then she was off, sprinting through the glen with a quick glance and wave back before continuing on toward her beau.

Only when she was out of sight did Aleksandr's breathing return to normal.

. . .

The Quinlan village was unlike anywhere Aleksandr had been, neither in his imagination nor in the dozens of books he devoured. His closest comparison was the elven forest of Lothlorien from *Lord of the Rings*. This was one of Far's favorite books, in fact, so it surprised Aleksandr how troubled his father was in this serene woodland.

Their first few days had been rough, to put it mildly. The night they arrived, Far had been cool, collected, and ready to do whatever it took to rescue Mora, even if it meant methodic, patient planning was in order; not a natural strength of his, but one he could draw upon in special circumstances.

The next morning, he'd risen in a rage, demanding Aleksandr get dressed. They were leaving.

Uncle Jon asked what had happened, but all Far would say was he'd changed his mind. Aleksandr saw the truth reflected in his heavy eyes: He'd dreamt of her. Aleksandr matched the look to a feeling, for his father appeared as he himself felt every single morning.

Remaining with the Quinlans was their only reasonable chance, and Aleksandr gasped with dismay that only he had the power to make his father stay.

I'm failing her. I'm failing you, Aleksei.

No, Far. I trust them. They mean what they say and they will *help us get Mora back.*

We don't know them. They seem like nice people, but nice *isn't going to help your mother. The longer we wait—*

You're scared, and so am I, but this seems our best chance, and I don't think we're gonna get a lot of extras to get this right. Do you?

Far shook his head, hands at the back of his neck. *I keep trying to compare you to how I was at your age, but there's really no comparison, is there?*

Aleksandr grinned with an expression of light exasperation. *No, and you didn't answer the question, Far.*

Resigned sigh. *You know the answer.*

Aleksandr had thrown himself into his father's arms then, pressing his tear-stained face tight to his chest, both men feeling the other was providing the bulk of the strength in their relationship.

Both right.

Both wrong.

FINN AND PADRAIG'S RELATIONSHIP HAD UNDERCURRENTS OF resentment running through from their first day of instruction. Padraig exhibited the patience of saints and insisted moving slowly would ensure the best outcome. Finn finally acquiesced to staying, which required some compromise landing them much closer to *let's get on with it already.*

He wants to meditate, Aleksei. I'm ready to visit ancient Egypt and watch aliens build the pyramids.

Jon and Anne fared better, at least.

Anne had grown up in a close-knit bayou community, the type where the village raised the children and everything else. It was nothing for her to fall into helping prepare food or launder clothing. Her relaxed posture and increasing smiles even suggested she was happier here than she'd ever been in Louisiana.

In a tribe primarily consisting of women, where the only males were an old man confined mainly to the cathedral and a young one often away on missions, Uncle Jon's presence was a welcome balm. Their dwellings needed a number of minor repairs and shoring up, and Jon eagerly offered his services.

From day one of his decision to journey with them, he'd

sought ways to make himself useful. The tribe finally gave him a tangible way to do so.

Aleksandr knew more than his father realized about the treachery of his uncle. He understood Jon had done terrible things to his mother, perhaps unforgivable. But he was here now, seeking repentance, and if they could not, or would not, grant it to him, then none of them deserved peace. Absolution was a gift primarily for the injured as opposed to the aggressor. More power could be found in the light than the darkness.

He also knew his unusual wisdom scared his father, so he kept most of these thoughts safely to himself.

When they found Mora, however, if seeing Uncle Jon caused her pain, Aleksandr's loyal heart would prevail over wisdom.

Aleksandr felt the forest's presence shift the moment Fiona passed the invisible protective barrier and exited out into the wide world.

With a glance at the setting sun, he jogged off toward the village to join his family for dinner, fennel forgotten.

4
NICOLAS

Richard swung open the door of *Ophélie*, squinting through his wrinkles with impressive exaggeration. "Why, Master Nicolas, we wondered if we might *never* see you again! What a blessed day!"

"Don't be insolent," Nicolas returned, pulling his elderly butler in for a quick, fierce hug.

"I would *never*," Richard answered, grinning. "To what do we owe this immense pleasure?"

Nicolas stepped around him, and the door closed. "Going on a trip, Richard. I'm here to pack a bag for Mercy and me. I won't be here long, unfortunately."

Richard's eyes lit up. "It's been a spell since you traveled last. Where're you two going, if you don't mind the interrogation?"

"From you? *Never*." They started up the stairs. The creak of old timber under Nicolas' feet produced abrupt, powerful nostalgia. He shook it off before the sentiment could settle. "Truth is, I don't know. I suppose I'll figure it out before I get there."

"That's exactly what you used to say to me when you were still more boy than man," Richard mused, stopping at the landing, letting Nicolas go on ahead, alone. "I like the sound of it on you now. You need an adventure, Nicolas. I gave ya a hard time at the door, but truth is, you've been suffocating for a while. It's my job to worry over the household, not you, but I can't help myself from doing both anyway. This house ain't going nowhere. You go where you need to go, and we'll all be here waiting when you feel it's time to make your way back."

Ophèlie HAD TWO STUDIES, ONE ON THE MAIN FLOOR, WHERE THE original Charles Deschanel must have conducted most of his public-facing business and where Nicolas, generations later, performed his when he could be bothered with the responsibility. The other was on the third floor, at the end of the hall of master suites, intended for the heir's private business.

It was here Nicolas found Oz, nose buried in his laptop.

"Ozzy!" Nicolas barked when Oz didn't look up.

Oz's face registered shock, but also, near immediately, unbridled excitement. "Nic! Jesus, how long has it been since you last shaved?"

Nicolas shrugged. "Your mom likes it."

Like old times. They both relaxed.

"If I'd have known you were coming, I might have been better prepared to walk you through the household accounts. If you have some time, I could type up a brief."

Nicolas flopped down in the chair across from him, spreading his arms and legs toward akimbo. "You can stop right there. I've never so much as glanced at the ledgers beyond the bottom line. You know that. We pay accountants for that."

Oz crooked his head and tilted back in the leather chair. "You're paying my full salary to stay here. I'm not going to sit back and do nothing. And you know, you shouldn't put so much trust in one place. Your father knew that, and he had auditors auditing auditors, auditing auditors. He always had five people doing the same thing five times, diversifying his confidence. With capital and investments like yours, you should be taking a similar approach."

"I've spent thirty-one years attempting to be *nothing* like my father. Any other wisdom you want to impart before I leave?"

"Leave? You just got here!"

Nicolas slapped his feet against the cypress floorboards and rose. "And I've already been here longer than I meant to be. Sorry, Ozzy. It's obvious you have a lot you want to catch me up on. I've never enjoyed the business end of things, so I deliberately chose not to be good at it. I don't anticipate that changing." He turned toward the door. "Come join me while I pack a couple bags, and we'll see what you can cram in before I jet."

Oz shuffled behind him, flinging more questions. "Packing? Where are you going? How long are you going to be gone? Where's Mercy? Have you heard from Finn? Or Amelia?"

They entered the master suite bedroom. "Let's try one question at a time," Nicolas said, moving toward the closet. "No, I haven't heard from Finn. The burner phones y'all gave him ring the firm, remember?"

"Right. Well, then he hasn't called. I'll talk to my father, and see if it's safe to call him and check in." Oz held back, eyes toward the ceiling, mouthing mental notes. "Amelia or Jacob?"

Nicolas pulled a leather satchel from the top shelf and emptied the remnants on the floor. "Nope."

"Well, how about the most obvious question, then: Where the hell are you going?"

Glowering at Mercy's side of the closet in utter confusion, Nicolas began pulling outfits randomly from their hangers, dropping them in the case. "I don't know."

Oz leaned against the closet door, shaking his head. "I'm sorry… you don't *know*? How are you going to get there?" He craned his head in. "Have you been drinking again?"

"If I had, I'd probably know where I was going," Nicolas muttered in reply, tossing more clothes down in a haphazard heap. He turned toward his side of the closet. "I need to take Mercy somewhere. She's not getting any better, and Aunt C thinks I need to get inside her head, somehow, but I can't do it here. Or The Gardens."

Oz paused in thought. Nicolas imagined his friend's hero complex, long buried, whirring into action. "Have you asked her where she might like to go?"

"Whenever we talk, the only thing that comes out of her mouth is more nonsense about the religious relic growing inside her. The old Mercy is buried deep."

"What about…" Oz hesitated, creasing his brows. "What about taking her where she was happiest? She lived thousands of years. Surely, there's a place she considered her favorite?"

Nicolas, once again reminded what a terrible boyfriend he was, didn't know the answer. He shrugged, defeat creeping further in.

"Nic, you like to pretend you're an asshole, but you're the best friend I've ever had. You'd act bored whenever I went on about a girl or something that didn't interest you, but you always remembered what I said later. You used to surprise me with how much you could retain. I'm willing to bet you *do* know who Mercy is, and if you'd step out of your self-pity for a moment, you might realize it."

Nicolas stopped packing. Snapping back at Oz would feel good. Barking at *anyone* would feel better than the agony of helplessness descending upon him. But coming here, by even admitting he was ready to help Mercy, meant accepting others might be able to offer some useful advice.

He sighed, opening his mouth to suggest taking her to Farjhem, then stopped.

A late night, months ago, filtered back to him. They'd made love on the gallery, against the crash of thunder, a sensory explosion. Afterward, she told him she was happy. *I don't remember the last time I felt this much at peace.*

Really? An old broad like you must have a few moments in the memory bank?

She'd smacked him. Kissed him. Laughed. *Sure, many, many years ago, in my early days with Aidrik, we spent years on the Isle of Skye. I know now this time was an illusion, but then... ah, then, I felt, for the first time, like myself. Like a true disciple of Emyr, yes, but also like Clementyn, a singular being who had something of value to offer this world.* She'd sighed, rolling toward him, her cape of silver hair falling over her breast. *You're going to laugh now, aren't you?*

Not unless you're about to tell a good joke.

"Skye," Nicolas said, swallowing the lump at the back of his throat as the memory trickled off. It settled down toward his belly, and his breath caught. He grabbed a shelf to steady himself.

"That's a start," Oz said. "And if it isn't the destination, maybe getting there will lead you to the right one. Like a scavenger hunt."

Nicolas turned away. The pain swelled, and he didn't wish to share any more than he already had. Not even with Oz. "Where's Lucia? And the kids?"

"Downstairs," Oz answered. "It's Luc's day to lead the homeschool instruction."

Nicolas nodded. He knelt in front of the bag, preparing to close the zipper, wondering what he was missing, or if it mattered. If any of it would even make a difference in the coming days, weeks, months. "Give me a few minutes up here. I'll meet you downstairs to say goodbye before I head out."

Nicolas cast one last glance around the bedroom. He'd either packed too much, or not enough. Time would tell.

He found everyone in the downstairs study. Lucia leaned over the desk where Oz's kids, Christian and Naomi, were head down in studies, the latter with her tongue wedged between her lips in fierce concentration, reminding Nicolas of Oz in their grade school days.

Oz stood behind Lucia, one hand at the small of her back, teaching Naomi about the rules of adding with zero.

He looked up to see Nicolas, who nodded, gesturing toward the front door, signaling his readiness to leave. Lucia glanced up and offered a brief smile, before returning to the children's studies.

When Oz joined him at the door, Nicolas couldn't help himself. "When you said she was helping with homeschooling, I didn't realize you meant she was teaching *your* kids, Oz. Usually, that's done by the, you know, parents. Something you wanna tell me?"

Oz blushed, but quickly recovered. "Whatever you think you know, you're wrong. It's just the two of us adults here, and we're doing the best we can to keep the household going in your absence. Lucia stays for Livia, because Livia, as a halfling, is at huge risk out in the world. She's protected here. And, there's always a chance the other Empyrean children will return. She wants to be here if and when they do. But Lucia is restless by nature, so she's happy to divide the schooling with me, to keep busy. When she's teaching, I work on the Deschanel trust. When I'm teaching, she works with Condoleezza on the household management. Between the two of us, we get things done."

Nicolas smirked. He patted his friend on the arm. "I'll bet you're getting things done, Ozzy."

Oz brushed his hand off and rolled his eyes. "Always about sex with you." He dropped his eyes, rolling back on his heels. "When Adrienne died, a big part of me went with her. I don't need anyone else, and I definitely don't *want* anyone else. The kids are my whole life, and it will stay that way. Lucia's been a good friend, and I hope I've been the same in return. More than that, I can't offer."

"Whatever you say," Nicolas answered. He wanted to tell Oz that Adrienne would *want* him to move on. The crazy girl had had her cousin Amelia brainwashed to accomplish just that. But bringing up his pain would be a poor thanks for all he was doing to help. "I'm not planning to bring my phone, so you're empowered to make whatever decisions you need to on my behalf."

Oz offered a side-mouthed smirk. "That's a dangerous offer. Never know what you might return to find."

Nicolas shifted one foot out the door. "I'm fucking serious, Oz. I trust you. You've always done the right thing. And no one knows the Deschanel estate like you do. Not even me."

His friend was visibly taken aback by the seriousness in his tone. "Okay, Nic. I'll do whatever is needed. Try to drop a post-card from time to time, though, yeah? So we know the world didn't swallow you whole?"

Nicolas nodded and moved in for a quick embrace, sensing the tug to be far from this place, and back at Mercy's side. He forced a quick smile, afraid if he didn't show some of his old self, Oz might call in the cavalry. "We both know the world is no match for Nicolas Deschanel."

"It isn't actually the world I'm worried about."

Nicolas paused briefly before heading down the steps.

5
ANASOFIYA

Anasofiya. Wake up.

You need to work on your timing, Wraith. I was having the most wonderful dream.

I know. I saw.

Then you should know better. It's so rare now I get visits from Finn and my son.

Those visits are dangerous. They cause you to retreat further when you need to be preparing for emergence.

So you keep saying.

And so you also know, Anasofiya. These thoughts come from me, and so they come from you. It isn't possible for us to be out of accord.

Riddles, Wraith. We've talked about this.

It's refreshing to see you in lighter spirits for once.

A visit from my family will do that. Unfortunately, those feelings are fast fading, thanks to a certain inconsiderate intruder.

You've slept for days.

What of it?

I have news, and it cannot wait.

Get on with it, then.

The magic binder is gone.

Leif?

Is there another?

What do you mean, gone?

Departed. No longer with the other drekar under this roof. Unlikely to return, so Cyler seems to believe.

Are you certain?

You are. And so I am.

ANASOFIYA AWOKE, SPRINGING FORTH SO ROUGHLY HER PHYSICAL bindings instantly bruised her wrists.

"But that means..."

Yes.

STARLIGHT FLOODED THE ROOM, CASTING A SPECKLED LIGHT SHOW across the wood floor and up across the patterned quilts.

She was alone, or as alone as she could be, given her dark friend nested within.

Even asleep, she'd sensed Agripin's insipid, inexplicable presence. His neediness. The swaggering emperor who'd held all the cards had remained behind in Farsengel as if he'd ceased to exist altogether. The being casting tender sentry over her was another creature entirely. One, she was certain, was far more dangerous than his overconfident predecessor.

He was gone, but not far. Nearby. Across the cabin, talking with Cyler and the others. Not as many as before. They'd lost some.

Most. Most have departed your mate. They do not subscribe to his disjointed mission.

He is not *my mate.*

Aye, Anasofiya, but he believes himself to be. This puts you in greater danger than any the Senetat may still pose.

He killed Aidrik. Murdered *him to self-preserve. We both know he only lives because I can't break free.*

You can. You will. You could have before but chose not to. The choice has always been yours.

I didn't choose any of this.

You made the choice when you stepped upon the rotting chair at Ophélie *and chose death over courage. Your original sin. Every moment since has been a product of this choice, this sin. Aidrik awakened something in you, unlike anything the world has witnessed.*

A gift I'll use to avenge him.

We will.

Now, hush. Maybe if I close my eyes, they'll visit me again.

THEY WERE IN FINLAND, SOMEWHERE. ANA PICKED UP BITS AND PIECES from outside conversation but hadn't bothered to search for clarity. It didn't matter if they were in Finland or Nigeria. She'd bide her time to any backdrop.

The dream of her husband and son had shaken her; more, even, than she wanted to admit. She'd carefully pushed memories of them to the fringe of her mind because being a wife and mother softened her. She was someone else with them, someone she looked in the mirror and was proud of. But that individual wasn't capable of the vengeance she planned against the creature who'd ripped their world apart. She could not be both at once. Anasofiya had reached, and then stayed, deep within her own darkness and pulled forth her Wraith, an extension of her soul that had lived dormant within her all her life, awaiting the key moment to appear.

Wraith was neither wholly good or bad, just as darkness

was neither. It was both. It was whatever she needed it to be, and often she was not conscious of her need. But Wraith *was* aware, sometimes helpfully, other times frustratingly, but always constant. Her only companion, her sole outlet, and the best, perhaps only, one for the task ahead.

The magic binder, Leif, was gone. Maybe, probably, Wraith was right that she could have broken free sooner, but to what point? He'd have bound her again, and her energy was not without limits.

Now many others were gone as well. She sensed Birger and Astrid still present, and one other. Dagr? Or maybe Stian? No, both. Cyler, too, of course, though it was evident to everyone but Cyler apparently that Agripin had no further use for the young Empyrean. Why Cyler stuck around was a mystery, but Ana suspected it was a blend of love and misguided purpose.

Cyler could be your ally. He doesn't know your heart.

You must be joking. Also, I thought I asked you to leave me be for a while.

He wants what you want. For Agripin to return to his senses.

Have you been drinking? I don't care if he comes to his senses or not. He can choke on them. When the moment comes, we won't be sitting down having a conversation.

Think on the surface, not so deep, Anasofiya. Cyler does not know your heart. This is your advantage.

He knows I'll kill Agripin at the first chance. He's not stupid.

His heart is torn in two. He will search for any answer, no matter how unlikely. Use his vulnerability as the weapon it can be.

He'll fight to the death to protect his master.

And what is his defense against the darkness of the etheric summoner, Anasofiya of the Darkness? How soon you forget the work you made of nearly every last being in Farsengel.

My wrath is reserved for Agripin alone.

This is why you cannot allow the memories of your dear ones to infiltrate. The kindness in you would sacrifice everything you desire.

Killing Cyler—or any of them—makes me no better than him, *or the Senetat. You often forget the importance of humanity.*

I'm not here to remind you of your inherent kindness. I'm your weapon, Anasofiya, not your therapist. I am you. I am the darkness in your soul, and the black corners of your heart. It isn't evil guiding you, but a power that does not come from your humanity. That part of you was nowhere to be found in Farsengel. Find that place. Go there. Only then will you achieve what you most desire.

Footsteps carried down the hallway. Agripin was returning, and if he thought she was awake, he'd engage her. More pleas, cries, platitudes.

Her lids fluttered closed, and, wiping a tear from the corner of her eye, pushed thoughts of Finn and Aleksandr down deep.

6
ALEKSANDR

Aleksandr lay under the *crann bethadh* and thought of his friend, Fiona.

First, he considered the oddity she was on his mind this much at all. Only family had occupied his thoughts to this degree thus far in his life. While he supposed Fiona was family, in some faraway distant sense, so then were the Empyrean refugee youth he'd spent time with—more time than this—in New Orleans. He cared for their well-being, but they did not rent much space in his mind.

Or his heart.

Fiona was twenty-six in Quinlan years, which were essentially no different than the human measure. Quinlans aged at roughly the same rate as Children of Men. Immortality was not among their gifts.

Aleksandr, in contrast, was not even a year old but had aged to maturity in weeks, now resembling a man of twenty or so, with a life wisdom that, while limited, matched his appearance.

His growth would slow now, for years, but even at his oldest, he'd never look older than his father was now, twenty-seven. The passport procured for him declared his age as twenty-one, to account for any further aging on their voyage. If asked, he was to say he was Finn's brother, not son. Were he to appear out in the world with Fiona, people would whisper about her penchant for younger men.

All things considered, nearly two decades of living separated him from Fiona. More than anything, he wished he could understand the many transformations she'd endured during those years; the slow realization of the woman she'd become. His growth had been fast. Turbulent.

And not yet over.

"What do you see from down here, Aleksei? The solution to all the world's problems?"

Uncle Jon cast a shadow over the knobby roots, and then over Aleksandr himself as he drew closer. Aleksandr peered up at him through slanted eyes. His uncle grinned.

"See?"

"You spend all your time here. Or with Nora's girl. Fiona, right?"

Aleksandr looked abashed as he pulled himself forward to a sitting position. "Whenever I try to help around the tribe, they shoo me off."

"I wasn't suggesting you're slacking," Jon said quickly. "Only asking about your choice of venue."

He felt silly telling his uncle, a man of science, that he lay here because the warmth of magic set him at ease. "Peaceful, I guess. And keeps me out of everyone's way."

Jon nodded, an awkward gesture replacing his lack of

response. "Supper will be at dusk, but in the meantime, your friend is looking for you."

Aleksandr brightened before he could censor his emotion. "Fiona?"

His uncle offered a knowing grin. "I'm supposed to tell you to meet her in your secret place? Do I want to know what that means?"

"Probably to talk about Mabon," Aleksandr mumbled, but his heart was already ten steps ahead, leading him down the path where the fork in the road split before the cherry tree.

THEY WOUND THROUGH THE MEANDERING PATH OF THE HIDDEN woods, stepping over mossy roots and dodging raindrops slipping through the canvas of trees.

Aleksandr followed Fiona, unsure of the destination, but enjoying, for once, not knowing.

Fiona slipped on a patch of slick leaves, and Aleksandr rushed to steady her. She smiled, then pushed forward, embarrassed. "I haven't taken this path in a long time," she explained.

"Why not?"

She thrust through a trove of lush green, and the branches snapped back, showering Aleksandr with the gathered drops. "Sorry, kid. It's... well, I suppose it's more a place I enjoyed as a child, and I'm not a child anymore."

Aleksandr rushed to keep up, brushing off the dew. "Why are we going there now?"

She paused, and he sensed her smile all the way back where he stopped. "I figured since you were still a kid, you could use a playground."

That was it. Aleksandr launched forward toward her, intent

on tackling her, mud and all, but this time, she was ready for it, off like a shot, sprinting forth in a nimble leap, out of his grasp.

"I bet you love having someone to harass," he called after her, panting, catching branches to the face as she peeled through the forest.

"Is it that obvious?"

Fiona skid to an abrupt stop. The dense flora opened into a clearing. Overhead, ancient oaks created a ceiling from the rain and stars.

In the center of the dell stood a wooden structure, roughly ten feet tall, listing slightly to the left. Vegetation rimmed the glassless window, slithering up and over the roof like an emerald cocoon.

"What is this?" Aleksandr asked, dropping his head down long enough to catch his breath.

"It was mine, years ago," Fiona said. She sighed, softly, but he heard it. "Flynn helped me build it. Said he so rarely got to use his hands to create anymore, and spent two weeks putting it together. I came here to get away. To daydream. Sometimes to do my coursework."

"Have you brought Declan here?"

Fiona passed him a peripheral look. "Of course not. And don't ask me why not, Aleksei. I'm on to you and the questions you already know the answer to."

Aleksandr grinned. "Maybe it's less that I know the answer and more that I wonder if you do."

"Stop sounding like an adult."

"Does it threaten you?"

"You couldn't threaten a mosquito."

"They never bite me. I don't think that's a coincidence."

Fiona stepped forward, tentatively, running her fingers along the moss-laden windowsill. "This used to be my escape. Then school became the replacement. Then Declan. I wanted out of this hinterland veil so badly, then, that I abandoned this place. Now I feel as if I belong to neither world. I can't leave the tribe, and I'd never be completely me in the outside world. I can't walk away from my duties, and I certainly can't walk away from Declan."

"I've never belonged to any one world. I think maybe that's okay. As for Declan, you know my thoughts."

Fiona said nothing in response. She glanced down at her feet, then lifted her head back, face to the canopy of trees. "Have you ever been in love, Aleksei?"

He narrowed his eyes. "I'm just a kid, remember?"

"I'm serious."

Aleksandr frowned. "I spent the first few months of my life on the run, and ever since then I've been hidden away."

"Remember how you said fate didn't matter? That we should all do what we want?"

Aleksandr nodded.

"Do you still want to know about the prophecy? About your role in it, and what it means for your future?"

"If you don't tell me, no one else will."

"They don't want you to know because everything is supposed to fall into place on its own, but you have a right. You might be okay with your life as it is, I don't know, but you deserve to have a choice. And part of that choice is having the knowledge to make one. I've been thinking a lot about your words, Aleksei, and we all should have a choice, even if in the end we choose our pre-destined one."

"The world won't end if we don't fall in line," he offered.

Fiona smiled sadly. "Let's go inside."

Aleksandr followed her. In the center of the room, a table with two bench chairs, covered in vines, that appeared older than the structure. Another piece of furniture in the corner housed old, damp books, unprotected by the elements. An old lamp without oil sat between the items.

"You can't hate me, Aleksei. I won't allow it, no matter how shocked or angry you are after you hear this. I didn't create the future for you."

The earnest look she wore sobered him. "I couldn't hate you."

"Don't be angry with your father for not telling you, either. He knows the stakes are high but refuses to see your part in the outcome. And that's at the center of all of this, isn't it? If we are fighting for our freedom, does the line end at our choice? Or does it begin there?"

"You're scaring me, Ona."

"I don't mean to, Aleksei, but what I'm about to tell you *is* scary. Some people are born, and they live their life and die, and the world eventually forgets them. *Your* life mattered before it was yours. We've all been waiting for *you*."

Aleksandr's brow rose. "You've been waiting. For me?" He could do nothing more complex than repeat her words.

"For you. And for the female heir, who hasn't been born yet, as far as anyone knows. But if you follow the path set forth thousands of years ago, she will be your mate, and the two of you will, together, save all of us. The new mother and father of a united tribe."

Aleksandr swayed, reaching toward the table to steady himself.

Fiona rested a hand on his arm. A chill passed down his spine and traveled back up toward his heart, which had first skipped and was now racing as if he'd run miles at top speed. "You okay?"

He nodded. "Tell me everything."

• • •

Fiona began with what seemed a fairytale. She told of two races, the Empyreans and Tuatha de Danann, with complementing strengths and a powerful alliance. The breaking of the association began a series of cascading events, leading to centuries of turmoil for both races. An agony that seemingly had no end.

Then the goddess, Morrigan, of the original Tuatha, emerged with a prophecy. One involving the descendants of the four original tribes of the Tuatha, now known as Quinlans, and those with the blood of Empyreans in their veins. The rejoining of the four tribes and the Empyreans would result in two heirs: a male and a female. The birth of the child of the heirs would mark the re-creation of the sundered alliance and the end of turmoil for both races.

Before Fiona had finished her long and sordid tale, Aleksandr gathered his role in the matter. By the time she said her final words, folding her hands over her lap in nervous anticipation, he'd already escaped into his own head, searching for another answer, a better one.

He'd spent the past weeks insisting to Fiona she was nothing without her free will, and now he would have to choose to sever his own in order to save everyone he loved. Everyone.

"I'm sorry, Aleksei. Truly, I am."

Hot tears burned behind his eyes. He turned his head away from her, from her words, from her truth. "But I'm nobody."

Fiona's warm hands landed on his shoulders. She rested her face between his shoulder blades. "You're so much more than nobody, sweet Aleksei. And you are so much more than the result of a prophecy."

Tears spilled over his lids, cutting a cruel path down his cheeks. He wanted to turn, to take her hands in his, to say *something.* Aleksandr was afraid of his own chaos as he faced her in his vulnerability.

The prophecy could end everything. The Deschanel Curse. The Empyrean wars. The hunting of Quinlans. I have the power to end all these terrible things, and start a new legacy.

"I've never thought much about my future, but I never considered… couldn't imagine I wouldn't have a choice in it," Aleksandr whispered. He wiped his tears on his forearm, drawing a light breath.

"You *do* have a choice."

He laughed, sniffling. "Right. Choosing to let everyone I love suffer, when I could save them, is a choice?"

"It is," Fiona insisted, gently. "It's one choice. Don't forget what you told me before, about leading the tribe."

"If you walk away, no one will die. None of them will suffer."

"They might. How can I know? And how can we be sure the goddess' words are even true? We trust in them, but there is no proof, no guarantees. What if they were only words or the shared hallucination of a group of individuals who want desperately to believe there's true peace ahead?"

"So you're suggesting I err on the side of selfishness and just hope things work out?"

Fiona's arms slipped down from his shoulders and around his waist. She held him, and he met the dampness from her own tears. No one but his mora had ever shown him such tender intimacy. "I can't tell you what to do. All I can do is remind you of what you reminded me. Our lives aren't guaranteed. Nothing is. In the end, all we have are our choices."

"You're choosing to stay with the tribe. To give up Declan," Aleksandr accused.

Fiona paused, pulling back. "Maybe not."

"What do you mean?"

"I've been thinking a lot about our talks and have decided maybe you're right. I should tell him who I am. He might run me off his property, but if he can accept me, and still love me, then I'm going to leave and be with him. Either way, I need to know. Both our lives have been on hold for too long."

Aleksandr pivoted in a snap. "Really? You're serious?"

Fiona nodded, wringing her hands over her lap. "I was hoping you might come and be with me when I told him."

"You don't think that would be weird?"

Her eyes—often chestnut, but at the moment, a glowing shade of flaming amber—betrayed her brewing fears. "I don't want to be alone if he turns me away."

He won't, Aleksandr wanted to say, but was weary of everyone around him promising things would be fine. *There are no guarantees,* as Fiona had said. He could not even be sure of his own self.

"Of course, I'll come," he assured her, squeezing her knee. Focusing on Fiona's needs felt safer than addressing his own conundrum, but he also, more than anything, wanted to be a part of seeing her happy. "But if you guys start kissing, I'm gone."

"Afraid of a little kissing, are you?"

Aleksandr twisted his mouth. "Of course not."

Fiona grinned. "Have you ever kissed a girl, Aleksei?"

Blood rushed to his face quicker than he could hide it. He rose, brushing imaginary debris from his trousers, then looked around, as if realizing he'd forgotten an important engagement. "When did you say you wanted to talk to Declan?"

Fiona gave him a knowing smile before looping her hand through the crook of his arm. "Tonight after supper, unless you're busy?"

He shook his head, all his focus having shifted to

tempering his rising pulse and inexplicable mortification at how visible it seemed.

"The sooner, the better, right? Before I lose my nerve."

"And besides," she added, once they were safely in the womb of the forest once again, "I hear your father's training is coming along better than expected. You might be off to find your mother before you know it."

7
CYLER

Decisions brewed in the dining room.

Words flew across the marble table, ones Agripin should be there to counter, or append his own opinions to, but there was no prying the emperor away from his empress.

Cyler would have to represent them both.

Astrid, a creature Cyler had always found to favor calm over chaos, had worked herself into a frenzy, her velvet dress flashing back and forth across the checkered tile as she cried out in angst.

"This is no longer about freedom! We cannot claim it is if we allow sister and brother Empyreans to be robbed of their lives so we, and we alone, can live in secrecy!"

"Astrid, no one disagrees," Birger soothed, though he stood several feet back, either in understanding he could do nothing to quell her, or in respect of her need to vent.

"Two more died today. Will two more perish tomorrow, or will it be four? Or six? We are not great enough in number to withstand such an annihilation."

"What do you suggest?" Stian asked, hands folded across his chest. He leaned into a floral-carved hutch, wearing a weary expression, sagging as if keeping open an invisible portail.

Astrid ceased her relentless pacing. Her long braid fell over her shoulder, resting in the crook of her arm. "I have no simple suggestion, so if you seek one, you'll be disappointed."

"But you have one," he pressed.

"I see only two options before us," she answered. "We either turn ourselves in, and become martyrs for our kind, or we gather our drekar and fight, ending this once and for always."

Cyler stepped forward into the dim light. "You don't really believe turning yourselves in will save anyone, do you? You'll be made examples of, and Oriana and her minions will continue doing as they please." *Fools,* he added, to himself only.

"I'm with Cyler," Dagr agreed, though he appeared pained by the admission. "Turning ourselves in changes nothing. *Does* nothing. The subjugation of Empyreans has been at the center of our strife for millennia. Would we really shrug and let it continue with our backs turned?"

Cyler countered, "I wasn't suggesting you fight, either, by the way."

"I said we had two choices. I did not say they were both amenable," Astrid said.

"The bondage of our race must stop," Stian added. "We know the mark is no instrument of Emyr. He would see us all free. We are His chosen."

Dagr had more points to make in the conversation and almost cut Stian off. "For thousands of years, this has been the way." Cyler could almost see the steam billow from Dagr's nostrils, so eager he was to fight. "No force strong enough to quell the Senetat ever came forth. Now we are more united than ever, and the Senetat is no more, replaced by a group bearing little resemblance to our past leaders. Tell me again why there's more than one choice?"

"Then we fight, as we always believed was the outcome," Birger said. "You are correct, Dagr, history has never seen us more united. Though I fear after the events at Farsengel, we will struggle to gather the drekar back under a common cause."

With an uneasy glance in Cyler's direction, Astrid said, "Agripin divided us with his blind love and false loyalty. Nothing went as planned. Farjhem is less ours now than it ever was."

"We no longer need Agripin if he is not leading Farjhem," Birger replied. "And he isn't, as you said, by his own recklessness. His involvement was our best plan, but not our only one."

Cyler spat and swaggered farther into the kitchen. "He saved every last one of you with his decision to let Aidrik take the fall. You accuse him of problematic loyalty while failing to see the hypocrisy."

"Agripin is making decisions for himself now," Birger said. The voice of reason. "He has forsaken, or perhaps forgotten, our broader mission of restoring peace, finally." He looked toward his companions. "We must depart soon if we are to repair the damage done in time to halt further destruction."

Astrid tugged on her braid, holding her breath. She nodded, but said nothing, struggling with the crushing emotion embedded in the depth of her heavy eyes.

"So you're going to leave? And that's it?" Cyler demanded. He was seething. No sense hiding it.

"Our mission is bigger than your master. In fact, his involvement in it is negligible at this point," Birger countered. "Not to mention unnecessary."

"Agripin deserves better." Even as he said the words, Cyler realized he meant them more for himself.

"*Anasofiya*, as mother of one of the heirs, deserves better," Astrid said. "If we could take her with us, and return her to her mate, we would. But Agripin would not allow this, and we have a more pressing battle ahead. So we leave you in charge of her well-being."

Cyler sniggered, backing into the counter. "You've picked the wrong creature. I care not whether she lives or dies."

Stian pointed to Cyler's rear. "And your master evidently possesses the same care for your future, allowing you to continue on with your mark while our kind continues to fall."

Heat rushed to Cyler's face. "I'll remove it with or without his permission."

"Then why haven't you?"

"That's my affair," Cyler hissed.

Stian lifted his shoulders. "Betrayal often is, fledgling."

"Easy," Astrid warned, then turned a strained smile on Cyler. "Protect yourself, Cyler. Agripin is not in his best frame of mind and is not capable of looking after you. Do not await his permission or his blessing, for you'll find death before you find either. His mind is singular and unchangeable."

You know nothing about your emperor, Cyler started to say, then, with a careful glance toward the other Empyreans studying him, he said only, "I'll do as you ask." *Not for her. For him. For myself.* "But her head is not on my conscience, should she find herself loose of her bindings and out for blood."

"We will seek out Leif before the others, and send him back," Birger promised. "I share your fear. Anasofiya will soon determine a method of releasing herself, and while I believe she *should* be free, if she finds herself as such while here, instead of safe with her loved ones, the results could be catastrophic, like Farjhem."

"You don't say."

"Please know your goal is not to harm her, but to convince Agripin to release her to her clan. Her son, the heir, needs her. His compliance and understanding of his role in our future depend upon it."

"You've witnessed my success in convincing him," Cyler muttered, chiding himself for trying to counteract their misguided optimism. Birger and Astrid would never surrender their hope of a better world, and his frustrated thoughts would only continue falling on deaf ears.

Birger jumped back into the discussion. "Our goals are more aligned than you may think. Since you wish to protect your master, you must protect his empress."

"You overestimate anyone's ability to reason with him on this matter."

"In the end, it will not be a matter of reason. We will send help back for Anasofiya. We owe her that much, and she's given us half the gift of our salvation, in Aleksandr. Above all else, you must keep her safe until Agripin can be convinced to release her, or we can find a way to do it ourselves."

Cyler waved him away, gestured them all away, and disappeared into the sitting room for some much-craved solitude.

Birger and Dagr left that afternoon. Astrid and Stian remained behind, awaiting word to leave, they said, though Cyler strongly suspected it was to keep an eye on the escalating events in Savonlinna. More, to assess whether he was capable of the task ahead.

In the evening, Astrid fell to her knees on the bearskin rug, her face a white mask of tears and grief.

Stian laid a hand on her shoulder. He shook his head, his pale face conveying more than any unspoken words.

Another one, then, thought Cyler. *Or are they killing them by the twos and threes now?*

Cyler knelt to reach into his boot, ripping his dagger from the holster. He pressed the sharp blade into his flesh, envisioning the sleek cut, the precision carving.

Thoughts of his master gave him pause.

Why do I hesitate?

You love him. More than that.

Aye. If he loved me, he would have insisted upon this years ago.

He fears losing you.

At the juncture we now straddle exists a hundred ways he might lose me.

Then let it be your choice.

8

NICOLAS

Colleen clutched her hands under her chin. "Dear, you will love Skye! The isle is where I fell in love with your Uncle Noah, and it holds so many fond memories for us."

Nicolas perked his brows. "I'm sure it's awesome, but this isn't a romantic getaway."

"With all due respect, you don't know *what* this trip could turn into, Nicolas."

"I don't even know what the fuck I'm doing. If Skye is even where we should be going."

"You will. Take a deep breath and accept you are not in control. Not fully," she soothed.

"I'd sure like to know who is, so I could punch them in the face and demand a refund."

Colleen watched him. "You're a warlock, nephew, not an agent of God, or Emyr. We're only passengers on this journey, not conductors."

"If you really believe that, why bother with the Magi

Collective?" Nicolas passed his hand around the room in a sweeping gesture. "Why bother with any of this?"

His aunt smiled. "Because without passengers, there would be no journey."

Uncle Augustus had offered the use of Deschanel Media's private jet. Nicolas didn't mind flying commercial, but in Mercy's fragile frame of mind, isolating her from the general public seemed safer and kinder.

Convincing Mercy to leave had taken nothing short of outright manipulation. He'd reminded her the situation in Louisiana was becoming toxic, and no place for a baby. She'd smiled, patted his hand, and declared he was absolutely right, and how thoughtful of him to consider that with all he had going on.

Nicolas had swallowed back his disgust, and looked at her, instead, with eyes that had beheld her when he'd loved her all those months ago, by the riverbank.

Mercy closed her eyes the moment they were settled on the plane, but Nicolas watched the crescent of the river and the fading grid of his city as they slipped into the clouds. In all his travels past, he'd never wondered or worried about when he might return.

Back then, the stakes had been as large, or as small, as his wayward, wandering spirit.

Several seconds of every minute left him questioning if he even wanted to be here... if this wasn't so far out of his league as to outweigh whatever feelings he had for Mercy.

The answer remained just outside his reach, dangling. Taunting.

What did he even know of love? How could someone like him define such a nebulous concept?

His father, Charles, never pretended Nicolas was ever anything more than a decoration for the bloodline. His mother claimed to love him, but her affection came in packages titled with *I loved you as best I could.*

I loved you as best I could had shared similar words as *I couldn't love you more*, but they were not the same thing at all. *I couldn't love you more* spoke to the vast, immeasurability of the nature of the emotion, something no scientist could adequately measure. *I loved you as much as I could,* by stark contrast, was a reflection of the inadequacies of the one granting the affection. Another way of saying they weren't capable of the level humanity expected from society.

How could he define which sort of love drove him now, when his exposure had been dotted with halfways?

"This must be hard for you," Mercy whispered. He glanced over to find her head rolled back, eyes glassy. She was smiling, so he was assured she couldn't possibly have interpreted his internal conflict.

"How so?"

Mercy's hand traveled to her flat belly. A sigh passed through her, head to toe. "I know the child isn't yours, but I see you as your Christian family saw Joseph."

"Mary's husband?"

"Jesus was not his child, but he didn't hesitate to love him as a father. You may not be the biological father of my child, Nicolas, but your role in his life will be as critical as mine. It warms my heart to know you're coming to accept him. I didn't expect that from you, but I feel as if I'm seeing you for who you really are, for the first time. Who I see is someone more amazing than I'd ever imagined."

Nicolas swallowed, his breath catching halfway through.

She'd said more words in a handful of seconds than in weeks, and, while they were revealing about her current frame of mind, they left him with more questions than anything else. He was now even less sure about his plan to spirit her away to her past. He wished, not for the first time, he'd not been left alone to face her demons.

With a forced smile, Nicolas slipped his arm over Mercy's shoulder and pulled her face to his chest. Her slow, hot breaths burned his heart. *I loved you as best I could.* "We're in this together," he assured her in a shaky tone, wondering whose words they were, whose voice. "Whatever happens." *I couldn't love you more.*

"I hear the worry in your voice," Mercy replied with a yawn, snuggling in closer. He longed to share her peacefulness. "It isn't necessary."

"It's nothing." *It's everything.*

"Leave it at *Ophélie*, Nicolas. What lies ahead for us is so much more beautiful than our mortal minds could ever conceive."

9
ALEKSANDR

"Have I told you how proud I am?" Aleksandr panted, several paces behind Fiona.

"Only a hundred times!" she called back, cutting a secret path through the forest. He realized he could stay here for years and still be surprised by the number of shortcuts and hidden pathways.

"He will love you even more once he knows the truth. I'm sure of it."

Fiona's loose ponytail whipped through the branches as she expertly bobbed and dodged hidden obstructions. "You've never even met him, kid. Now hush, I can't run and talk at the same time."

Aleksandr snapped his mouth shut, contrite, and let his thoughts wander to the events ahead.

He knew admittedly very little about Declan Murphy, other than he was a couple years older than Fiona and a strict man of God. Of his personality, Fiona had only said he was *everything she could ever want.* She had never elaborated or defined what "everything" meant to her.

Seeing Declan through Fiona's eyes left Aleksandr feeling as if they were about to meet the most perfect specimen in all of Ireland.

Declan co-owned a pub with his father, and lived above the establishment, alone. They closed early on Sundays to allow for evening worship, and Fiona's plan was to catch him as he locked up for the evening, before he left for the cathedral.

What she planned from there, Aleksandr wasn't privy to and could not guess. Would she be relying on Aleksandr to help in convincing Declan? Or was he only there because she was secretly afraid?

He didn't have a clue what she expected from him, but he feared letting her down.

Far gave him a strange look when he said he was going into town with Fiona. Remarked with a grin on all the time he'd been spending with her. Aleksandr couldn't share what they'd *really* been talking about, for not even Fiona's mother knew about Declan. Until Aleksandr had come along, Fiona had held the secret close to her heart.

That she'd loved the man for nearly a decade was astounding to Aleksandr and spoke more to Declan's quality than just about any other thing. He suspected, though, that her mother knew more than she let on.

Moonlight appeared overhead as they exited the protection of the forest. Fiona came to an abrupt halt, drawing in a refreshing breath as she fixed her wayward ponytail.

"We have to hurry," she directed. The rose blush of exertion painted her face. A sheen covered her forehead. "We're a couple minutes later than I'd hoped." Under her breath, she muttered, "My fault for not leaving sooner. I'm going to be all sweaty and awful."

You've never looked more beautiful, Aleksandr thought but

didn't say, more fearful of how the words made him feel than how they might resonate with her.

Five minutes later, they stood outside the Killianshire Public House. The interior of the building was dark. Fiona sighed, lamenting he might already be off to services.

Then he emerged; a man older than Aleksandr's own father by a couple of years, though unmarked by life's difficulties. A youthfulness suffused his smooth, unlined skin and his smile when he saw Fiona spoke of innocence even Aleksandr himself no longer felt.

"Fiona, my treasure!" the young man exclaimed, taking her hands in his. He hadn't noticed Aleksandr standing several feet to her left.

"Declan," she demurred, blushing even darker than the color from her run. "I hope this isn't a bad time. I was hoping we could talk."

"Oh, aye? Can it wait till after service? You could join me, you know." The last had the light ring of chastisement.

Fiona shook her head. Aleksandr could, briefly, in her fluster, catch her thoughts: *If I don't tell you now, I'll never find the courage again.*

Declan apparently gathered the heaviness in her eyes and slowly turned, unlocking the door to the left of the pub entrance. "A'right, then. Upstairs." As he slipped the key into the lock, he added, "He with you?"

"A friend," Fiona said quickly.

"Why's he here?"

I'd like the answer myself, Aleksandr thought, but boldly stepped forward. "Fiona has some things she needs you to know, but she's afraid to tell you for fear you won't believe her.

I'm here to help in case that happens because I can vouch for everything she's about to say."

Declan turned and flashed him a bemused, dismissive glance, then unlocked the door.

They marched up the stairs and emerged into a modest flat. The apartment consisted of one large room, bedroom, living room, and kitchen in the same space. A small door at the back likely led to a bathroom.

Declan's good humor had faded. When he turned, his figure took on a defensive stance, arms crossed, stiff. *He thinks I'm her boyfriend on the side,* Aleksandr thought with a short, brief thrill.

"Who did you say this was again?"

"Aleksei. He and his father are staying with my family for a short time," Fiona answered, shifting and shuffling her feet. "He's my friend."

Declan shoved his hands through the front of his hair, latching them to the roots. "Friend. Right, then."

"I should go," Aleksandr said, backing toward the door. The tension in the small room could not be measured by any instrument, but his sense of it was acute. It burned. "Fiona, I'll just be on the bench I saw—"

"Stop, Aleksei! I need you."

"Ah," Declan said, leaning into the wall.

"Not like that," Fiona cried. She dropped her head and drew in several short breaths. "This has nothing to do with Aleksei. I see why you might be confused... let me start at the beginning."

Declan glanced between them. "I have eyes." He placed his hand on his chest. "And a heart. Yes, you'd better begin at the start, but please don't draw this out, Fiona. I've waited eight years for you to either come be with me forever or walk out of my life. I haven't even met your mother! Have never seen where you live." He closed his eyes. "I don't have the heart for further suspense."

Fiona glanced to Aleksandr for help, but he shifted away before their eyes could meet, understanding, even in his limited experience, how any shared looks or perceived alliance would only make matters more difficult.

"There's a reason I haven't come to be with you, Declan. I couldn't tell you because I was so afraid of losing you. But you're right, this cannot go on forever, and I want to believe our relationship is stronger than what I'm about to tell you."

Declan crossed his arms again and nodded at Aleksandr with a smirk. "He's hardly legal, Fiona."

"I should really go..." Aleksandr started.

"You stay put, Aleksei!" Fiona commanded, balling her fists at her side. "Declan, if I wanted to leave you for another man, I'd have done it years ago. I wouldn't have kept coming, day after day, year after year, *praying* to the goddess one day I could tell you the truth of who I am."

Declan appeared ready to make another witty retort involving Aleksandr and his age, but the sight of his love in distress seemed to calm his building anger. "Have I ever led you to think I couldn't love you for who you are?"

"You love me for who you think I am," Fiona replied, her voice growing more faraway as the confession loomed closer.

"I'm not a terrible judge of character, Fiona. But you tell me what it is you think I don't already know. I'm listening."

Fiona closed her eyes, drawing strength from somewhere within. "My background... where I come from... isn't anything like yours."

"Yes, you're a heathen. You weren't raised in the church. You're not even a Protestant. I've heard you talk about the goddess. I know," he teased, offering a tense smile.

"It's so much more than that." She opened her eyes. "My

world is more than a difference in religious and spiritual beliefs. I was raised for something other than a career and a family. There are expectations, sacred duties dating back thousands of years."

Declan shook his head. "You're losing me, Fi."

"I'm a druid," Fiona spit out, the words heaving forward as if expelling them from her soul. "At least, it's the closest comparison that will make sense to you. My people are called Quinlans, and we descend from the Tuatha de Danann."

Declan gaped at her. He uncrossed his arms and spread them wide. "The *fairies*. You're saying you descend from... the fairies. I heard that right?"

"Yes," she replied, without missing a beat. "As does Aleksei. Our role and presence in this world are meant to protect the ancient ways, and prevent the outside from coming in and questioning or changing who we are. Specifically, *my* role, when my mother is no longer here, well... I will step into her shoes."

Declan continued to stare at her, filling the space between all three of them with a heavy, uncomfortable pause.

Then, coming to his senses, he'd seemingly decided on a course of action.

He hurried to the dining table and lifted his wool coat, dangling it over Fiona's shoulders. "You're delirious, my treasure. I can't begin to hazard what's happened to you, but Father O'Connor will know how to fix it," he said, ushering her toward the door.

Aleksandr stepped in front of the door. "He's one of us." Declan's eyes widened, and for a moment, Aleksandr thought he might throw a punch. "Father O'Connor is a Quinlan, also, and if you go to him, Fiona will get in trouble for sharing this with you. Don't you understand, she's trusting you to keep her secret? She loves you so much and would risk everything to be with you."

Declan glared at him, then pivoted, positioning himself between Fiona and Aleksandr, hands clapped on her shoulders. He leaned in close. "I don't know what this young man has done to you, but you're not yourself."

"I have never been more myself than I am at this moment," Fiona whispered. Tears rolled down her cheeks. "I've loved you, Declan. Oh, how I've loved you. But I've given you only half of me, doing you a powerful disservice. You know my laughter and my whispers. You know what it is to kiss me, and to receive my love. At my core, though, I am so much more. Ancient blood courses through my veins. If you truly know me, this will never change. I'll never be less than this, and I cannot turn my back on it, or deny it. I'm descended from the magic of this earth and am an integral part of it."

"You're putting me on," Declan answered. "*Why*, I can't fathom, when I have *loved* you—"

"I am doing no such thing!" Fiona cried, pupils flaring. "Declan, I come to you, arms open, soul bared, with the truth, finally!"

Declan's mouth hung wide. He focused past her to where Alcksandr stood, helpless. "What sort of drugs have you given her?"

Aleksandr began to respond when Fiona, in a rush, broke free of her beau and crossed the room, drawing a deep breath. In her haste, she tripped. In a moment Aleksandr would never forget, she fell backward, toward the open window and the street below.

Later, he would tell himself that, even with the consequences, he would do it again.

He had no other choice.

Time.

Stopped.

Declan's incredulous expression locked.

Fiona's chestnut hair flowed back from her head in a diagonal cascade, blowing out the window in the evening breeze, locked in space like a wax figure.

Aleksandr bolted forth and pulled her to safety, settling her into a wooden chair several feet away.

Time moved forward once again, but everything had changed.

"Sorcerer," Declan accused, in a voice barely a whisper. He'd recovered from the pause in haste, drawing directly from his only source of confidence in the matter: his faith. "You have the devil in you!"

Aleksandr trembled from the weight of his slip, but Fiona's hurt had turned to rage.

"He saved me, and you call him a sorcerer! It's this brand of ignorance that keeps your so-called church so separate from our world. You think he's a sorcerer, Declan? You think he has the devil in him? Well, watch the devil in me, then!"

Fiona rose, dropping her head back, her hair dangling like a cape. As she leaned forward, her hands rolled toward the hearth. A fire appeared from nothing, roaring tall.

"Those flames come from me, from nature," she called, still facing her creation. "There is no devil in me, or my friend, or anyone I love. Nature lives and breathes through me, as it breathes through all of us. My people simply know how to cultivate it. To use it. To sustain us. To give ourselves back and, in turn, strengthen it."

Fiona turned, her eyes imploring. "Can you see? Declan, please tell me you can understand this for what it truly is, and not for what your own fear would have you believe."

Declan stepped backward. He ran into the wall, hands spread against the peeling paint, pushing as if looking to escape through the tiny, splintering cracks. “Who in heaven *are* you? You’re not the woman I’ve loved since childhood. And if you’ve always been this way, and kept it from me, you are truly a witch, indeed.”

More tears pooled in her eyes. “You can believe so easily in a God you cannot see, but it’s a great stretch to believe and accept what you can? This is why I feared telling you, but deep down I believed… I truly believed you would see my heart. That you loved me enough to suspend your fear.”

“I can’t see anything except the devil running rampant in this room!”

“What do you know about witches, Declan?” Aleksandr prodded. His voice choked, furious at the ignorance pouring from the man who was supposed to love his friend. He struggled to match this creature against the one Fiona had held on a pedestal. “For that matter, what do you know about anything? This amazing woman loves you, and would do anything for you, and you point at her with fear? She deserves better than this.”

“Get out of my flat.” Declan’s voice was calm, but Aleksandr sensed the current of rage below the surface. It wouldn’t take much more to bring it forward. “Now.”

“If I leave, this will be the last time you see my face,” Fiona returned, gathering herself. As she approached him, Declan flattened himself against the wall. “I won’t beg your understanding, and I won’t show up asking for another chance. I will simply be gone, and it will be as if I never existed.”

Declan’s eyes finally reflected the agony visible in hers. “You never did exist, if this is who you really are.”

Fiona’s face contorted in the start of a sob, but then she

bolted, out the door and down the steps, holding the hem of her emerald dress as she fled the scene.

Aleksandr gifted Declan with one last potent glare before following her, torn between the desire to give the ignorant man a piece of his mind, and the need to be with Fiona.

FIONA RACED THROUGH THE FOREST AT A FRANTIC PACE, DESPERATE AS Aleksandr trailed. She discarded her cape in her distress, and then her shoes. He caught both, wondering what she might release next.

At last, she stopped. Aleksei found her crumpled in a heap at the base of a large oak.

"Fiona," he sighed, wrapping her cape around her shoulders as she moaned, knees embedded in the mossy roots.

"Why did I let myself believe?" she cried, pulling at her hair, her shirt, her skirt. "Why!"

"I shouldn't have pushed you." He crouched behind her, and she fell back into him, her body trembling with sorrow. "I am so sorry, Ona."

"Better you did. I should have done it sooner, before giving my heart so fully. Oh, what my mother would say if she knew what a fool I'd been! He turned out to be just like my father."

Aleksandr held her in share silence. He recalled her mentioning briefly how her father had been a man of the church, and when Nora discovered her pregnancy, he'd fled from the truth of who she was, taking their son and leaving Ireland. *She told me no one born out there could ever accept what we are in here. But Declan is different, Aleksei. He's given all of himself to me. He isn't like my father or the others.*

Fiona sagged in his arms, and he carefully spread her cloak over the roots, laying her across it.

Her soft, vulnerable eyes gazed up at him, damp with tears. "Do you think I'm a fool for believing?"

He shook his head in answer, unable to speak. His racing heart had stolen his breath.

She pulled him down next to her, wrapping herself in his arms like a cocoon. He enveloped her without words, his confusion pulsing with the muscle in his chest.

10
ANASOFIYA

Ana awoke naked.

Both legs were bound to opposing posts of the bed, her ankles swollen from the tight binding. Her arms were still stretched uncomfortably behind her neck.

Agripin hovered over her, his gaze both appraising and predatory.

"I've waited so long for this. For a mate worthy of me. We've settled with our past selves and can become the future, together. Something great and powerful. There's nothing standing between us now."

"Except my consent." Ana writhed beneath her bindings. The blood rushed north, its effect as dizzying as the reality now upon her.

Another feeling. A swoon as the room faded in, then out, and again. The pain of her bindings throbbed in her ears like a heavy heartbeat.

Had she been drugged?

Agripin grinned, a sinister effect dividing his face. "What is that saying from Children of Man? It is better to ask forgiveness than permission?"

Cyler appeared in the doorway. Slow shock came over his expression as his eyes darted between the vulnerable Ana and his master.

"Are you still my acolyte?" Agripin asked.

"Aye," Cyler said, eyes again falling upon Ana. "You know I am."

"Then take her for me."

"Take her? You're not serious."

"Is there humor in my eyes, Cyler?"

"Aggie, come on. She's not my type."

"When has that stopped you?"

"She's tied up! To do this makes you no better than Oriana."

"Oriana's pets are with her of their own volition," Agripin argued, a perplexing defense.

"An illusion," Cyler barked. "Nothing more."

Agripin shifted, pressing himself tight into the small corner. He crossed his arms over his chest. "You do this, or you leave me and never come back."

"And why... would you want to watch me assault your empress?"

"Questioning me is the same as denying me."

Ana's consciousness slipped away, but not far enough. No, not far enough to miss Cyler tentatively unbuckling his trousers, pulling his limp cock into his hand.

"I can't," Cyler started to say, eyeing the organ, but then Agripin fell to his knees before him, taking him in his mouth. Cyler's head rolled back, and an excited moan escaped.

"Now you can," Agripin said moments later, once again rising.

Ana's eyes opened in time to see Cyler hovering over her, apology in his eyes but a desire to please his master burning hotter.

As he entered her, she gasped, a pitiful whimper burgeoning from deep within her soul. Ana reached for her Wraith and came up empty. The only sounds in the room were her own soft cries and the staccato grunts from the creature thrusting atop her.

Cyler stopped. "What if..."

"You'll not evigbond with her," Agripin said with confidence. "She is mine. This is how I prove it."

"By forcing me to mate with her?"

"Fool. By spilling your seed within her and then walking away without a permanent bond. When I do the same, she will be mine, always."

Cyler started to protest but his master whispered something in his ear, and instead, he continued. His movements grew faster, quicker, more desperate.

From the corner of her eye, Ana witnessed Agripin fondling himself, getting off on her humiliation.

His death would not be quick. Not merciful. She would drag it out for days. Months, if she could find the self control.

Cyler released one final, stilted groan, spilling inside her.

Agripin smiled in satisfaction. "And? Was I correct?"

"I feel nothing except shame," Cyler muttered, flashing one final, apologetic glance at Ana before fleeing the room, pants around his ankles.

"Mine, then." Agripin flicked his tongue across his lips.

Ana closed her eyes, and then realized she needed to see this. Every insulting moment. She'd feel this and allow it to fuel her rage.

Agripin slipped inside her, splitting her mind in two.

And as he came, declaring his claim to her, Ana found the core of her hatred and held on for dear life.

WITH A GASPING START, ANA AWOKE. BETWEEN HER LEGS, A throbbing dampness.

But she was not naked. She had not been violated.

That was one hell of a nightmare.

Not a nightmare, Wraith replied. *A divination. What you saw has not yet come to pass, but it will.*

If Agripin wanted to force himself on me, he'd have done it by now.

No. The emperor is many things, but he is not a rapist by trade. As you evolve, so does he. You have both shed your past selves and developed into someone new. The creature he becomes is capable of far more treachery than his predecessor.

I'm not sure I understand what you're saying.

Agripin made choices that led to pain for others, but he was not a monster before the events at Farsengel. His decline is now self-fulfilling; he becomes the monster you accused him of being. And he is both Victor Frankenstein and the monster, all at once, battling for position. The monster will win because it is easier to descend into darkness than emerge from it.

How do you know all this?

Same way you know, Anasofiya.

I'm not a prophet. I can't see the future.

No, but another can. And this one has sent you the vision for a purpose.

What reason would that be? And who?

Both answers will come to you in time.

If you know, then why don't I?

You do know. You just haven't found your access to the truth. But you will.

When?

Soon.

AGRIPIN HUNCHED IN THE LEATHER ARMCHAIR, SNORING. ANASOFIYA attempted to murder him with her eyes. Failed. Having fallen short of her initial goal, she instead thanked Emyr for this brief time of solace.

The house seemed lighter. Specifically, two bodies lighter.

Birger and Dagr had departed the day before, for reasons she didn't know or care.

Except, now she did know. And it concerned her a great deal.

Astrid's grief seeped through Anasofiya's vivid, sordid dreams, highlighting images of Empyreans being senselessly slaughtered all over the world. Oriana had taken the reigns of Farjhem, leading without scruple or critical direction other than the public and universal recognition of her worth and power. She cared nothing for the lives she'd sacrificed if they led to her enemies being rooted out and justice meted.

Anasofiya recalled the sinister vibe radiating off Oriana at her coronation. The snake-like hiss of the word "sister" rolling over her tongue.

Only now, in horrifying retrospect, did Ana recognize Agripin and his sister were two sides of the same demented coin.

And now Anasofiya had two names on her list.

Why stop there?

Wraith, you pick the most inopportune times to show.

I show when you wish me to. I am you. You are me.

Anasofiya's shoulder ached with fire and ice. "These fucking bindings," she muttered, shifting to a less imposing position.

You could break free at any time. You choose not to.

And then what? I can't kill Agripin if I'm dead.

He would never kill you. You know this. He loves you. I know this, and so you know this.

I don't give a fuck what the disgusting creature feels or thinks. All of this is his fault. All of it! Not only Aidrik's destruction but now the sanctimony has reached new heights, propelling his sociopath of a sister to a position of power. She's murdering all of us. What a waste. Strictly the result of one being's supremely delusional narcissism.

You have always been so colorful, Anasofiya. Since you were a young girl. Darkness has never become you, not fully.

Anasofiya wondered how a being cut from her own soul could possess such sentiment. She wouldn't indulge it.

Apologies, Anasofiya. I forget myself. And here I'd advised you to put Finnegan and Aleksei aside.

I can't delay, Wraith. You said I could choose to free myself? How?

I know the answer and thus, you do too.

Stop with the riddles!

My words could not be more simple.

If you're my minion, then work for me! Tell me what to do! Stop making me guess when it takes all my energy just to live!

You're doing it.

Doing what?

Your anger. It guided you in the direction of my emergence. Toward the destruction of far more than your hands alone could have laid asunder. Concentrate your ire. Feel Astrid's pain. Experience the deaths of your own. Remember how you felt as Cyler, and then Agripin, came after you in your prophetic dream. Do not simply think of your anger, or imagine it, but be *it. Absorb it as your own, and turn it into tangible, usable energy. Your darkness is not me; it is you. Having the ability is important, knowing how to use it, is vital. Instead, as quickly as you discovered this, you turned your back on it.*

Anasofiya listened.

I feel your vengeance, but you've tempered it. Compartmentalized it, and morphed it into an idea, no longer a feeling. You've placed it in a safe location where it cannot hurt others. But your vengeance will not be satisfied with simply conceptualizing the pain of your energy. If you truly wish for retribution—true, raw revenge—you must cease this fear of yourself.

I don't fear myself, Anasofiya replied. Finally, she considered her outlook on all she'd done. All that had happened. *I fear losing myself.*

You fear that surrendering to this will cost you your humanity.

Yes. I fear there will be no going back. That the woman who stood beside Finn and promised forever, the woman who brought a beautiful son into this world and nurtured him, will cease to exist.

You are you, Anasofiya. You will always be you.

A shifting reality, Wraith. I am no longer the same woman I was before I stood and watched my evigbond destroyed in Farsengel.

No one is ever the same after a new grief. Agony.

It is not the pain which changed me. You know this.

Where you can only experience, I can consider. I would never allow the complete loss of the Anasofiya who created me. You can trust this.

Can I?

I daresay I'm insulted.

I mean no insult. But you know this because you are me, and I am you, right?

Touché, Anasofiya.

If I created you, wouldn't the loss of the true me become the loss of you?

You created me. If you cease to exist in physical form, as would I. But our sentience is only linked, not dependent. I am aware of all you see and know, yes, but am also conscious of things on my own. I love you, Anasofiya. You are my creator. I would not allow your destruction.

Then help me in avoiding the ruination of our people. I didn't know, but I see now, this is bigger than me. Agripin must be stopped—he will *be stopped—but the problem isn't only about Aidrik. I've let my hatred be tunneled, but I think... I believe... it's stifling me.*

Aye. Stifled and confused. The answer has been within you all along. See, the power did not leave you at Farsengel. That was only the inception. Your strength grows, as I grew, within you, cultivating until you were ready to know me.

Hot tears burned Anasofiya's eyes. The first she'd allowed herself since Farsengel. She feared them, even more than her own darkness. *I miss him so much, Wraith. I was so hurtful to him in the end. I took anger out on him that belonged with me.*

He knows. No one has ever known your soul as Aidrik did, Anasofiya. Not Finnegan. Not Aleksei. Not I. He knew then and still does.

I won't let his death be in vain. I won't let it be senseless.

You won't.

I can't.

I know, Anasofiya.

She choked down a stifling breath, holding back rising panic. To the right and left, her wrists were bruised under the silver, and she had only herself to blame. *I've wasted so much time. What am I doing here? Brooding? Biding time? For what?*

You are on a journey. One which is only beginning.

Blood rushed to Anasofiya's face, and her head fell back on the pillow, overcome. *I can't sit back anymore and wait for the world to present an answer. Empyreans are dying. Finn and Aleksei could be in danger.*

Astrid and Stian will depart soon. Then there will be no one to stop you.

How many more will die before that happens?

Not everything is in your control, Anasofiya. You are but one mass of energy on this vast planet.

Fuck off with your reverse psychology, Wraith.

Welcome back, my darling.

11

FINNEGAN

In the two hours Finn had spent with Padraig, the draoi Quinlan designated as his "trainer in all things draoi," he had come to one very definitive and simple assessment of the man.

He was one insufferable son-of-a-bitch.

For starters, he seemed to get off on speaking in the types of riddles no one could actually answer, doing so with a cheeky smile that said, *I speak for the goddess, you know.* Finn, never fond of riddles, found his mind wandering to more pressing topics, which in turn provoked Padraig's anger in the form of frustrated huffs and arms crossing and re-crossing.

The situation got so tense, Finn had to keep Forbia away from the sessions; otherwise, she'd spend the whole time with her teeth bared, growling at the draoi trainer.

"If you don't take this seriously, say so," Padraig grouched.

Finn knew if he didn't respond with humor, his own mood would take a darker turn, and they'd get even less far than nowhere. "Of course, I take it seriously. You just haven't produced the ruby slippers yet."

Padraig's look rode a line somewhere between confusion and annoyance. He knew Finn was poking fun at him, but he didn't get the reference.

"We both have our puzzles, apparently," his trainer muttered, leaning against the oak table in the room's center.

Finn pursued his own thoughts on the matter. "Let's try this without them. If you're not clearer in the instruction, how am I supposed to be precise in the results?"

Padraig stiffened, setting his jaw. "I don't know how I can be more precise."

Finn smirked. "Really. 'The goddess works through you, so you must work through the goddess. Feel her in your veins as you travel, not through space, but through time, to the place of your destination. Your heart is the vessel. Your soul is the guide.'"

"Yes, those are my words, but the problem isn't in them. It's in your interpretation, Finnegan."

"Then help me understand because we're getting nowhere."

"Hopeless," Padraig said to himself, quietly but clearly intended for Finn's ears as well, resuming his favorite activity: pacing the room. "This is why we raise draoi within the tribe. Society has already done a number on you, and I'm not sure I'm up for the task."

Finn stood. "Then I've lived up to my end of the bargain."

"Where are you going?"

"To see Nora. The deal was I would try to find Amelia and Jacob, with your assistance. If you can't handle it—"

"Sit down."

"Why? So you can remind me again what a Neanderthal I am?"

Padraig breathed out a long sigh. "I'm sorry. You're the

second civilian draoi I've had to train in recent months, and neither of you is what I expected."

"Then we have more in common than you think because none of this is what I expected, either."

"No. I suppose not." Padraig ceased his pacing and studied Finn as if he were a peculiar specimen. "It's as simple, or as complicated, as opening your heart. You've done this before, even if you're not aware. When you fell in love with your wife. And when your son was born. You did it without realizing. Besides, that's what it's like for those of us who were born in the loving shadow of the goddess. We open our heart to her without realizing we've ever done so."

"You were raised that way, as you said," Finn replied. "I don't know anything about the goddess and have no emotional connection to her. So maybe we should try another angle."

"On this, Finnegan, I believe you underestimate yourself." Padraig smiled. He approached him and fell into a squat. His finger poked Finn's chest. "She has always been inside you. She lives there, waiting, all these years, for the moment you'll feel it."

"And how do I do that? Feel it?"

"The goddess, Finnegan, is love. You are a man who has known passion and love. You've known the vulnerability, the sacrifice. That absolutely terrifying and empowering sensation of losing yourself and turning everything within over to that love. Pull yourself back to the first time you laid eyes on Ana, or the moment your son emerged and entered the world. Let it all go except that, and when there's nothing left but that tremendous power of love and acceptance, then you ask for the goddess."

"That sounds almost too simple," Finn countered. For the

first time in the days they'd spent together, he felt he had been given a direction that made sense.

"Because it is," Padraig responded, rising.

AND IT WAS.

FINN HAD NO EXPECTATION OF TIME EXCEPT AN ASSUMPTION THE results would not come easy. Nothing important ever did.

Yet no sooner than Padraig left him to his own thoughts, and he'd let his mind wander toward the moments where his heart had felt the lightest and heaviest at once, did a new sensation sweep through him, from head to toe. The awareness included the impression of being overcome with a lightness of breath, but there was nothing unsettling about it. It was a welcome rush of euphoria and an inexplicable comfort amongst what could only be described as confusion.

Help me, he pleaded, as Padraig had instructed him, words mixed up somewhere in the riddles that he'd somehow remembered when the moment came. *Goddess, I ask for your assistance now.*

Finn's feet were in the air. No... only the feeling of being knocked over, feet over head, but he hadn't moved. The single pane window in the hut still reflected his face, and the chair where he sat remained upright.

Again. There it was. He squeezed his eyes shut to bring balance to his overworked equilibrium. It didn't stop this time, that spinning sensation, the same as when he was a kid flipping over the monkey bars in the schoolyard at recess. Over and over he'd go until the dizziness won out.

When his lunch threatened to rise, the movement abruptly stopped. He knew he should open his eyes, but *something* had changed. The smell of aging pine and fresh construction. Grout from recently laid tile.

And the sounds. Or startling lack of them. The sharpness of silence recalled memories of him waking in the early morning hours at the old Victorian back home in Maine. A time when not even the dogs stirred, and it was only Finn and his thoughts. The Atlantic lay still, at the peak of low tide.

Boom. It echoed across the marble—yes, he was sure now, this was not the oak floor of the hut he occupied a few moments ago—and a musty breeze passed by him. The scent of logs on a dying hearth was tinged with the decaying filth of an untended city avenue. *Bourbon Street. I've come back to New Orleans somehow.*

Finn opened his eyes, expecting to find himself the lone patron remaining in a hotel lobby, the Bourbon Orleans perhaps. Instead, he gazed into the most elaborate shrine he'd ever seen.

I've been here before. I've seen this. But it was... different.

He scanned the room, turning a circle as he surveyed the scene. Elaborate Norman and Gothic carvings arched up toward the tall raised ceilings. Behind him, a nave draped in crimson silk was adorned with dozens of golden candelabras, sparks of tiny light.

A church, then.

No, larger. Much larger.

A cathedral.

Turning back toward the shrine, an etching in Latin caught his eye. It had been years since he'd studied Latin, or used it in earnest, but the words came to him as if in his native language.

In the thousandth year of the Lord, with the seventieth and twice hundredth with the tenth more or less complete this work was made which Peter, the Roman citizen, brought to completion. O man, if you wish to know the cause, the king was Henry, the friend of the present saint.

All the teachings came back to Finn.

He'd been here before, as a child. They'd traveled north in Scotland to see his grandparents but first stopped in London. It had been his mother's idea to come here. She couldn't leave without seeing Westminster Abbey one more time before she died.

Had she known then she would lose her life young?

Finn pushed thoughts of his mother aside, returning again to his recognition. This was Westminster Abbey, and he was standing before the shrine of Edward the Confessor. His death in 1066 had led to the Norman Conquest, changing the geography, politics, and culture, of the English landscape forever.

Henry III, in the thirteenth century, had revitalized and romanticized the legend of The Confessor, rebuilding the church with Gothic inspiration, and hiring Italian designers to create the tomb he believed Edward, who had always desired a pilgrimage to Rome, would have wanted.

So, judging from the details in the shrine, and the architectural style, it was at the earliest, the thirteenth century.

That didn't narrow it down much.

Finn jumped when a deep, resonating bell sounded twice. Nearby but not within the cathedral. Morning or afternoon, he briefly wondered, then understood it must be early morning for the air to be this still.

"Are you misplaced?" a baritone voice inquired, bouncing off the stone emptiness. "Abbey is closed. How did you find your way in?"

The man, in full sight now, appeared sixty but had the gait and crouch of a man two decades older. He wore the full vestments of the Catholic church, a variation of the ones Finn remembered from his childhood. These were laden in rich velvet and cloth of gold.

"I'm... I'm sorry," Finn croaked, clearing his throat. He found his voice. "I didn't realize."

The man waved him away, but it was less dismissive and more what Finn interpreted as an archaic form of *no worries.* His eyes scanned the intruder, frowning at... could be anything, Finn guessed. His strange clothing. The accent and sudden appearance in the abbey at two in the morning. "Our Lord would not wish me to turn you away. Would you be after the sacrament? I'm not prepared but a few moments would find me so."

Finn shook his head, and in the process of doing so found he was lightheaded. He gripped a wooden railing. "No. I... actually, I have a strange question for you."

"Are you ill?"

"No, I don't think so. It's that—"

"Share with me your name, if you will, my brother in the Lord."

"Finnegan St. Andrews."

"A clan name, from the sound of it. You don't sound Scottish."

"It's a long story," Finn replied, now completely overcome by the realization of what he'd done. He, with very little effort, had traveled across time and had found himself in London, in Westminster Abbey, though not the abbey he remembered from his own time.

"Take a seat," the man urged, ushering him toward a red satin cushion atop a prayer bench. "Are you sure you're not ill? I can point you toward succor, but as to my own health, it is not what it once was, as you may well see."

"I'm not ill, I just... can you please tell me..." He trailed off, understanding this would be the moment he lost the man's assistance, where everything would go to hell if he was not careful. What were the jails like in whatever time he'd landed?

"Ah, my own name! I have fallen short on my duty. I am Abbot Richard de Ware. You are not from here, though if you were, you'd have been familiar with my name and face for going on eight turns of the calendar."

Finn brightened. He may have found a better path toward his question. "And what year did you arrive, then?"

The abbot leveled him squarely in his gaze, likely wondering how a young lad in London couldn't subtract eight. "In twelve sixty-two, the year of our Lord. I arrived on Holy Saturday and delivered my first Eastertide mass. Two days hence will be my eighth, by the grace of our Lord."

A quick calculation... 1262. That made it 1269.

Imagine that, 1269.

What did Finn know about that year?

Henry III was King, but not for much longer. This would explain the fresh construction in the abbey, which was completed just prior to his death.

What else?

The Baron's Wars were probably still being fought.

Come on. History is my subject. Why am I here? Think!

Finn couldn't think. He couldn't focus.

He had landed himself in the year 1269.

One.

Two.

Six.

Nine.

Holy hell.

"Son? You most certainly *are* ill, and I'm afraid I have to ask you to find succor elsewhere. I can direct you ...arise! I cannot have you bringing disease to these blessed... see you to the door... pray for you..."

. . .

Finn's entire body was heavy with an unknown weight attached. His arms and legs were rooted in place as if by an unseen magnet.

And then there was the matter of the stinging slaps to his face.

"You're awake! Finnegan! Are you all right? You did it, by goddess, you did it!"

"Get off me," Finn managed, the heaviness coming free of his arms as he flailed them in front of his face, forcing away his friendly assailant. "Back off."

Padraig did as asked but didn't cease the slew of questions and affirmations. "We did it! You did it, but my words clearly made the difference. Did you find them? What did you see?"

"Please," Finn pleaded, blocking the view of his excited trainer with his hands, like a child who believes if he cannot see his parents, they cannot see him. "Not now."

"What do you mean not now? Did you find them? If you didn't, we need to try again. Strike while the iron is hot! Is that not what your people say?"

"Not. Now. Padraig."

This time, something in his tone must have struck the intended chord, for the draoi backed out of the room, mumbling more about his desire to hear everything.

Finn ignored him.

If he didn't close his eyes and block out the world, his brain would explode.

12
MERCY

Emyr welcomed Mercy with open arms, beckoning her home.

No matter it was only a dream. For Empyreans, a visit from Our Father could come in many forms, and none should be disregarded.

She'd passed the first test. Becoming human was not, as she'd originally believed, a punishment or a denial of her faith, but the fulfillment of thousands of years of unfailing piety.

In those early days as a mortal, Mercy had first wished for her own death. When she lay dying, her mark activated by the volatile, draconian Senetat, she understood, truly and finally, that the promise of her faith was no more than an illusion. She was not the first, nor would she be the last, to find herself dedicated and enamored to this false reward.

Realizing she had feelings for the most reckless of all Children of Men did not help matters. Observing him vacillate between loving her and feeling trapped by those same feelings reduced her self-worth to nothing. Even knowing what she knew then—or believed she'd known—about her false dogma, she would have rather returned to living in blissful ignorance than face the bleak truth: her life meant nothing, and in another half-century or so, it would cease to exist entirely.

That Nicolas had failed himself, and her, by submitting to his own carnal weakness with Eydis came as no surprise. Mercy, was aware now that, since her early days, she had always sought validation for her beliefs and felt no satisfaction in being right about him.

And then Emyr began to visit.

Initially, his appearances were subtle. She would see his figure, the phoenix with wings spread in a wide V, in the forming clouds, or in a bowl of grits Condoleezza forced her to eat when the weight fell off her. Her absent mark began to experience phantom shudders as if His wings fluttered against her skin once again.

Then, as she began to document her life, for the purposes of assisting with the instruction of the Runean children, her own words ceased to flow across the page. His replaced them. Promises of significance to come, and appreciation of her fealty.

Mercy's conception shocked her most of all. Surely she was not worthy of that task! Of such an honor! To carry the child of Emyr, as the Virgin Mary had once carried the Christ child? Who was she, but one Child of Emyr in a sea of faithful?

Our belief is not true faith if we leave it to question. Aidrik's words, often frustrating but also equally on point, returned to her as she'd stood before the gilt mirror in Nicolas' master suite, admiring the curve only she could see.

Nicolas pretended to see, though, bless him. He had gaped at her, in a confused sort of horror, unsure whether to hold her or ship her off to an institution. In the end, he'd chosen to be a man.

And in that very, single moment, Mercy realized none of

what had transpired between them up until then—not the heated, sweaty entanglements that drove the bulk of their courtship, not his indiscretion with Eydis, not even his whispers of love—mattered. Every moment now was a transcendence of all the memories that had come before. The two of them were on this new trajectory, together, and Nicolas would see his own reward for this new role, as Joseph surely must have been recompensed by God for raising his son.

Her son would have a spiritual father, and an earthly one.

Nicolas' head bent against the leather headrest, his breaths light and measured. He'd fought against sleep, so worried for her, but eventually succumbed to his own exhaustion. She watched him; the beautiful curve of his well-formed mouth, slightly parted; that dark hair, messy against the sunlight streaming through the jet window, reminding her of how he looked after their coital exertions.

Mercy had agreed to accompany him on the journey, not as a result of being convinced of his urgency to leave New Orleans for the baby's sake, but of observing his own need to get away.

She wouldn't tell his dear, sweet heart that none of this mattered. The Son of Emyr would be born no matter where they lay their heads, and would thrive in any environment.

Telling him would do more ill than good. Mercy suspected Nicolas was on the verge of a complete mental collapse. He was already showing signs of detachment from reality. Soon, he might extend beyond her help, but she would do what she could, as long as it did not come at the expense of protecting her son.

She would need to tread more carefully around Nicolas. To shield him.

"Sweet dreams, prince," she whispered with a fond smile, both hands wrapped in a protective caress over her flat belly.

13
ALEKSANDR

Aleksandr didn't dare chance a glance at Fiona. No need to see her, anyway, to catch the shame radiating from her.

They knelt side-by-side in the great hall, before three stern figures: Father O'Connor, Nora, and Finn.

Father O'Connor had spent the last thirty minutes recounting the desperate, flustered words of Declan Murphy, who'd fled to him after the confession of a certain Fiona Quinlan.

"Reckless!" Nora barked though her voice was barely above a whisper. "What were you *thinking*?"

"We searched all night for the two of you," Aleksandr's father added, hands rooted in his hair. Dark circles rimmed his eyes, spidery red lines speaking to his restlessness. For the first time, Aleksandr noticed fine outlines around the edges as well. "All over the forest."

"I'm sorry, Far," Aleksandr mumbled, eyes still burning a hole in the canvas floor.

"What did you think was going to happen?" Father

O'Connor attempted, in a softer tone than his niece. "Declan is a God-fearing young man. He believes in magic, sure as day, as any Irishman, but not as anything more than adversarial. For him, magic is synonymous with the work of Satan."

"I thought maybe he could love me for me," Fiona sniffled, wringing her hands over her knees.

"Have you learned nothing from the stories of your father?" her mother answered. "Or the heartbreaking tale of my mother and father? I have been separated from my brother Noah nearly all my life because of the inability for our worlds to mesh!"

"Not everyone is my father."

"Thus far, my theory has held solid," Nora replied. "Certainly, I wish things could be different, but they cannot. And now you've drawn attention to us. Do you think he will leave well enough alone at his confession to Flynn?" She shook her head. "Fire in the hearth. And time shaping? Great goddess!"

"I stopped time to save her life," Aleksandr said, eyeing Fiona's white knuckles from his periphery. Oh, how he wished to take her hands in his, to calm her.

Memories of her sleeping in his arms caused a fierce blush to rise to his cheeks, one his father immediately noted with a tilted head.

"And for that I thank you," Nora said, nodding his direction. Her eyes didn't leave her daughter. "I don't blame you, Aleksei, for it was my Fiona who put you in that position in the first place."

"Actually, I put her there," Aleksandr pressed, chancing a look up. "I convinced her Declan would understand. This is my fault, not Ona's."

"Aleksei," Fiona chided.

Nora's stern gaze traveled between the two offenders, settling once again on her daughter. "You think I didn't know about your dalliance with the village publican? Nothing escapes my notice, Fiona. Not your late nights in the forest, not your evenings in his arms. I said nothing, for it was your lesson to learn, and not mine to teach. But this carelessness affects us all."

"I know," Fiona admitted, head hung in contrition. "I'm sorry."

"We are already at risk after the attack on Amelia and Jacob."

"You never mentioned that," Finn accused, turning toward Nora.

Nora sighed, exchanging a glance with Flynn. "We didn't want to alarm you, with all you have to deal with on your own. Jacob and Amelia were caught and tortured by an Empyrean scout who was collecting bounties for Quinlans. Jacob came into his powers in time to stop the assault and free them both, but Amelia almost died. When Padraig happened upon them, she was in the care of an Empyrean enclave still friendly to us. Her survival wasn't guaranteed, and before they could fully nurse her to health, she and Jacob departed with another Empyrean. We don't know why, or where they went, but presumably, this scout was still after them. And surely he pulled information about us from one of their minds during the incursion. Our magic only keeps us safe when we are in the mood. It does little for us when exposed, which inevitably we must sometimes be."

Finn looped his hands behind his neck. His eyes closed. "So you mean to tell me Amelia may be dead? And there are those nearby who want to kill us, and you're still allowing Fiona and others to venture into town?"

"I am saying we aren't sure," Nora answered. "There's a lot of we don't know, and cannot know, until we have Amelia and Jacob back in our care."

Fiona jumped in. “I haven’t sensed any danger in my travels.”

“None except the one you brought to us?” Nora accused.

“I may be able to massage Declan’s memory,” Flynn said. “He was in too dangerous a pique last night to attempt it, but he might be more malleable today.” He tossed his head in dismay. “A dangerous business. One I’d as soon have avoided.”

“Leave him be,” Fiona pleaded. “It’s over. I’ll never see him again.”

“The precaution is not for his sake,” Nora answered. “But for ours. Should he choose to share what he’s seen beyond the church walls, we may find ourselves in even more dangerous times.”

Back in their hut, Finn threw Aleksandr a sweater. “You must be freezing,” he said, moving to the stove to heat the kettle.

“Thanks.”

“I’m not going to lecture you, Aleksei,” his father said, pausing at the small cast iron stove. “You’re my son, but you’re quite capable of making decisions.”

“Thank you.”

“But I wish... I would ask... that you not ever scare me like that again.” Finn’s hands gripped the counter as he bent forward, lowering his head. “I had no idea where you were. With your mother gone...”

Aleksandr shuffled across the floor to his father, wrapping his arms tight around his waist. His face fell against Finn’s back. Forbia curled herself at the base of their feet. “I know. I’m sorry, Far.”

Finn enveloped his son’s arms with his own, embracing him in the reverse hug. “I know you are. And you were helping your friend. Sometimes we go about things from the wrong angle, but what's done is done, right?"

Aleksandr nodded and turned to face his father.

Finn frowned. "I said I wouldn't lecture you, and I won't. But can I ask you, man to man, what were you thinking?"

Aleksandr dropped his eyes to the floor. He felt no further shame than he had when Nora and Flynn were laying into them, but he lacked the experience to answer his father's question.

"I wanted to help her. She's the most bea—" he stopped short of finishing. "Fiona's my only friend, and I want to see her happy."

Finn leveled his gaze. His mouth twisted. "I'm not talking about what happened in town."

Blood rushed to Aleksandr's face, a sensation he was now growing painfully accustomed to. "Oh."

"Yeah, oh. You spent the whole night in the forest with her."

"Nothing happened... I mean, it wasn't like that."

Finn smiled. "I believe you that nothing happened, but that's exactly how it is. I see your face when you look at her, and, for me, it's like looking in a mirror at the first time I saw myself after I found your mother."

"She's my only friend," Aleksandr repeated, as much for himself as his father. Forbia snorted, and he shot her a look.

"I'm happy for you, that you've found one. She seems like a nice girl," his far answered. In an attempt to break the tension and start the conversation on his terms, Finn poured steaming water into two mugs, covering the fragrant tea leaves.

He handed one mug to Aleksandr. "But I see you're developing feelings for her that are a lot more than friendship. Does she know?"

Aleksandr started to protest, to insist his father was way off base with such a wild assumption. But as he recalled the heat of her breath against the corner of his neck, and her tiny hands wound through his as she slept cuddled to his chest, he found himself unable to make such a strong protestation.

"I don't think so," he said finally, gazing down into the steaming liquid. "Anyway, you don't have to worry about me forgetting my duties."

"Your duties?"

"The prophecy," Aleksandr replied, before realizing his father wasn't aware of his own knowledge on the topic. It was too late to turn back, though, so he went on. "I know what's expected of me. I won't let you down."

Finn's face went blank, his eyes heavy but unreadable. Slowly, he set his mug of tea down on the small table between them. "Aleksei. You could *never* let me down."

"I only mean—"

"Stop. I can't imagine what must be going through your head right now. I didn't want you to know about this, until..."

"I know. Until Mora was safe."

His father nodded. "Yes, and even then... Aleksei, you have to understand, I don't expect anything of you except that you'll seek out and find your own happiness. I can't tell you what that means, because only you know, and you'll understand when it lands on your lap. Your mother... I didn't see her coming at all, but then she was there, and everything changed."

"What would make me happy is my family safe."

"A burden that should *not* be on one person's shoulders. Let alone yours," his father answered. He stepped forward and knelt at Aleksandr's feet. Finn reached up, enveloping his son's face. "Aleksei, you have the right to seek out your own happiness, and make your own decisions. Do you understand me?

No one can tell you what choices to make. No one should take away your right to choose your direction. No one."

Aleksandr's eyes burned. He nodded, thinking of the many conversations he'd had with Fiona about free will. Words he was no longer sure he believed, after witnessing Fiona attempt to exercise hers and fail so miserably.

"Whatever path you choose, I know you'll do the right thing. For *yourself*, because you deserve to find your own way," Finn said. He swallowed, as his voice caught, choked. "Don't you ever let anyone pressure you into doing anything that doesn't make you happy."

Aleksandr leaned his head against his father's. He cried freely, unfettered by his worries about not being strong enough for others, particularly Fiona, whom he now knew, and was beginning to wholly accept, held his heart in a way not even his mother and father had.

"You can talk to me, Aleksei," Finn said. "I know it's not always the coolest thing to talk to your dad—"

"Far, you're the coolest guy I know."

Finn grinned. "That's because you don't know all that many guys."

"I know the only one who matters."

"You're the best thing I ever did in my life, Aleksei. You and your mora. I never want you to feel alone."

"I don't."

"And if you really care for Fiona, don't let this prophecy bullshit stand in your way. If you need advice, you can come to me, though if you wanna know about... ehm, *specifics*... I'll have to draw the line there because you're still my son, and will always be my baby."

Aleksandr laughed. "Thanks, Far."

"Promise me, Aleksei," Finn said, growing serious again.

"That you won't let anyone stand in the way of what matters to you. Not now, or ever."

"I promise, Far," the younger man answered, not adding that what counted to him most was knowing he was the agent of his family's flourishment, not their destruction.

That no matter how his heart ached for Fiona, he would do what his conscience could most live with.

14
ORIANA

Ahh, power. Delicious, unlimited, maddening power!

Oriana had never, not in all her years in Farjhem, desired the crown. She was a queen in her own right, ruling over The Menagerie in her ivory gowns and unbreakable rules. She lacked the interest, and the desire, in democracy. Rule was absolute, or it was nothing.

And yet, now the crown *had* landed on her lap. She'd had no other choice as she saw it. Either she would scoop it up and set their world back to rights, or her damnable brother would run it into the ground. Even worse if Nerys managed to scramble her way to power, with her saccharine goodness and unreasonable designs toward peace for all.

Harmony was a foolish notion, one meant for fairy tales and bedtime stories. The nature of all sentient creatures was selfish, tainted with everything peace didn't stand for. There was so little to be gained by seeking that elusive dream, and those with the good sense to understand this, like Oriana, thrived in the world as it was, not as she wished it to be.

The Menagerie was the sum total boundary of her

universe. She wished nothing more than to spend the rest of her days there, amongst the flamboyant flora, and the truthful, hedonistic natures of all who flocked to her. Many believed her a villainess, presiding over her epicurean kingdom without scruple. If they had a mind to listen, she would tell them she was living the only honest life among them. To be herself, to exist amongst those like her was the only way to live purely.

Yet to return to that world below meant the need to secure the world above.

Her brother, Agripin, had fled with the drekar somewhere Oriana could not see him. Without marks, they were untraceable, and none of her scouts had brought back anything of use.

And so she had done the one thing she knew would get their attention.

She did not take joy, exactly, in extinguishing the light from those of her kind. Her lack of interest in government and politics did not mean she didn't care for the prosperity of her race. Without this success—or in her words, clientele—The Menagerie would cease to exist with such potency.

But Oriana lacked the patience and, yes, she would admit it, the tactical experience to attempt anything other than an immediate attack to the jugular. Nothing would root the drekar out like an assault on their ethics.

For, how could they claim to stand for freedom, when, to do so came at the expense of their own people?

Oriana's scouts had been useful in that regard, at least. They'd managed to filter word down to Birger, through various means, who undoubtedly carried the news back to his compatriots. And Oriana had been aware all along of Astrid's special variety of empathic senses. She felt every single death.

Every. Single. One.

Ten Empyreans had died for the selfishness of the drekar. Ten. Tomorrow it would be twelve. Then fourteen. Then twenty. Oriana's patience ran thin. She ached to be back in her own kingdom, where everything around her was true, real, and not disguised by intrigue or false intentions.

Whatever it took. She would kill them all if she had to.

Every last one.

"GRAND EMPRESS," THE FEMALE IN THE CRIMSON ROBES SAID, kneeling before her.

"Rise," Oriana commanded. "Remind me who you are again." She hadn't bothered to learn names because they'd never mattered to her in The Menagerie. Those who entered chose their own identity.

"Eldre Maxima, Your Grace."

"Ah, yes, I remember now. The one who hid under a pile of bodies like a coward to escape the halfling."

Maxima lowered her head. "Yes."

"Cease your cowering. I'd have done the same. What good is bravado if it comes at the cost of everything else?"

Maxima smiled, but slowly. "I felt I had more yet to do to assist Farjhem."

"And what do you bring to me today, to that aim?"

"Word that the drekar have received your messages. Clearly and loudly."

Oriana crossed her legs. Her jeweled wrist fell over her knee as she leaned forward slightly. "And how did you come across this information?"

"Our scouts have intelligence from all over corroborating this. They are assembling again. The drekar plan to come to you and beg your forgiveness. To swear fealty."

"Is that right?"

"We've received confirmation of an increase in activity."

"And what makes you think this means they wish to

surrender? They could as easily be plotting my head on a platter."

Maxima stood, straightening her crimson robe. Her red hair was piled high on her head, wrapped in gold rope. "Our scouts have spoken to some of them directly, Empress. They're afraid but believe in your mercy and kindness."

I'd like to see you present proof of either's existence. "I see. And when do you expect them to arrive?"

"I know not," Maxima confessed, appearing uncomfortable once again. "But they're ready for the deaths to stop. As... as are we all."

Oriana stood, a signal dismissing her visitor. "They'll stop when I force them. And not a moment sooner."

Maxima bowed, backing from the room. Her hatred of Oriana was palpable, but the empress wasn't offended or threatened by the sentiment.

Hatred empowered her. Sustained her.

15
CYLER

Cyler awoke to a heated exchange between Astrid and Agripin.

That someone other than Anasofiya was able to rouse Agripin from his languid stupor was miracle enough, but that it should be Astrid, and not he, Cyler, peaked his interest most of all.

"Come with us, Agripin," Astrid pleaded. They stood in the center of the kitchen, a healthy distance separating them. Stian hovered in the far end doorway. "There's nothing for you here."

"You speak of things you know nothing about," Agripin spat. "You say there's nothing for me? There's nothing for *you*, is what you mean. Leave, then. I never invited you."

"It is we who invited you," Stian reminded him, in soothing, overly reasonable tones. Cyler noted that Stian had no center to his personality. He was either straining or as cool as a still lake.

"To a bloodbath. To anarchy," Agripin volleyed back. "I had the good sense to get us as far from Farjhem as possible, and I plan to move us farther still. What can you claim to have done, you peacekeepers, other than throwing us into war?"

Astrid glided closer, but Agripin whipped back as if being struck. She stopped, straightening her posture. "You should not have brought her to Farjhem. Her role was not to be your plaything, but the mother of our male heir. Of all our futures! She should be safe, in hiding, with those who would see to her well-being, not bind her against her will. I shall not lay blame for all of this at your feet, but events transpired as a result of that misstep."

"None of which I could have known as you kept me in the dark," Agripin snapped. "You think I don't know I was your plaything? *You* chose not to reveal the true purpose of the heirs and the prophecy, deliberately keeping me away from such knowledge while purporting to make me your leader. And now we are here. And you may leave."

"Let us take her. We've received word of where her mate can be found. We could deliver her safely to him, where she belongs. They are safe. Protected."

Cyler noted Astrid was careful not to reveal *where* Finn was hiding.

"You will not go near her!" Agripin boomed. He seemed to propagate, and tower over his audience. "I will destroy you where you stand if you take another step in this direction! Leave us!"

Astrid noticed Cyler standing silently behind his master. She cast him a glance, sad but hopeful, and in the few seconds that passed between them, he understood the mantle of reasoning with Agripin had been passed once again to him.

He would be alone.

"As you wish," Astrid said, bowing as she backed away. Stian took her arm, casting a sad look back at the fuming emperor.

"You're going to let them leave?" Cyler questioned, making his presence known.

"And good riddance to them," Agripin sneered, then pivoted in the direction of Anasofiya's room, leaving the conversation, and his once-friends, behind.

"What of me?"

"What of you?"

"Aggie, you can't be completely unaware of what's going on in the outside world? To our people?"

Agripin stopped. "That doesn't concern us. We have more important things at hand."

"Like *what*?"

"Observe your tone, Cyler. My patience with you wears thin."

Cyler's pent-up anger and frustration roiled to the surface. He not only couldn't stop it, he didn't try. "I might be next! You will possibly awake tomorrow, and my mark has been activated. Does that not matter to you?"

"Does my authority mean nothing to you? I've told you my thoughts on the situation many times over."

"Aye, you said it would draw suspicion in Farjhem when we were plotting under their noses, pretending to play nice. I didn't like it, but I understood it. Then. But we're no longer in Farjhem, Aggie. I don't even know if Farjhem still exists after what your untrained lover did!"

Agripin's shoulders stiffened. At his side, his fists drew up. "If you choose to stay in my service, you will continue to respect my authority. My wishes. You will cease to slander your empress, and will treat her with the same respect you *used* to afford me. If you're incapable of such fealty, you are free to leave. I encourage you to. For I'll accept nothing less than your full and complete obeisance should you indicate a preference to stay."

"Aggie—"

"You have until morning to decide. I am taking Anasofiya somewhere safer. A place no one will intrude on us with their unwelcome thoughts or presence. You may join us, or not. You know the requirements."

"Will you, at least, tell me why you keep her here? You used to talk to me. You used to trust in me."

Agripin slackened. His stance shifted, and, for a single moment, he was the old Agripin again. "My singular learning from this mission has been that faith is an illusion. You are a good soldier, Cyler, and have served me well. But I can trust no one except my own self. You want to know why I hold her close to me? If you truly knew me, knew my soul as you claim to, the answer would be clear."

"So I've failed you. That's what you are implying?"

"Or yourself. Sleep on it. Rest your crazed mind, and remove your bloodlust from the equation. You claim to love me, but can you do so when the world around us no longer matters?"

Cyler had no answer. Agripin departed, returning to his wordless sentry.

THROUGH FRUSTRATED TEARS, CYLER SLID THE DAGGER FROM HIS BOOT —a gift from Agripin, all those years ago when he'd located him, lost and directionless outside The Menagerie. Everything, then, all he was and would be, existed toward his desire to stand in the duke's service. How Agripin had found him that night—more importantly, *why*— was a mystery that hadn't mattered to Cyler until they stood upon the precipice of the end of everything.

He observed the sharp glint of the moonlight dancing over the Empyrean steel as he tilted it side to side.

"I'm sorry Aggie, but you've turned mad. I'll continue to serve you, but I will no longer do so blindly," Cyler whispered, as his tears slid down the length of the blade.

Before he could lose his courage, Cyler reached his hand around to his ass and carved off his mark in one deft slice.

It was over as quick as it begun. Cyler stood in the quiet cabin, the sensation of warm blood sliding down his leg to a pool under his heel, forcing his mind to shrug off all other conflicted questions.

16
NICOLAS

A driver met them at the airport in Glasgow. Nicolas had arranged for their own rental once in Portree. Although the vehicle awaited them at their cabin, he feared his ability to drive the several hours to the Isle of Skye in his current frame of mind, which had not ceased racing, even in his dreams.

Mercy's demeanor was unchanged, and she continued wearing the mask of foggy, serene bliss without giving voice to her thoughts under the surface.

How Nicolas would combat her growing beliefs was beyond him. He held tight to his aunt's words about the answer arriving when he most needed it. He'd certainly needed it since Mercy walked into his life.

By the time they arrived at the cottage on the outskirts of Portree, it was past midnight. Nicolas, having dozed only sparingly during their voyage to Scotland, was ready to drop. Mercy, though, had found a second wind the moment she crossed the threshold.

She dropped her bag on the couch and sashayed through

each room, gliding as she inspected their digs for the next however long. In preparation for the open-endedness of their trip, Nicolas had paid cash for the property, so it now belonged to the Deschanel Trust.

"Do you like it?"

"Did you happen to notice the placard near the door? This home pre-dates the Jacobite Rebellion. Do you know how hard-pressed it is to find many buildings on Skye from that era? The English raped this island when they overthrew the clans. The beauty you see around you is not untouched."

"I didn't know that," Nicolas replied. History had never been an inspiring subject for him though he could say that for any subject requiring his focus but no immediate reward. "Were you here during that rebellion?"

"No. Aidrik counseled me to avoid the wars of Man. No good could come of our involvement, not when Men are determined to destroy one another in the name of greed, religion, and uniform living."

"Aidrik was a wise fellow."

Mercy turned and smiled, sadness tinging the corners of the gesture. "That's why they called him Aidrik the Wise. But it's also why they feared him."

"You didn't."

"Not fear, no, but his confidence often intimidated me. He never hesitated because he could see outcomes ten steps ahead. For example, he knew I would eventually grow disenchanted with his unfailing pragmatism. Actually, at the time of this revelation, I still had nothing but stars in my eyes."

Nicolas stepped into the kitchen. A bottle of wine, surrounded by several bottles of water, sat atop a silver tray with a thank you note from the sellers for a quick and easy transaction. He smirked at the wine, and went for the water, grabbing one for Mercy.

"Makes me wonder how Ana managed him," Nicolas said, handing her the bottle. "She's never been one to deal well with lectures, even when they come disguised as wisdom."

Mercy accepted the bottle with a grateful nod, downing half the contents immediately. "Aidrik appeared for Ana when she most needed him. As he did for me, and so many others. Who's to say how the longevity of their union would have been? Then again, she was his evigbond, something I could never claim to have been for him. Many believe evigbond is far stronger than any difference of personality."

The old Mercy, the one who had loved Aidrik, and even deified him, shone through with her words. Her current sad smile melded with Nicolas' memory of Aidrik showing up at *Ophélie* after she'd believed him dead for years. How she appeared to want to smother him in her arms and murder him at the same time.

Nicolas' own jealousy had reared forth at that moment. It was then he'd realized he couldn't let Mercy walk away, even if he hadn't quite known yet how he loved her.

"You spent a lot of time with him here. In Skye," Nicolas said.

"Oh, aye. Many, many years. This was before the Anglo-Saxons fought for territory. The Bronze Age, Men called it, though, for us, time and eras ran far longer and far slower. Establishments were scattered across the isle, such as the hunter gatherers in Staffin, but for the most part, this land was untouched then. A playground almost solely reserved for the two of us."

Nicolas guided her toward the couch and settled her in, covering her with a blanket. A rush of excitement passed through him at how easily she shared these stories. Because of the honesty of the moment, he was determined to keep her talking.

He knelt by the hearth and assembled the kindling and sheets of newspaper. "How many years were you here?"

"Most of our years together as a duo were spent in the hills of Skye," Mercy answered, wrapping the blanket around her. She drew her knees in and took another sip of her water. "Our world seemed so much simpler then. We lived for Emyr and had no worries about anything the world threw at us, for we knew our reward was promised. Everything we did was in tribute to the life given us. Everything." She closed her eyes, taking herself somewhere far away.

Nicolas searched for the question that would keep her engaged and talking, but then she patted the cushion next to her, inviting him.

"Even inside, the air is different," she mused, allowing him to pull her in. He settled the blanket over them both, inhaling the light oiliness of her hair and skin after a day of travel.

The rain arrived. It changed from sprinkles to a steady, driving hammer, raining fists upon the roof and earth around them. Mercy pressed herself tighter to his chest. A chill passed through them both.

The onset of the storm awakened something that had been slowly birthing within Nicolas, a realization he'd come to, but never fully acknowledged. "I want to know everything about you, Mercy," he whispered into her hair, resting his chin atop her head. "I know I've been a shit listener and an even shittier boyfriend, but I think... no, I believe, I can do better."

Mercy pulled her head back against his chest, looking at up him. "You brought me here, didn't you? You must have known it would bring me peace, which means you *have* been listening. The Nicolas I met on Deschanel Island wanted to ship me out on the first plane, and never would have given it another thought."

Was he that same Nicolas? In many ways, he sensed he

was, and the shift that had occurred within him felt isolated to whatever had passed between them. He still watched the world through the same defiant eyes, but the glasses, a newer model of sight, fell over his gaze where she was concerned.

"I feel so unsteady," Nicolas admitted, wrapping his arms around her belly. She folded her arms over his. "No one I ever cared for actually *needed* me. They never needed anything *from* me, but I guess they knew better than to ask. My sisters, Oz. I've always taken more than I've given."

"I can see how you would think so," Mercy answered, tracing her fingers over the knuckles on his right hand. His breath faltered at the intimacy, far more powerful than any sexual encounters they'd had. "But your energy, Nicolas... Emyr pulled me to you for a reason. You bring more to your relationships than you release. A bright light in the darkness."

Nicolas chuckled. "That's a nice way of saying I'm an asshole with a colorful personality."

Mercy smacked his hand, a playfulness he hadn't witnessed in her in months. His heart skipped; his throat felt dry and full of yarn. "Don't put words in my mouth."

"This is the most you've talked to me in weeks. Maybe I just like hearing you speak, even if it is to make fun of me."

Mercy pressed her face to his heart, sighing. "I'm sorry for that. But I thought you couldn't understand what I was going through, and worse, that you didn't believe me."

Nicolas swallowed back his shame.

"Then you told me you wanted to take me away, and I knew you'd come around."

"I want you to be happy, Mercy. That's why I chose Skye. Because you said you were happy here once."

"I'm happy here now."

Nicolas wished beyond words she could break free of the instabilities and uncertainties overcoming her. That she could, suddenly, pronounce she understood none of this was real, except the warmth of Nicolas as he held her in his desperation.

He searched for more words—any words, anything other than discussing the phantom child of her god—but her breathing slowed and then she was asleep in his arms.

"Goddammit, Mercy," he slurred, drunk on his own emotions. "I really do love you."

17
FINNEGAN

Padraig wasn't especially pleased, but Finn didn't much care. He needed a day off, and he needed that day to be with his son.

While he'd been visiting other places and times, his son had been growing up. And he was missing it.

"The sooner we can secure all our futures, the faster you can protect his," Padraig had said, maddeningly, and Finn found himself close to hitting him.

"I won't get so wrapped up in the task that I miss his life, either," Finn snapped back. "It's only a day. We're further along than you thought we'd be, you said, so I'm taking the day."

Padraig threw his hands up in surrender, not agreeing but apparently unwilling to engage.

Finn took advantage of his trainer's pacifist nature and exited without another word.

. . .

He found Aleksandr under the *crann bethadh*, reading *Don Quixote.*

"Shouldn't you be training to save the world?" his son asked, peering over the top of his book.

"Ha. Shouldn't you be chasing your girl?"

Aleksandr frowned. "She wanted to be alone today. I guess I don't blame her."

"I kicked my date to the curb, too. Wanna hang out?"

Aleksandr brightened, lowering the book to his lap. "Heck yeah!"

They wandered the forest, meandering paths Finn was as yet unfamiliar with, ones his son appeared to have expertly memorized.

How long had they been here? Did time pass differently within the boundaries of this wood?

"It's not as big as it seems," Aleksandr explained. He skipped over obstructions Finn couldn't see until he was upon them, veering off path only to find another. "I want to show you something."

"I'm your willing student."

"Skipping one class today for another," Aleksandr replied, chuckling. "Some student you are."

"Your Uncle Jon used to scold me about school all the time when we were boys. Would you believe I wasn't the best student? I thought I could learn more by doing."

Aleksandr shot him a look over his shoulder but didn't respond.

They came upon a clearing at the end of the path. In the center stood a weather-worn structure, overtaken by vines but still standing strong on the foundation.

"Is this where you two sneak off to?" Finn teased.

Aleksandr blushed. "You really don't know what you're talking about."

"I know well enough. But I didn't take the day off to come tease you about a girl."

"You missed me."

"That, and I thought we should talk."

"Far..."

Finn put his hands up. "Not about that. Unless you want to."

"I don't!"

"Okay, we won't. I won't bring it up again. *Today* anyway."

"If Mora were here..."

"Well, see, that's what I want to talk about," Finn replied, gesturing for his son to enter the house. He did, and Finn followed. Although the structure was grown over and the definition of the word *derelict,* the atmosphere was inexplicably welcoming. "You and I are partners. I was wrong to keep things, explanations, from you, even if it was for the right reasons."

"I'm not mad. I know why you didn't tell me about the prophecy."

"Yeah, well, I had my reasons, but they weren't good enough. Much as I hate it, you're growing up. You *have* grown up, and you're not a kid anymore. You have a right to be a part of any big decisions we make. I believe you're mature enough to handle it. Would you agree?"

His son nodded, but the nervous apprehension didn't leave his face.

"I'm starting to get antsy, Aleksei. You know I've been that way since we left New Orleans, but I can't help feeling we're wasting time here while your mora..." Emotion choked the end of the sentence.

"I thought the time travel worked?"

"It did, in the sense that I, you know, traveled through time. Under any other circumstances, my mind would be blown because, holy shit, time travel, ya know?"

Aleksandr giggled.

"But I haven't found Jacob and Amelia, and I'm not cool with spending the next few weeks, months or longer, hoping I eventually land where they are. How many thousands of years and how many locations, would I have to travel before I did? I don't know what Agripin plans to do with your mora, but I don't trust him. Not after what he did to Aidrik."

"If you don't keep training, Far, what would we do, then?"

"That's the thing, Aleksei, I don't know. I don't have a clue. But it isn't in my nature to do *nothing,* and that's how the time here has felt to me. Like I'm doing nothing while your mora suffers, alone."

Aleksandr paused thoughtfully, in such a way that Finn had the strange impression his son knew the answer but believed it would be accepted better if he gave the appearance of considering it. "I think Mora would suffer more if something happened to us. She knows we're safe."

"But she isn't," Finn replied. "And how do you know? That she knows that."

"I can still sense her. It isn't as clear as before because she's far away and not herself, but if she thought we were hurt she would be crazed as she was in Farsengel."

"And you think if we leave here, we will no longer be safe."

"I don't know what will happen," Aleksandr said with a light shrug. "But that's the problem, Far. We don't know what waits for us at the end of the journey. If we go in, and we're outnumbered, and we fail..."

"Even with the Quinlans' help, failure is still on the table. They're a small tribe of peacekeepers."

Aleksandr shook his head. "This isn't everyone. Fiona said

they could raise an army for us. But they won't do it without reassurances. Last time they trusted Empyreans, their whole world imploded."

"What if I can't do this?"

"You can."

Finn studied his son, searching for signs the young man couldn't handle the knowledge thrust upon him He found none. "This is all still so new to me, Aleksei. Barely more than a year ago, I was a lobster fisherman, responsible for no one but myself. I'm still a kid in a lot of ways, too. I wouldn't take back any of this, not a moment, but forgive me if sometimes I flail around like a blind man whose cane has been replaced with rope licorice."

Aleksandr grinned. "I couldn't ask for a better far. Mora would be really proud of you right now, for your patience. You can do this, Far. Dad. Fiona told me that even though Padraig is hard on you, he's shocked how quickly you were able to time travel. It means you're strong. Only Jacob was as strong."

"Or stubborn."

"Definitely stubborn."

"He's driving me up the wall," Finn said with a chuckle. "Padraig has to be the most obnoxious man I've ever partnered with. If I was back in Maine, we'd have already come to blows by now."

"But it's working."

"Not the way it needs to," Finn replied. "Our planet is four and a half billion years old. We don't exactly have the time for me to visit all of them... and cross every inch of the earth."

Aleksandr scrunched his face. For the first time in their excursion that day, Finn saw the boy in his son again. It chilled and warmed him, for opposing reasons. "When you time travel, what do you think of?"

"Padraig has been giving me possible candidates for where they might've gone. But the truth is, he's as clueless as I am."

"So, you're thinking of a place each time?"

"Yes."

"What if... what if instead of a place, you thought of a person? Of Jacob and Amelia?"

Finn leaned forward. "How do you mean?"

"Don't focus on the destination as a place. Think of it as a person. You want to get to Jacob and Amelia, so think of *them* as the endpoint."

How had he not considered this? "Aleksei, that's a brilliant idea."

His son performed a faux flex, but the blush gave away how proud he was to have contributed. "I don't know if it will work, but it's worth a try, right?"

"Of course, it is. You get those smarts from your mother."

Aleksandr watched him, eyes full of adoration, an infinitely pure love Finn often wondered if he'd truly earned. "And you, Far."

It was Finn's turn to blush. "Enough serious talk. How about we go into town, have a pint or two, and forget our troubles for a few hours?"

"I'd love that!"

18
AGRIPIN

Years—many of them—had passed since Agripin last traveled through Siberia. Its utter vastness, the strangeness of isolation and queer people, had left him unsettled. The sensation had ridden him through his journey, whispering in his ear, daring him to stop, set up camp. He did not. Could not bring himself to.

Those residual memories, like a family ghost he could not entirely shake, drove him toward this icy landscape when the need to move on from Finland pushed him out of their comfortable solitude. He could not be the only being who had felt these inexplicable tremors, just under the surface, beckoning, when Siberia came to mind.

That same draw would keep away all those who did not belong there.

He did not belong in that special place, nor did Anasofiya, but this very fact caused him, perhaps blindly, to select it. Maybe all others seeking them out would pause only briefly at the tundra borders before moving on.

The drekar had no known outposts in Siberia. The nearest

was Mongolia, and he'd driven them far north of there, wishing to leave no trail. Astrid and Birger would be along, intent on ripping Anasofiya from his arms. He would die before allowing this transgression to occur, but he preferred to avoid having to make the choice.

Cyler had dutifully scouted ahead, finding a cabin twenty miles from the nearest village, paying the owner triple in cash what it was worth, then wiping his memory. The property was as off the grid as one could get, with solar panels for energy, and a hand-pumped well for water. This particular land sat where taiga met tundra, and vegetation was on the cusp of drying for the season. The climate, so near the Arctic Circle, threatened a constant freeze. With the sun setting not long after noon, and not rising again until seven the next morning, the nights would be long.

Anasofiya thrived in darkness. Agripin had known this the very moment he first met her, in her dreams. That she was an etheric summoner took him longer to ferret out, but he'd never met a creature so in tune with her own darkness, and yet, so afraid of it. Her strength and fear worked decidedly hand in hand, without her ever really accepting or knowing they existed in tandem.

To understand how she came to be aware, how she got here, Agripin also needed to trace his own journey with her. A wild ride that included his mad descent from indifference, to mild interest, to an obsession which had the power to carry him forward or cease his breaths forever.

Agripin prided himself on this ability to fulfill the outside expectations of his enigmatic nature. Was he on your side, or had he become your formidable opponent? Did he fancy you, or wish you gone? He'd enjoyed dangling Anasofiya on the end of this frayed rope, allowing her mind to circle around his intentions and make dozens of interpretations to satisfy her own growing fear.

The truth about his feelings for Anasofiya then was quite simple: He was fascinated by her, this creature of darkness, who had seen so few years but encompassed the soul of the greatest of ancients.

But he did not love her. No, not then. He did not even truly love her when he marched her evigbond to the scaffold, allowing him to die before her eyes.

His feelings, after that pivotal moment, had evolved. Agripin did not wish her dead. He even manipulated matters to save her life. A gift she would never appreciate, but he hadn't done it for her.

While he knew he'd pushed her to the precipice—that the act of witnessing Aidrik's murder would be the very catalyst needed to activate the dormant darkness and save them all—he had not foreseen the shift within himself. From detached ally to the possessed warden. From merely admiring her with the gift of distance, to craving her presence, her body, her mind, her broken soul.

Why attempt to attach words or explanation to this near-immediate phenomenon? Pointless. No one around him could understand or appreciate the surging turmoil within Agripin, the monumental shift that had occurred without his permission or intervention. How his pulse, his very life force, was now connected to her own.

Agripin had been reborn. He was only just learning what to make of the creature he'd become.

Cyler tended the small fire in the other room because the isolated cabin consisted of only three rooms. A tiny bedroom, suited more for a closet, with only a tables-width of space at the foot of the twin bed occupying it. The living room and kitchenette combined to make the second room, and a third, a bathroom, was not en suite but a detached space off the narrow back porch.

Their limited space, thankfully, meant the fire warmed all within the walls.

In Savonlinna, Agripin offered Anasofiya some measure of space, retiring to a leather chair in the corner of her room. Their reduced circumstances did not allow for anything less than intimacy, so he curled next to her on the small bed, imagining the words he would need to compel her.

Such words might not even exist.

Agripin, as he had since he secreted her away from the destruction of Farjhem, lost himself in reflection of his inexplicable need for his empress, the allure, and dangerousness of it.

Many, many years he'd wandered. In the beginning, his desire for companionship was potent, only tempered by the lack of a suitable mate. During his burst of youth, Aanya was the closest he ever came to that sort of love, but in hindsight, he could see his father had been right all along: Her kindness did not make her worthy of his side.

He needed a mate who could match him for wit but recognize his authority. One with no shortage of sexual appetite, but someone who could also withstand his need for long absences. And yes, most importantly, a creature who possessed a skill so rare he could cherish it the way a collector treasures an exceptional find. Another mystic would not even be uncommon enough. He desired the absolute best of the best, the upper echelon of his race. A creature others of his kind would covet until the end of time. An expression of Agripin's dominance in every sense of the word.

Eventually, Agripin had come to accept that his ideals were

loftier than what the world could provide. No male or female he had encountered came close, though several, like Cyler, filled a piece of the void.

He hadn't seen any of this in Anasofiya, at first. He couldn't get past her halfling status, even if her mix leaned more toward Empyrean. Once his mind caught up to what had fallen into his lap, everything had changed. The odds of her accepting him as anything other than an adversary bordered nonexistent.

Persistence came in many forms.

Agripin was so occupied he missed the exact moment she awoke and was entirely unprepared to find her eyes burning holes in his skull.

"This is not the space I imagined for you, but it's where we'll be safe," he explained, despite no question being posed.

"Your imagination doesn't interest me." The sound coming from his obsession was hollow, with a gravelly quality. As if she'd recently emerged from the earth.

"Can I get you anything?" The question, one he'd posed a hundred times since their retreat, had never once been answered. He'd been forced to guess at her needs and meet them without guidance.

Her lips peeled back in a sneer. Red hair clung to the corners of her dry mouth, skin splitting as she grinned, a menacing result. "Nothing you'd be willing to give so easily."

Agripin chose to overlook the implication buried in her words, and instead decided to capitalize on her first bout of talkativeness. "You're safe here. Your mate and child are secure, as well. You may be operating under the assumption I'm here to betray you, but you couldn't be more wrong."

"Your intentions also hold no interest for me," she answered, licking her chapped lips. "You've *already* betrayed me." Physically, she had wasted to a wisp of her former, robust self, but he could not guess at what regression, or growth, had occurred internally.

"Cyler, water!" he cried out the open door. "I could have left you there to die. Or to be dragged out and tortured for your crimes."

"How benevolent of you."

"Don't you wonder why? Even a little?"

"No."

Cyler appeared, thrusting a glass through the open door, avoiding eye contact. Agripin accepted it without breaking his focus on Anasofiya.

He brought the cup to her lips. As with all other times he'd fed her or given her drink, her spirit disappeared entirely with the gesture, retreating somewhere he couldn't reach her. Agripin suspected she couldn't bear to be so beholden to someone she greatly loathed. At least, she had the good sense not to turn away needed sustenance.

Glass emptied, her hardened glare returned. "I have a question for you, Agripin."

He set the tumbler on the windowsill, perking. "Anything."

"Do you still believe you'll escape this alive?"

Agripin forced down the laughter that attempted to spring forth, instinctively. Reminding her of his own freedom, and her lack of it, wouldn't warm her to his cause. "Neither of us knows what the future holds."

"But I do. And fully understand what I can do. What I will do. Do you?"

Agripin brushed the back of his hand over her brow. She didn't cringe at his touch. Her gaze didn't falter, and the lack of fear startled him even more than her words. "I know you've been through a tremendous tragedy. If I could bring Aidrik back, I would."

"Don't mock me," she snapped. "And don't ever speak of him in my presence again. Don't you dare."

"Fair enough," Agripin replied. The room had grown noticeably warmer, not gradually, but in a matter of seconds. "I do have other details I would wish to tell you, but I can tell you aren't ready."

Her sinister grin returned. "No, Agripin. It is you who isn't ready."

A chill struck him, such a stark contrast to the burning heat he now realized radiated from her. "I'll leave you to rest. I regret our waste facilities are not advanced. A trip to the restroom requires a short walk through the cold, but when you are in need of relief, call me. The house is small enough I'd hear your whisper, so there is no need to strain yourself."

"I'm saving my energy," she answered. "As you should be saving yours."

"I'll return in two hours with supper. This darkness outside will continue for much of the days here, but I can light a lamp should you need it."

Anasofiya regarded him from her pillow, head pressed to the side, hands bound above her head. She smiled. "I'll be just fine in the darkness."

19
ALEKSANDR

The morning of Mabon, Aleksandr joined his uncle and cousin for breakfast. He'd been so wrapped up in his world with Fiona that he'd hardly seen them. With Far deep in training, Aleksandr wondered if they felt abandoned here in this strange world.

Seeing the small changes in the space between Jon and Anne, the decrease in hesitance, the growth of intimacy, he realized how much had changed for them as well.

"Where has Nerys been?" Aleksandr asked, ashamed to not know the answer.

"She left two days after we arrived," Jon answered. "Something about a spiritual pilgrimage. Didn't say where, but said she'd be back before we moved on."

"Ahh."

"You really scared your dad the other day," Anne scolded lightly, eating her porridge.

"You never ran off to be with a boy?" Jon asked her, with a peripheral grin.

"You know I never did," she answered, dropping her eyes. "But if I had, I'd never have let my mother worry so."

"I was helping Fiona," Aleksandr defended. "Or so I thought."

Anne dabbed her mouth with a cloth napkin. "We haven't seen her in a few days. Is she okay?"

Aleksandr shrugged.

"Well, check on her! God bless America!" Anne cried. "Goodness, Aleksei, she's your friend."

"I'm not so sure she wants to see me."

"Trust me, she does."

"If she doesn't come out tonight, I'll go to her," Aleksandr answered, then quickly shifted the conversation away from his conflicted heart. "What have the two of you been up to?"

Anne and Jon exchanged looks. "Helping wherever we're needed," Anne answered for both of them. "Jon has been working on small repairs to the homes. Loose table legs, wobbly bed frames, things like that. He even reinforced the altar for tonight, didn't you?"

Jon nodded, grinning through a large swallow of porridge. "We'll see how it holds up."

"And I've been assisting Nora and Deirdre, mostly," Anne went on. "They're teaching me the Quinlan way of preparing food, which is to only use what you can find in nature. I showed them how to make a roux, and I fear nothing will ever be the same here again."

Aleksandr realized this was her attempt at a joke, so he laughed. "Sounds like you two have been keeping busy."

"It's a good busy," Jon said, lacing his hand through Anne's. "Productive kind."

The air shifted as his uncle and cousin watched each other, and Aleksei suddenly felt as if he were intruding on a private moment.

With a smile, he excused himself, thinking a short nap sounded like a great idea before the evening's festivities.

Aleksandr slipped on the burgundy robe given to him by Nora, noting the burly heft of the fabric but also, in contrast, how his spirit felt somehow lighter wearing it.

She'd left him a basket filled with dried herbs, plants, and seeds. When he'd asked what he was to do with it, Nora's eyes twinkled, and she advised him to observe and take it all in. Magic ran in his blood, too. He would know.

Days before, Fiona had explained, *Mabon is a time of mysteries. A time of balance. For us to both honor our goddess, Morrigan, and all the goddesses before and after her, but also to take the time to enjoy the fruits of our harvests.*

Earlier that same day, he'd seen two of the Quinlans, Nora's sisters, adorning a circle of stones with pine cones, acorns, and legumes. Later, his far told him they were decorating the burial grounds to honor their ancestors.

"Padraig schooled me," he confessed. "I know no more than you do about what's gonna go down tonight."

"Have you seen Fiona?"

Finn wrapped an arm around his shoulder, shaking his head. "I'm sure she'll be out tonight. Padraig tells me they look forward to this all year."

Anne fetched him that evening, donning a deep red cloak of her own. "Come! The festivities are starting."

She laced her hand in his, tugging him out of the hut he shared with his far, through the path of crunching leaves, toward the smell of burning spices and the rich earthy tones of the *crann bethadh.*

Aleksandr's breath caught as he took in the whole of the scene.

Torches blazed, stuck in the ground. A bed of autumn leaves, fallen and dead for the season, were no less beautiful as their earthy notes glinted off the torchlight.

Root vegetables had been strung together in beautiful decorations, looped around the branches of the great tree, spiraling around the bark and up into the lower branches. An altar large enough to seat half the tribe occupied the center, adorned with a rich feast of venison and herbed squash and apples.

But it was the swirl of red and orange, brown and yellow, dancing, twirling, as the Quinlans surrendered themselves to their celebration, humming an ancient hymn in harmonious unison, that landed the hardest against his heart.

They honored the dying land, and the cold months ahead, but Aleksandr had never seen anything so electric. So *alive*.

He was torn from his reverie as Nora looped his elbow through hers, spinning him as she danced across the gilded earth. She guided him toward the altar, where a pitcher of fresh cider rested next to an arrangement of wooden mugs. "Have some," she offered, pouring him a drink.

The apple and cinnamon overwhelmed his senses, only adding to the irresistible reverie of light and rich scents of joy and offering.

"Tonight, light and darkness are one," she whispered, backing away. "We honor them both, in this passing of warmth to the cold of winter, as we thank each for having a role to serve in our lives." In her eyes, Aleksandr saw Fiona's reflection, could imagine Nora in her youth as she once was, and as she seemed on this magical eve.

In a grove to the left of the great tree, Jon and Anne embraced, the red and orange of their mantles creating a seamless blend. He drew another sip from his cider, the blur of light and darkness as the Quinlans spun to the lure of their songs and offerings sending him to a light stagger. His heart was full, but the cause of this wholeness wasn't there to feel it, and experience it, with him.

Aleksandr closed his eyes, swaying to the soft music, drunk on the moment. Tears appeared in his eyes, and he didn't know where they came from, but he surrendered to them, overawed.

From behind, soft arms wrapped around his waist. He drew in the familiar and enchanting scent, letting his other senses make the identification, even though his heart already knew.

"Where have you been?" he asked. The words, now on his tongue, seemed an accusation. *How could you abandon me when I was on your side?*

"Come with me," she beckoned, but Aleksandr refused to turn. He couldn't look at her. His heart couldn't handle it. The freedom of Mabon had both released him from that pain, and also solidified it and given it roots, a realization he could never un-realize.

"Aleksei. Please."

He still didn't turn, but this time, he allowed himself to be led by the hand, eyes closed, following the sound of the hypnotic refrains and the cloying autumnal aromas. The energy of love radiated from all directions.

Fiona tugged him gently, pulling him farther away from these comforts until they were no more than a subtle vibration passing over the surface of his skin.

When, at last, she halted, she asked him to open his eyes.

Aleksandr relented.

Fiona's mahogany curls reflected against the moonlight and took hold in his chest, burrowing into his heart next to the memories of her resting against his skin, her breath tickling his neck.

Aleksandr swooned, and she caught him.

"Let's make our own offerings," she said, handing him back the basket of herbs and plants he didn't remember dropping.

Fiona knelt at the base of a small sapling, frail in comparison to the vast *crann bethadh*, which now seemed miles away. "Thank you, blessed goddess, for the continued health and prosperity of our people. For the food on our plates and the shelter over our heads. For our continued health and joyous spirits."

Aleksandr repeated her words, as if in a trance, his soul still loose and unattached.

"Equal hours of light and darkness, we celebrate the balance of Mabon and ask the Gods to bless us. For all that is bad, there is good. For that which is despair, hope reigns supreme. For each moment of pain, equal moments of love. For all that falls, a chance to rise again. May we find balance in our lives as we discover it in our hearts.

"And thank you, most of all, for showing me the balance in my own life. For bringing a light to my darkness. For leading Aleksei to me," Fiona whispered, scattering the remaining contents at the base of the tree.

Aleksandr stood abruptly. The blood rushed to his head, and he pressed his hand into the bark of the tree to stabilize himself. "Don't say that!"

"Say what, the truth?" Fiona replied softly.

He stumbled over the root of a nearby tree, grasping forward. "I need to go back."

"Aleksei."

He stepped blindly forward, unsure of his footing. Aleksandr had no direction, except away.

Then her arms were around him again. Steadying him. "You're safe with me."

"You left me," he charged, realizing only then that he was crying. Had been for a while. *If this is love, I want nothing to do with it!*

"I needed to think. So did you."

"And was it worth it?"

"Don't look at me like that. Not all of the thinking was about you. I spent so many years believing in something that wasn't real. During that time, I never thought of myself as a romantic, or an idealist, but my behavior reflects me as being both. Maybe those things aren't so bad, really, but they were in this case. I let myself be blinded by hope, ignoring reason altogether."

Aleksandr swallowed.

"I didn't mean to hurt you by being silent."

"You didn't," he lied.

Fiona sighed. "I did, and I'm sorry, but I needed to know where I went wrong. I'm still not completely sure, but I know being here with you is right."

"Did you forget our futures are already pre-determined and that people may *say* we have a choice, but truly there are no options? No choice if we aren't selfish and horrible people?"

Fiona stepped before him. She lifted his hand and pressed it to the side of his face, covering hers over like a soft veil. "The other heir isn't even born yet, Aleksei. You're free to love whomever you wish tonight." Her other hand came up, touching his opposite cheek. "Do you love me, as I think you do?"

"Don't ask me that," Aleksandr choked. "You know I do. You know I love you."

Before they took another breath, Fiona's lips met his, and the world stopped. Time ceased to be linear, as all memories of her flooded him, in random order, every moment he'd known love for her, and in return.

"The winter ahead will be cold, in more ways than even we know, but tonight I am yours, Aleksei, and you are mine. Maybe that's enough."

"It's not enough," Aleksandr gasped between her lips, a confession he was no longer unsure of because it was real. Truth could be terrifying, but it was solid, as firm as the ground they stood on. "It will never be enough."

"Then we'll cross that path together when the time comes," she vowed, pushing his wrap back over his shoulders. The light sound it made as it crushed the leaves awakened him, pulling him from the reverie he'd been unable to shake.

Aleksandr freed Fiona of her own robe, lifting her in his arms and pressing her gently against the bark of the tree. Their tree.

The confusion of his youth fell away as he loved her by the protection of the goddess and the moonlight.

20
CYLER

Inevitably, it was Agripin who drove Cyler to Anasofiya's bedside.

Their blowout began with an innocent question. Cyler needed to know how long Agripin planned to live like this. Their resources were not unlimited, and winter would be settling in soon. Cyler could arrange for more provisions, but it was not a decision he could delay.

"You think I don't *know* what you did?" Agripin accused, flinging the empty water glass at the wall, with all the disregard of tossing a towel aside. The thick tumbler merely crashed to the ground, without breaking.

"What are you talking about?"

"You prance around here now, smug. Walking on air. You think I've missed the change in you? That I'm so preoccupied with the empress that I don't see how *different* you've become? Aye, and I know why. I know why."

"Truly, I'm shocked you've noticed a damn thing about me," Cyler retorted before he could stop himself. Agripin, even then, as always, had the power to make his blood boil the way no other creature could.

"Your childish notions of attention have no place here," Agripin snapped. "I've given you everything, Cyler. I rescued you from a future under the thumb of my hedonistic sister. I gave you the world you wanted. The one you most desired. I asked for only one thing in return. One!"

No, you asked for everything. And I willingly gave it. "Would you have watched me die?"

Agripin scoffed, waving dismissively. "You would not have died! My sister wouldn't dare. She would not deign to anger me."

"She loathes you, Aggie. I'm only shocked I was not her first target! You think she *respects* you? She's stolen your crown and kingdom, you fool!"

Agripin struck him. Cyler crashed into the wall, unprepared for the severity of the blow.

"So you're no more than a jealous creature after all," Cyler accused, cradling his throbbing jaw.

"The next time, you'll not be around to make an assessment of what I *am*."

"You're proving everyone right. They called you a despot. Aye, I see now you are. You never intended to grant my freedom. You would have seen me die before relinquishing your control."

"I might yet witness it if you continue speaking," Agripin warned, but the fight had left him. He grabbed his cloak from the rack and fled out the front door.

Cyler gaped at the entrance for an untold time, considering the implication of the words spoken between them. The subtle power dynamic had always been at play, a silent factor in the master-soldier relationship. By never speaking of the intricacies, Cyler could imagine Agripin's care for him to be far more than simply a commander. The lack of confirmation gave him peace.

And now Agripin had, for all intents and purposes, confessed he would rather see Cyler dead than free.

Cyler didn't recall his next steps or how he ended up standing at the foot of Anasofiya's bed, sounding off his thoughts to the sleeping empress.

"I no longer know who my master is. I fear the monster he's becoming," he said, needing to hear the words aloud. Seeking new strength in this raw truth.

"Becoming?" Anasofiya opened her eyes, smiling. "Cyler, your master has always been a monster, only in a different colored vest."

Cyler started hitting the wall behind him. He never considered she might wake or engage him. "You say that because of what he did to you. But you didn't know him as I did. You never had the honor of seeing him in his glory and wonder. You can't fathom the sadness in this shift."

"Unbind me, and you can pour your heart out," she prodded.

"You know I can't."

"Won't. Even after Agripin is willing to toss you aside as if you're nothing, you insist on remaining his dog."

Cyler snorted. "And yet I'm not the one tied to his bed."

"Whether the binding is physical or mental, we're just debating semantics."

"Serving Agripin has always been a choice."

"Yes. *His* choice."

Cyler glared at her, questioning his judgment for ending up in a conversation with her to begin with.

"I have nothing against you, Cyler. You've done as asked, and my quarrel isn't with you. But don't come to me and whine of the creature your master is becoming when we both know you've chosen to be blind to it all along."

"Yes, I believed in him. Before I even knew him, I had faith in him. You can't know that level of fealty, halfling."

Anasofiya regarded him with something nearing sympathy but bordering closer to cold disgust. "What reward have you been given for this loyalty? I'm asking this question honestly, not to rile you up. What reward, other than being near him, has he given you?"

"Being at his side was enough," Cyler admitted. He didn't quite know why he was opening himself up to the empress, whom he felt, at best, indifference for and, at worst, loathing for taking Agripin away from him.

Perhaps it was that, standing above her. Finally, the shift of power was his. With her, he was in control as he had never been with Agripin.

"What do you believe in, Cyler? If you answer Agripin, so help me, I'll rip free—"

"I'd like to see you try," he goaded. "I believe in self-preservation."

"Everyone believes in that. It's ingrained in the psyche of all creatures. What else?"

Cyler wanted to put a boot through her impudent mouth, but her question sincerely gave him pause. "When I was young, all I wanted was to see battle at Agripin's side. As I aged in his service, I never thought of my goals as independent of his."

Her soft tone jarred him. "I suggest you start thinking of them that way, and soon."

"You think you can drive us apart? I see what you're doing. It won't work, wench."

"I don't need to do anything," Anasofiya answered. "The deed was done when you let him execute Aidrik. Yes, you allowed it, Cyler, for while you may not have much power over him now, you once did. More than you realized."

"Executing Aidrik was the only option once the Senetat discovered us. Someone had to take the fall to protect the rest of us, and yes, I chose Aidrik over my master," Cyler defended. "My loyalty was to Agripin and his prosperity, not to you or your mates. I counseled him toward the only way out."

"Nonetheless, at that moment, your master changed," she said in her most reasonable tone. Too much for a woman who'd been bound for weeks, powerless. "Both of our realities have shifted beyond what we wanted for ourselves, Cyler. We have that, at least, in common."

"He'll never release you," Cyler told her. "And don't look to me to convince him otherwise. I do not have that authority, and even if I did, I have no reason to exercise it."

"I said we had something in common, not that we had any chance at friendship," Anasofiya said with a slow smile. "The longer he keeps me bound, the more of a danger he poses to you. He's insanely jealous of anyone who might come near me or threaten his power over me. That isn't only my take on things. You know this, too."

"I swore an oath to him," Cyler said, weakening, realizing, as the words flowed, he meant to leave. That had been his plan since before they landed in Siberia. He only needed the push.

"An oath of service is not a one-way promise," she reminded him. "You've more than lived up to your end of the bargain."

"It also isn't meant to hold up only when times are easy," Cyler countered, but for every word he spoke aloud, hundreds more churned internally, convincing him of the truth of his situation.

"Okay," she said, watching him. "Then if you want to help him, really help him, you'll separate him from his madness.

That may be your only chance to save him if you are really so bound to your love and fealty."

Cyler stared at her incredulously. "How do you propose I do that, in his current frame of mind?"

"*I* am his madness, Cyler. Release me, and you release your master."

"He would kill me, without a second thought."

"Come with me."

Cyler snorted. "With you? Why? Where?"

Anasofiya propped herself up on her elbows and looked Cyler square in the eyes. "Take me to Finn."

21

ORIANA

Oriana stretched her weary body over the ivory settee, exhausted with the weight of everyone's compounding ineptitudes.

Empress, let us try another tactic.

Perhaps we need more scouts.

Yes, scouts. We'll increase our scouts.

Have we tried to palaver with them?

If we continue murdering our own, who will be left to govern?

"Out of my sight! My presence! I'll have your marks activated if you say one further word!"

The Senetat, who was supposed to exist to serve *her,* shuffled off in shame. Had they more sense, they'd have considered looking less relieved to be free of her attendance.

Oriana did not outright dismiss the last claim, though. The logic there, at least, was sound. More scouts would do naothing against the iron will of the vagrant drekar, and she had no desire to talk.

Fretting over the future of their race, though, that was logical. And had she any long-term designs on ruling this dying race, the appeals might have resonated with her.

Not that any of those robed fools would be sad to see Oriana retreat into her basement kingdom. They thought her an autocrat, with an irrational temper. They feared for the future of Farjhem with her on the throne.

She enjoyed their tension far too much to let them in on her secret. Let them dangle. Let them squirm. Let them rue the day they did not bend to her whims, without question.

In this world of sunshine and rebirth, their fear of her remained her solitary joy. Nothing had gone her way since taking the mantle. Did no one appreciate the sacrifice? She had placed her own life, her own empire, on hold to save a race that couldn't be bothered to find their own way.

Why had the drekar not shown their craven faces yet? Oriana had gone directly to her most aggressive plan, not wishing to waste time, confident the deaths of their own would be the catalyst to stir them to immediate martyrdom.

She planned to accept their fealty and execute them on the spot, showing mercy by killing them quickly, as an expression of her relief and gratitude to end this. Then, Oriana could leave Farjhem in the hands of her most trusted pet and retreat to the world where she belonged.

But she could not return until the drekar were extinguished... and they would not be extinguished without luring them to Farjhem.

No flaw existed in her plan. So, what, then?

"Empress." The impudent one, Maxima, appeared at the double doors of the great hall.

Without pulling her gaze away from the ornate tableaus in the ceiling, Oriana waved a hand at the eldre.

"I have a thought that may interest you," she ventured,

footfalls echoing across the marble. The sound was like thunder in Oriana's aching skull.

"By all means, let us not wait a moment longer."

Maxima's footfalls grew closer, her step neither tentative nor quick. At that moment, it occurred to Oriana what grated her most about the creature: Maxima did not seem to fear her.

"Well, get on with it."

"Your—our—efforts to lure your brother and the Runeans, while brilliant, may not have appealed to them in the way intended."

"Clearly, you are a masterful observer."

"What I intended to say is," Maxima pushed, stepping closer. Too close for Oriana's comfort, and far too close for a subject to a master. "Perhaps we are attacking the wrong Empyreans."

"Wrong?"

"We may have miscalculated their humanity," Maxima replied. "They claim to stand for freedom and posterity, but their actions of late prove it to be wrong. Unfortunate, but they've revealed that hand, and now we can course correct."

"You're failing to get on with your idea."

"We must get our hands on one of them. One of the drekar," Maxima answered, growing excited. "Particularly one of the leaders. They may not care about the lives of those bearing a mark, but the loyalties among and within the drekar, run deep, spanning thousands of years. Murdering those with the mark, you see, is doing nothing. Will never do anything."

Oriana leaned her head toward the eldre. "And you've come to know this, how?"

Maxima bristled, but it was unclear why. "The Senetat has always made a business of knowing the modus operandi of our enemies."

"Is that so? Then why have they been allowed to run free,

gallivanting across the world, raping Our Father's good name?"

"With respect, we've caught and punished *many* drekar over the years."

Oriana rolled her eyes. "And yet, the ones who matter remain untouched. Taunting us."

"Past failures do not equal future ones."

"We'll see," Oriana barked. Her mind began to wander, toward the trill of her scarlet macaws, and elaborate palms and bird of paradise. How boring, how mundane and trite the dealings of politics were!

"Have you reached your point, Eldre Maxima?"

"Very nearly. I come to you now because we have received word Astrid and Stian, the terrakinetic, are on the move, preparing to cross into the British Isles. There are few drekar as treasured as Astrid. If we were to secure her into our custody..."

"Say nothing more. Do it. Act on it. You don't need my permission," Oriana snapped, impatient.

"Of course, Grand Empress. I'll move on the task immediately. I can tell the others to cease the genocide?"

"The genocide may or may not cease when I'm satisfied we've reached our intended goals," Oriana retorted, boiling with agitation over the eldre crossing a line from providing a plan to assuming she could give the empress orders as well.

Maxima backed away, too quickly for her station. Oriana couldn't resist one final dagger at the brazen creature. "If, however, you should return without Astrid, you'll find me not only disappointed, not only unappreciative, but a furious manager. Without mercy or understanding or regard for your life. Failure would indicate you have no regard for the lives of your kind."

"Aye, Empress. My life is yours, as is my loyalty. I submit to your mercy."

Before Oriana could loll her head back toward her comfortable vantage point of the ceiling, she caught something she was most certainly not intended to: disgust in Maxima's eyes. A sly, snake-like grin had appeared as she bowed through the open doors and pivoted to leave.

22

ALEKSANDR

Finn once told Aleksandr there was nothing as calming as a decent rainstorm. The drops pelting the windows and the ground outside, the canopy of sky shades of dark blue and grey, and tickling warmth from the hearth running straight to your bones.

Despite the wicked storm raging that afternoon, casting a murky darkness over the land that confused their sense of time, Far was as on edge as Aleksandr had ever seen him. His right foot tapped to an invisible rhythm. One hand clenched into a fist and unclenched, repeatedly.

"You've done this before," Padraig reminded him, affecting a soothing bedside manner Aleksandr actually found condescending. He was fairly sure Far thought so too from the white in his knuckles.

"And they weren't there," Finn answered through gritted teeth. Studying him closer, Aleksandr witnessed the trembling in his far's right foot when it came to a momentary halt. To Padraig, he seemed angry, but Aleksandr knew better.

His far was terrified.

"It was only your first attempt," Padraig said in a calm, reasonable manner as if people closed their eyes and ended up in thirteenth century London all the time.

"And I still have no idea what I'm doing."

"Which is why you need to practice."

"Practice! And what if next time I don't end up in a cathedral in the middle of the night, but instead a war zone?"

Padraig cocked his head to the side, twisting his lips. "Then you come back. I don't see the problem."

As the two bickered, Aleksandr's mind wandered to the night before and the moonlight reflecting against Fiona's milky skin. How he'd loved her, and then watched as she slipped into sleep, unable to find his own rest despite the peace falling over him like a comfort blanket.

I know I love you, Fiona, he'd whispered against her arm. Gooseflesh rose to the surface of her skin when she smiled in her sleep.

Loving her was a dangerous business, though, and Aleksandr had stepped over a threshold better left uncrossed.

What if it didn't have to be? The child in him asked this question after every strong argument to the contrary.

No child here, the man answered. *Children don't love like this. A man does.*

But what if it wasn't really love? How could he ever tell the difference between true love and youthful infatuation? He might appear old enough to be his far's younger brother, and he'd certainly matured very fast, faster than most, but the fact remained he hadn't even walked the earth for a full year.

Love is supposed to be scary. Mora said so, and Far did, too, in his own way. When people are scared, they cast doubts on what frightens them.

Fine, maybe he was afraid. Sometimes, he was his own

worst enemy. But no rationale changed the responsibilities ahead for him.

Black and white. That's how people who are unsure think, because it's safe. Ever try reasoning in the middle?

Aleksandr enjoyed thinking, and in the grey, thank you very much, but entertaining any avenues leading to a future with Fiona was reckless and would only make this more difficult than it already was.

Only if none of the avenues could give you what you wanted and *save everyone you care about.*

"You are a time traveler, Finnegan," Padraig was saying, his pitch rising higher and higher as he grew further frustrated with his apparently stubborn student.

See, time travel. Time travel is a very viable option.

Time travel?

Aleksandr turned toward the window. Somewhere beyond, Fiona helped her mother prep for the evening's supper. Was she thinking of him, too?

Focus. Who's acting like the child, now?

Time travel, the other voice repeated, as if it meant something.

Are you dense?

"Apparently," Aleksandr muttered under his breath.

A future with Fiona would be hard, sure, but what about a past?

A past. All at once the implication of his subconscious hit him full throttle. The problem of his love for Fiona was only an issue at the moment.

But ten years ago?

A hundred? A thousand?

Good thinking.

Well, sure, it was a lovely thought, but seeing as time travel wasn't one of his abilities, the idea was as good as useless. And even if his far could figure out a way to take him along on one of his own adventures, he'd never be able to talk him into *leaving* him there.

No harm in daydreaming. Where would you take her, if you could?

Aleksandr furrowed his brow. Hmm, where would he go? He'd inherited his love of history from his far, and most of what he read was an escape into the past.

Then, most of history was bloody and unstable.

The answer might be right in front of you.

Aleksandr hardly noticed his far squeezing his hand. He wanted to follow the previous thought, even if it led nowhere.

Where would he take Fiona if they had eternity?

He saw her, the deciduous leaves tangling in the cascade of chestnut hair as she flew like an elven princess, through the forest and into the glen, their own private escape.

The answer truly was right in front of him.

He would go back in time here. Right here.

Aleksandr's eyes closed, and he couldn't help surrendering to the beauty of this fantasy. Spinning her in his arms beneath the magical veil of the *crann bethadh*. Tracing kisses down her collarbone, coming to rest with his face against her heart.

Desire for this reality took a powerful and immediate hold upon Aleksandr, and, with the force of a hurricane, spun him upside down and around, stealing his breath.

It continued like a gale force, happening to him way too fast to register none of this was in his head anymore, but happening. Really happening.

The whirling stopped. Rich scents of seasonings filled his nose. A light wind passed across the surface of his skin, and he breathed it in.

"Aleksei! What the hell happened?"

Aleksandr re-opened his eyes, startled by the distress in his far's tone, and still reeling from whatever tumult had just overcome him.

At first, he didn't detect the problem. They sat, side-by-side, as they had for the past hour, in Padraig's hut. He hadn't spotted Padraig, but perhaps the draoi had slipped off to give Finn some peace.

Small trickles invaded the tough façade of his reality, one at a time.

The floor was dirt now, no longer solid wood.

Where the door should have been, an animal skin hung.

In the corner, where Padraig slept with his wife, Regan, lay a pallet of straw. No longer the strong oak frame with the cedar nightstand.

"Aleksei, answer me," Finn demanded, firmer now.

"I... I don't know." *You know.*

"Padraig was standing right in front of me and then he disappeared into thin air. I didn't even blink. He was just gone."

"And the door. The floor. Everything is different. And where did the light go?"

"This wasn't like before," Finn answered. He stood, taking a tentative step over the dirt under his feet. "When I went to London something specific happened. I didn't feel anything this time."

Aleksandr's pulse quickened. He found himself lacking his far's courage, unable to stand. "What did it feel like the first time?

"Like someone strapped me to a chair and turned the world upside down."

Sounds familiar, doesn't it?

Aleksandr didn't need to ponder the situation further. He'd done this, and he knew it. His strong desire to pull Fiona back in time to the only place he'd ever known real peace had drawn him exactly there.

Only one creature on earth had the power to time travel.

A draoi.

Hey, we got that out of the way!

"Obviously, we're not in Kansas anymore," Finn said to himself. Aleksandr wondered where Kansas was. "I don't think we should stay here, Aleksei. I can't explain why, but I have a strong feeling this isn't where we should be."

Aleksandr had different ideas. His heart raced around the possibility.

But his far was correct. This wasn't right. He didn't know if it was the *when* or the *where* or a combination of the two, but his sense of wrongness had quickly replaced the wonder in what he'd done.

"How do we get back, Far?"

"There wasn't a button or a trigger, I was just sitting in Westminster Abbey one moment, getting grilled by the abbot, and then I was on my back with Padraig standing over me foaming at the mouth. I don't remember doing anything to make that happen."

"That instills a lot of confidence."

"Now's not the time to be a smartass."

"Sorry."

Finn stepped across the dirt, peering around the room as if something might jump out at them. "The abbot thought I was sick, and he was going to kick me out."

"Were you scared?"

"Scared?" Finn paused. "Yeah, I guess I was. Everything about me was suspicious of the guy. I half-expected to wake up in a moldy jail on Fleet Street."

"Maybe your fear brought you back."

Finn gave a nervous laugh. "I'm pretty damn scared right now, kid. We're both still standing here."

He's not the one who brought you here, remember?

Aleksandr had a strong suspicion fear was not the only way to return.

You only need ask the goddess, Padraig had said, many times. *She will aid you in your time of need.*

Aleksandr found his courage and stood. One step, and then another, and he was at his far's side.

He threw himself that direction, wrapping his arms tight around Far's waist, fingers digging into the thick muscle of the older man's back. Finn, interpreting the gesture as fear, held him back, whispering how it would be all right.

Goddess, Aleksandr pleaded, picturing Fiona's face as he thought the words. *Bring us home. We don't belong here.*

"I'm sorry, Aleksei, I shouldn't have told you I was afraid."

His far's voice started strong and then faded, carried by a wind he couldn't see.

"You both disappeared!" Padraig cried in a near-shrieked voice. "Both of you!"

"Take it down a notch," Finn said, squinting at the sudden rush of light.

"What happened?"

"You're the expert," Finn answered, but the bite was gone from his tone. He watched Aleksei closely, taking his own stock of what had happened.

Padraig studied them both, frowning in suspicion. "Nora will have my hide if we're late for the festivities. We can talk about it later."

THEY ENTERED THE CIRCLE IN FRONT OF THE *CRANN BETHADH*, WHERE the tribe had already gathered to break bread on the second and final night of their Mabon celebration. The air was ripe with apples, spices, and distant rain.

By instinct, Aleksandr's eyes fell on Fiona. Her hand dropped to the ground on her left, motioning at the empty space. *For you.*

Finn nudged him. "Go on, kid."

Aleksandr blushed and rushed off toward Fiona. Her outstretched hands held a bowl of fragrant stew.

"I saved this for you," she said.

"Thank you." His stomach let out a fierce growl, but he couldn't eat if he tried.

Aleksandr could sit at her side forever.

23
CYLER

Cyler departed before his blood could cool.

He left without Anasofiya, despite her finest efforts to convince him she should make the journey. He didn't owe her an explanation about where his thoughts were with this decision. Let her guess, he thought. He couldn't care less what conclusions she came to on her own.

In the end, his destination was the same, another detail he'd failed to mention to her before departing. Anasofiya's logic wasn't lost on him. Removing her from Agripin's sway was the answer. She was not wrong there, but if Cyler had attempted to secret her away, they'd not have gotten far. Their transportation—Stian—was no longer an option, and Cyler's voyage would be on foot, overland, until he could reach civilization.

On the other hand, though a painful and sobering detail to realize, Agripin would not go after Cyler alone. He might or might not grieve his absence. The master had more important matters to occupy his thoughts.

With these views in mind, Cyler decided the only way to

free Agripin of his madness was to find Finn and put the task in his hands.

THEIR CABIN SAT TWENTY-FIVE MILES FROM THE SMALL ARCTIC TOWN of Salekhard. From there, he would need to cross the Ob River to Labytnangi, and find a train. In pleasing weather, this would be a task, but with the ground frozen solid and the wind chill on the negative end of the scale, it was also dangerous. His fiery Empyrean blood would only go so far.

Another reason dragging Anasofiya with him was out of the question. Agripin would rage if she were taken from him, but Emyr only knew how he might react if anything happened to her. Something irreversible.

Before Astrid left, she'd given him a location where he could leave a message for her, should the need arise.

That need had arisen. Cyler only hoped the channel still lay available to him.

More, he hoped, should they succeed in their task, Agripin would be capable of returning to the creature Cyler had walked all ends of the earth for.

THE LEGEND OF GRAND DUKE AGRIPIN HAD REACHED CYLER LONG before he ever beheld the prince. Under the Scholars' tutelage, he'd absorbed the details of the duke's glories in the Second Runean War, and tales of him seeking out and destroying the rebels once the war ended. For centuries, he'd wandered the earth, never returning to Farjhem, in order to protect and secure the glory of Our Father by ridding the earth of the rebel scourge.

Cyler learned later, much later, that Agripin had done no such thing, spending that time away in self-exile, as far from his father as time and distance would allow. He never rooted out a single enemy, though he located plenty of whiskey bottles.

At the time, though... ahh, how Cyler had admired the duke! Dreamt of a life in his service, at his side. When, at last, the duke made his triumphant return to Farjhem, coinciding with the graduation ceremonies of that centuries' batch of fledglings (Cyler among them), Cyler cherished his timing as fate.

He'd searched for ways to make his move. Knowing he'd have a limited amount of time to appeal his case to the duke, he had prepared and re-prepared his words. But nothing prepared him for the throngs of Empyreans vying for Agripin's attentions. His homecoming was a sea of Empyreans all wanting their own audience, their own earful of his adventures and wisdom.

In the end, he was never granted the adoration he'd waited so long for. In his hundred years, he had never known such powerful, soul-aching disappointment.

Fate, or perhaps something more sinister, landed Cyler a coveted invitation to The Menagerie, where Oriana had been determined to turn him not only into a member, but one of her most loyal. She'd thrown at him her most coveted pet, and Cyler was "initiated" upon a dais before all the other pets and members, experiencing his first sexual encounter with someone he did not know, in front of a crowd of dozens.

In his youth, Cyler had struggled against the rules set up in The Menagerie. Of human "pets" brought in under the guise of having avoided worse fates in the outside world. They'd been given such restrictive rules that the cost of their Eden was complete and total submission. Cyler's quest to right this injustice had resulted in his first true heartbreak, and, he was determined, his only.

Then Agripin had shown up, when Cyler least expected it, at his absolute lowest point, and lifted him, buoyed him and held him to his breast. Promises were made; vows exchanged. And while Cyler had struggled against Oriana's mixed ethics and moralities, he'd somehow never questioned Agripin's. That the duke could ever do serious wrong never entered his mind.

Centuries later, Cyler viewed his youthful foolishness for what it was: blind love. And now, once again, despite the promise made to himself all those years ago, his heart had been broken.

Is the worst of it that the old Agripin is gone, replaced by this mad version of his former self? Or am I, now, finally seeing him for who he always was?

Versions of this question had played across Cyler's stream of consciousness for weeks, his intention in the query evolving with further exposure to the duke's changes. The answer, neither before or now, was immediately evident.

And would not be, Cyler knew, until he could release his master from the madness.

24
ANASOFIYA

Anasofiya closed her eyes, riding the rhythm of Aidrik's slow breaths, the light rise and fall of his chest. The rest of him was entirely still, despite never being at rest.

"Are you happy, Kjære?"

She looked up. "Where's this question coming from?"

His strong, calloused hand stroked the length of her back. "I ask due to our change in circumstance. Now that Finn rests with us," he answered, his tone careful. "You wear his ring. This matters to you."

Anasofiya sensed evidence of insecurity, despite it being a trait he had never demonstrated in front of her before. She chose her words cautiously. "You gave me this gift, Aidrik. I couldn't live without him, but I also couldn't live without you. I never dreamed of a world where I could have you both. I can't think of a better gift."

"A day may come when I cannot look after you as I would like to," he whispered. His hand ceased. "Finn is a good man. Strong. His care for you genuine."

Anasofiya chuckled nervously. "We're about to bring a child into this world, and you're talking about leaving it?"

"Preparing for the future is not a luxury, Kjære. Children of

Men secure financial insurance policies. I have nothing comparable, except to ensure you are not unprotected."

"And there you go again, accusing me of being unable to take care of my own damn self," she teased, afraid of his words. What they might mean, if she peeled back the surface.

"You indict me of unflattering behaviors," he returned, briefly playful. "I mean not to scare you. Forgive me."

Anasofiya sat up, the last few moments catching up and no longer the least bit amusing or lighthearted. "Aidrik, you said be ready for the future. You didn't say prepare for possibilities. What's going on? Did you see something? What aren't you telling me?"

Aidrik silenced her questions with a kiss, a tenderness so rare it stole her breath and quelled her fears, for the moment.

AIDRIK HAD SOMETHING TO SHOW HER. HE WOULD GIVE NO HINT, only the gentle command to follow.

Finn and Aleksei napped back at the cottage, where Finn's grandparents had cared for them during their coalescence. Time there was nearing an end. Aidrik's demeanor had shifted. Ana was as tuned to his synchronies as her own.

When she followed him, through an untrodden path, weaving through the tall trees, she realized they'd not shared a moment alone since Aleksei's birth.

The distant sound of water escalated closer, and louder until Aidrik paused at the shore of a small brook. When she arrived at his side, he pointed to the left, toward a small waterfall pouring over two boulders.

"Our time here nears an end," Aidrik said. Ana leaned into him, lulled by the soft sound of the creek below. Though their stretch in Scotland had been restful, it had not always been so peaceful.

"Yes, I understand."

"We may not find a similar rest once we depart."

"I agree."

Aidrik paused. Steadied himself. If Anasofiya didn't know better, she'd say he was nervous. "I consider myself impervious to most of Man's weaknesses. On the eve of our departure, I already regret we have not had time to ourselves."

Ana turned to face him, lacing her arms around his waist as her lips grazed his chin. "We have some now."

He wrapped himself around her, pressing into her with a sharp tug. "Will you indulge an ancient wanderer his unflattering need?"

She rose to her tiptoes, resting her mouth on his ear. "With pleasure."

ANASOFIYA SAT ASTRIDE HER EVIGBOND. TEARS STREAMED DOWN HER cheeks, trickling over his scarred chest. She couldn't say where they'd come from, except that every moment now with Aidrik had the power to tap into the emotional reservoir she'd always kept buried deep.

To see him in his own ecstasy, this stoic, enduring creature, always brought her over the edge. The muscles in his abdomen clenched, flexed. His thighs spasmed.

"My Kjære. My eyes-like-the-sea," he breathed, head lolling to the side. One arm went slack, the other held her, easing her down to lie by his side.

He was asleep in moments, leaving her with a consuming vulnerability she couldn't shake. Every time she lay with him, her fears burned hot against her heart, and the release brought them out in the open, exposing Anasofiya to a heartbreak she feared more than anything in all the world.

She wanted to wake him, to beg him to reassure her the fears were foolish and unfounded. That he would be with her forever.

Of course, she knew better.

• • •

"Kjære."

"Mm?"

"You have been sleepwalking again."

"Have I?"

"Tell me."

Ana knew what he was asking and that he would accept nothing less than honesty. No one could detect evasion like Aidrik the Wise. "I don't know what awaits us ahead. If Agripin won't meet with you, how long will we wander? And if he does, what if he betrays us? I try not to dwell on these things, but it's hard."

"Aye. I also find myself challenged in this regard."

Now that he'd invited her thoughts, she couldn't slow them. "I hate the idea of Aleksandr living in exile. He'll never know what a regular childhood is, and he might never know what it is to be a normal adult."

"And you? Did you experience such a childhood?"

Ana considered this. "I guess it depends on your perspective of normal."

"Aye. And he has no other perspective. I, too, wish better for our son, Kjære. That is why we are here. Why we shall push forth and do all we can to leave him this gift. A gift not only for him but his future progeny."

"That's the other thing." She sat up, propping on one elbow. She needed to see his face when he answered this question. "Why do you always talk as if you're leaving us?"

Aidrik dropped his eyes. She gripped his chin, forcing eye contact.

"Tell me, Aidrik. You think I don't remember you're a seer? When you say things like this, it makes me believe you've seen something horrible in your future. And if that's true, tell me now. I can't bear to lose you, but I could tolerate it even less if it's to something senseless you kept from me."

"I have seen many things," Aidrik replied, his words rolling off

the tongue slowly, with purpose. "My gift has never been reliable. I never foresaw loving you. Needing you. And yet, I cannot breathe without you."

Ana squeezed her eyes shut, stemming tears. "You always deflect. And you know what to say to shut me up."

"I love you. I will always love you, no matter the future ahead, no matter our strife. Nothing can tear that love asunder. Nothing will cause me to part your side. Not time. Not betrayal. Not death."

She sniffled, turning away. "That isn't an answer."

Ah, but it was. In a single moment, her heart had come alive and broken.

"It is the only answer."

"Anasofiya."

"I don't know this memory."

"We are not within a memory. Not any longer."

"That's all you are now, a painful memory, and I'm only a woman filled with hatred and regret. Go away, stop taunting me."

"Kjære."

"This isn't real. Stop!"

"You are not the only one in pain. Would that I could be there to carry this pain for you."

"But you can't. Because you're no more than a figment of my imagination. No better than my Wraith."

"I am more real than your Wraith, Kjære. You inquired of me what would occur if I were to meet an untimely end. I never lied to you."

"You never properly warned me either. You left me unprepared for this! And why I am arguing with my imagination!"

"How could I? I went willingly to the dais, to ensure your salvation. Aleksei's. Finn's. You have always assigned me false deification. I am not a god. Not Emyr. I chose my death because it was the only

choice. What I would not have given to remain with you. What I would not have sacrificed, Kjære."

Anasofiya cried in her sleep, clutching her sweat-drenched pillow. "What do you want from me?"

"To remind you of my vow."

"What vow?"

"Have you so soon forgotten? I love you. I will always love you, no matter the future ahead, no matter our strife. Nothing can tear that love asunder. Nothing will cause me to part your side. Not time. Not betrayal. Not death."

"You think I could forget that day? It eats at my heart, reminds me of my own failings. That if I hadn't convinced us to go with Agripin or any number of incidental decisions I made that led to you walking up to the platform..."

"Your mind and words lead you in circles. I am here. I have always been here. Within you. I have never left your side."

"Please," Anasofiya cried. "Please stop taunting me. I have so little fight left in me."

"Your strength is greater than you have ever given yourself credit for."

"You don't know how close I am to giving up."

"Anasofiya. Open your eyes."

"Stop..."

"This is not a deception. I would never commit so hurtful a crime upon you. Open your eyes."

"Go away!"

"Kjære." A command.

Anasofiya opened her eyes.

"This is an illusion. Something of Agripin's doing," Anasofiya accused, backing into the wooden frame with a light thud, limited further by her bruising bindings.

Aidrik's broad smile filled her vision, blinding her from anything else in her surroundings. "Not an illusion. Agripin does not possess the skill. Did I not vow nothing would cause me to part your side?"

"Aidrik, no. It can't be. I saw it. I saw every moment of your death. I still see it, every second of every day." Blood surged to her head, and she fell back in a daze.

"Calm yourself, *Kjære*. It injures me to see you so pained. I wanted to visit sooner, but you would not allow it." Aidrik smiled patiently, running his hand over her brow. "How lovely you are, my eyes-like-the-sea. To behold you again..."

"I wouldn't *allow* it! What the hell are you talking about? I watched you die! I tore Farjhem apart in grief for you!"

"Aye. You and your Wraith wrought that destruction. A creation of your soul as much as your flesh. Your blood. Is the answer clear yet?"

"You crazy fool, I can hardly breathe! Do you think I'm capable of reasoning out your riddles? Tell me! And if you're really here, unlock me!"

Aidrik's eyes glistened. He spread his arms so wide they brushed the opposite walls. "I am here simply because you willed it so."

Anasofiya stared at him, wordless.

"You are an etheric summoner. The most powerful I've beheld. Agripin must concur, or he would not find it necessary to bind you so cruelly. You found your Wraith because it was a part of you from the moment of your conception. A chimera, if you will. And I? I am your evigbond. I was a part of you from the instant I laid eyes on you, and the bond was sealed. Death did not sever this.

"Alas, I cannot unbind you, Kjære. I have only now discovered the ability to become visible to you. The power comes from you, and you have work yet to restore yourself. My strength in this form wavers already. This much took weeks. You alone have the control."

"I... but... how?" No, that wasn't the question. She knew how. Wraith had been there at her birth, yes, but the strength Wraith drew *came from her,* like a font. A supremacy she'd awakened in Farsengel and then stifled again in her grief.

Yet, not fully. Wraith retreated, but never went away. Some part of her continued this growth, for Aidrik. As her evigbond, Emyr's most sacred bond, he *was* a part of her. His grief was hers, his joy hers. The love she felt for Finn had always operated on a different level than the symbiotic *need* she possessed for Aidrik. His presence in her life seemed as critical as the pumping of her lungs. When he died before her eyes, she thought she'd drawn her last breath as Anasofiya.

He smiled. Unlike the Aidrik of before, his face possessed no lines, no stress. Not even his phoenix scar remained. He had the countenance of an angel. "I can hear your thoughts now. I never could before. Do you know what a gift this is?"

Ana's chest burned, a sensation that radiated out through her belly, and into her skull, pressing against her orbital bones. "Are you really, truly here? This isn't a dream? Not my imagination?"

"I deceived you only once, Kjære. I have not done it since, and would never again."

"It was you."

"Me?"

"Who sent me the vision of Agripin assaulting me."

"Aye."

Inexpressible grief escaped her in the form of energy. A silent scream, soundless pain. Then the shrill keening of an animal, whistling through her lips. "I need to get out of here. Now. I can't... I can't *breathe*... Aidrik, get me out of here."

Aidrik stretched out next to her, his expression tragic. "I would give anything in the world to break you free myself."

"Tell me how," she cried, writhing. "Tell me how. Tell me *how.*"

Hot tears rolled down his cheeks, stinging her own. Real.

He was real. He was here. Aidrik.

Aidrik.

"You know how."

Tears mingled with sweat. Grief, with agony. "I'm not strong enough for this. I've never had that strength."

"You are. You have. You always will be."

"Tell me."

"You know the answer. It has always been within you. As I am. As Wraith is. As a darkness that burns as bright as the sun."

Across the small cabin, a door slammed open. Agripin had returned. The creature who had taken her whole world and crushed it under his heel.

Rage. Blind, unquenchable fury surged into Ana's hands. Next to her, Aidrik cried silent tears, pressing his face to hers. Whispering, over and over, *You know the answer.*

Yes, I know the answer. The answer is me. The answer is believing. The answer is strength. The answer is... the answer is...

"Don't leave me," she whispered through clenched lips. "Don't you ever fucking dare leave me again."

"Never."

"I might not make it. It's rising up within me, like a poisonous cloud. I can feel it, and I don't think I can stop it. Maybe this time, I won't return."

"You will. I will be at your side. Always. Close your eyes and breathe."

Ahh, Anasofiya. I see you've found my surprise.

Not yours, Wraith. Mine. Only mine. Now hush and get ready.

I have been *ready.*

THOUGH A GREAT DARKNESS HAD STOLEN OVER THE HOUSE, A brilliant light replaced it.

A light so bright, so deafening, that deer and elk for miles were stunned in their tracks, temporarily senseless.

Strange illumination so brilliant and unusual at this hour and season that scientists in Moscow would study the phenomenon for years to come.

Radiance so powerful the ground outside warmed to a thaw, confusing the ecosystem underneath which had burrowed away for the season.

Closer still, a fallen emperor fell to his knees, a powerful, unbelievable realization stealing over him.

So late.

Too late.

All this, Anasofiya saw through her Wraith.

And then again through her own eyes, as the bindings ripped free.

25
NICOLAS

Time passed slowly in Portree.

Mercy slept during the days, lost with her need to nourish the "child" growing within her.

At night, she came alive. Stories of her youth and travels poured out of her in endless supply, exciting a passion that made Nicolas' heart ache for who she had been before the world went to hell.

He listened to her in his drowsiness, willing himself to stay awake. Hanging on every word, wrapping around every syllable. What a mystery it still was to Nicolas, to love so deeply. The desire to understand another being so fully had never possessed him to this degree. Not even with Ana.

Nicolas considered staying like this forever, in suspended animation, but the burgeoning adult in him brought them here to solve the issue of Mercy's decline, not hide behind it.

On the afternoon he decided on action, he sat tentatively on the side of the bed where Mercy slept, soundless, prepared to spend the next hour selling her on the benefits of leaving the cabin for the day.

As it turned out, he needed to say nothing.

"I could use some fresh air," Mercy said, stretching.

Nicolas hadn't thought further ahead than convincing her, so he had no destination in mind. The Isle of Skye was a playground of beauty; therefore, he hardly thought he could choose wrong, but if this was to be the day Mercy had a breakthrough, he wanted the location to be perfect.

In haste, he texted Aunt Colleen for a recommendation. She replied immediately: *The Fairy Pools. Uncle Noah and I found our magic there.*

The navigation unit was useless; nothing in the directory even close to "Fairy Pools." Apparently reading his mind from across the globe, Colleen sent a follow-up text: *Find the road to Glen Brittle.*

Driving there took half an hour on the twisty, narrow roads. Nicolas searched for conversation starters, but Mercy's wistful smile toward the passing scenery quelled any desire to disrupt her.

As he maneuvered the car toward Glen Brittle, Nicolas wondered, had she been there before? With Aidrik? The Fairy Pools had never come up in her stories during the past few days, but their absence didn't necessarily hold meaning when Mercy had thousands of years to mull.

Nicolas slowed the car as they approached a sign that said *Glumagan Na Sithichean*. Below, in smaller text, *Fairy Pools.* Behind the sign was a gravel lot, empty save two other cars.

Mercy was out of the vehicle before he had a chance to turn it off. She navigated through the lot and down toward the start of a long, open path. At the trailhead, she turned to wait for him.

"You coming?"

Nicolas jogged her direction, zipping his raincoat up and over the bottom of his chin as the wind chill tore through him. Mercy, used to colder temps, a trait that apparently did not depart when her Empyrean self perished, had a light sweater tied around her waist. Her skin radiated the luminescent glow of summer.

Once Nicolas reached her side, Mercy started down the path. In the distance, the Black Cuillin mountains towered above a blanket of fog, jutting into the heavens. To the right and left, fields of heather stretched as far as the eye could see.

A family, and a couple, linked in arms, passed them on their way toward the pools, going the other direction. Presumably, the owners of the two other cars in the lot.

They were alone.

Mercy started at a brisk clip, then, as the ground moved from loose gravel to the rocky path, she escalated to a jog, followed by something resembling a skip. When they reached the first river crossing, she jumped, landing several feet ahead, giggling.

"You all right?" Nicolas asked from behind, amused.

"Couldn't be better!" she hollered back, gamboling on, off on her own. Nicolas let her go. He wasn't sure he could keep her pace, and more, he seemed vaguely like an intruder in her blissful moment.

He followed like this, several dozen paces behind, watching Mercy come further alive and into herself as she crested the hill. At last, a series of small, brilliant pools and falls came into view.

Mercy stood on a rocky outcrop, overlooking the crystal

streams of water. To her left, the mountains cast an ominous shadow, but it was eclipsed by the dreamlike quality of the air.

"Can you feel it?" Mercy cried, arms wide as Nicolas made his way toward her. "Is it just me, or can you feel it?"

"I can," Nicolas replied, letting her help boost him atop the tall cluster of rocks on which she stood. He *could* feel the magic. Surely, this was what she referred to. He couldn't identify a source, or even define what about the serene waters caused such a response, nor could he deny it.

"I've never been here before now," Mercy told him, answering his unspoken question from earlier. "This used to be Quinlan lands. We were at war with them. Still are."

"I thought Quinlans were in Ireland?"

"After the sunder between our races, after they re-emerged in the world, they spread out all over the British Isles. Eventually, they were forced into smaller, more condensed groups, closer to where they'd originated. *We* forced them there," she explained, glancing down at the flowing water with a sad expression. "We were horrible to them. I can see it now, with the teachings of our false Scholars a distant memory and a known fallacy. Emyr cries for the Quinlans."

"Humans aren't much better to those who are different from us," Nicolas offered. "We have a bit of a history fucking each other over, too."

Mercy nodded. "The gift of free will and thinking comes with tremendous responsibility. When put to the test, we all fail, every time. Even kindness cannot override the prevailing nature within all of us to destroy."

"That's pretty nihilistic, even for me."

"Nihilism rides a fine line with realism. An important one, too. For example, did you think I wasn't aware of your motivation in bringing me here?"

Nicolas watched her. "To the pools?"

"To Scotland."

"I was upfront that I thought New Orleans was toxic for you and... your child," Nicolas replied, carefully.

Mercy's smile spread slowly across her pale face. "You're a carnal creature, Nicolas Deschanel. I haven't been appropriately attentive to your needs. Sometimes a change of scenery does the trick."

Nicolas opened his mouth, but no words escaped. Not only was he touched by her, well, thoughtfulness, but he was also shocked at himself for having no sexual impetus, for once, something that hadn't even occurred to him until she attached this false motivation to him.

"You and I, we've been through a lifetime of heartbreak and joy in our short time together." Mercy touched her cool hand to his cheek. "Sometimes you're the asshole, other times that designation belongs to me. Right now, you're the one holding it together for both of us."

"You know how I feel," Nicolas said. Guilt knocked at the edges of his conscience. To entertain her theory would be to further deceive her, but he couldn't hurt her, either.

"Aye, darling." Her lips came upon his in the briefest and most tender of kisses. "You've told me many times. In these past few days, you've shown me."

"We could stay," Nicolas choked out. His sinuses felt a tingling pressure. No, he wouldn't cry. Tears hadn't solved a damn thing in his life, and they weren't welcome now. "Here. We don't have to go back if you're happy."

Rain drops landed on her hand first. Then he felt them on his scalp, a light drizzle that quickly escalated to downpour.

"Aw, hell," Nicolas muttered various expletives, angry at the heavens at this interruption to the verge of a genuine breakthrough.

Mercy backed away with a curious expression. “It’s Scotland. What’s a little rain?”

“We should go,” Nicolas answered, pulling his hood up and tightening the strings. “This isn’t a solid path. It’s not safe.”

Mercy ignored him and climbed out over the pools, crossing toward the side covered in wilderness. No paths or clear footing dotted the side of the water where she headed. “What happened to the Nicolas I met on the shore of Deschanel Island? The one who feared nothing?”

“He’s trying to be responsible. Maybe you should encourage this well-behaved Nicolas. We can come back tomorrow.”

Another step. Her foot settled, then slid, on a slick black boulder, covered in waterlogged moss. “Why, when we’re already here?”

“Mercy, it isn’t safe!” he called, then shook his head. With a sigh, he realized his words weren’t going to penetrate in her current frame of mind. She was all over the place, living moment to moment. He started after her.

His loafers weren’t a match for the wet rocks, and he lost his footing twice before he even made forward progress. Looking ahead, Mercy was almost across to the other side. Once she reached the rough bank, there was no telling where she might run. He could very easily lose her in that blinding endlessness of heather.

“Mercy, come on! Come back!”

It happened too quick, too terrifyingly fast for Nicolas to do more than gape. Both her feet became airborne, and she made no sound as they came up, and her head came down, smacking into the craggy edge of the boulder on which she’d just been standing.

“Mercy!” Nicolas cried, the sound piercing his vocal chords.

She hit the center of the larger pool with a splash, floating immediately to the surface. Nicolas forgot the dangers and scrambled down the bank, sliding, falling.

Like a leaf on a lake, her body was at first still and then began a slow drift across the surface. With acute panic, Nicolas saw which direction she was headed: downriver.

He backtracked to the path and watched in helpless horror as she fell over the first set of falls and traveled down the River Brittle.

Nicolas launched into a sprint, losing his footing but carried forward by his crazed momentum as he pressed down the path where they'd entered.

The muddled trail created obstacle after obstacle, but Nicolas flew forward anyway, with a fear greater than the one that had brought him to Scotland.

As the current outmatched him, every stride seemed like twelve of mother nature's.

He didn't stop.

Didn't falter.

But his heart screamed as Mercy was carried beyond his reach.

26

ANASOFIYA

Agripin's steps faltered in the kitchen.

Anasofiya's breaths were coming fast and heavy. Her eyes surveyed the room, vision the only sense that had stayed true to her during the confinement.

Her mind had not yet caught up with the reality of her freedom.

"Aidrik," she whispered. No response.

He was gone.

Not *really* gone, she knew now. Never all the way gone. Her evigbond was as much a part of her as her own heart and lungs. Knowing that empowered her enough. Aidrik could take his time to recharge and find new energy to return to her. He could draw from her whatever he needed.

This was her score to settle. Alone.

"Anasofiya?" Agripin's voice floated from the kitchen. Tentative. Unsure. "Did you see that?"

She didn't answer. The once-bound Anasofiya, at the mercy of his sadism, wouldn't have responded so the one no longer fettered would do the same. She wasn't ready for him to know the trouble he'd sown.

She awaited, with relish, the moment he would realize the painful turn of the tides.

Click. Click. Click. Click. The heels of his boots echoed on the tiled kitchen floor.

Breathe in. Breathe out. Breathe in. Hold.

Anasofiya, you are ready, my darling. You have always been. Show him how ready you are for him.

Wraith, I thank you, but this is my vengeance. You rest and look after Aidrik. Show him around the place, make him comfortable.

Aye.

Anasofiya slid one leg down the soft cotton. The sensation of oak on her feet sent a thrill through her, as she eased first the tips of her toes, landing softly and soundlessly on her heel.

She had very little room to work with. Only a foot, perhaps a foot and a half, separated the edge of the bed from the wall.

Click. Click. Click. Click. Agripin paused feet from the bedroom door. "Cyler? Have you returned to us?"

She pivoted. *Long breath out. Another one in.* The other leg came over the side, skin against skin as she laid her second foot atop the first.

Click. "Anasofiya? Is someone else in there with you?"

Anasofiya squeezed her eyes closed. *Long, slow exhale.*

Concentrating on the energy building within, the boiling vengeance developing for the creature on the other side of the wall, Anasofiya pulled herself up, planting her feet shoulder-width and chancing one, quick stretch of her aching arms. She slid them against the wall, rising to a triangle above her head, wincing at the difficulty.

Come on. Walk your disgusting, treacherous pile of bones into this room so I can witness the horror of knowing your own death is inevitable.

Click. Click.

"Are you going to hover outside my room all evening?" she challenged, still not playing her hand. She flexed her knuckles, dropped her arms behind her in one final, painful stretch. Later, she would be sore. She might not even be able to walk.

Now, though, she was alive with the power of her ancestors boosting her, coursing through every vein in her body.

Her sarcasm gave him the ease to drop his guard, and with one last click, Agripin stood before her.

Agripin's eyes strained to catch up with the image his mind had presented: his empress, free and towering, searing with an energy he hadn't seen since she'd brought down Farsengel.

"You have nothing to say now that I'm not lying at your mercy?" she charged, taking her first steps toward him. He held his ground, but his face peeled back, the first sign of the fear she'd craved.

"For your own safety," he managed to get out before finally doubling over, coughing, clutching at his throat as he gasped for air.

I shouldn't enjoy this so. But I do... oh, I do.

Anasofiya sent her darkness at him, wrapping him in it, stretching it around his soul. "My safety, you say? You aren't even fighting back." Her bare feet gripped the cool wood as she approached his cringing form. "Your whole life, you've done as you pleased. You've manipulated the worlds of others to your benefit. Mine will be the last, *Grand Emperor* Agripin."

He reached a hand up. The other still scratched at his throat as if he thought he might open another windpipe to find relief. "I... won't... fight... you."

"That's a shame," Anasofiya replied, frowning. She tilted her head, regarding his pain. His crippling defeat.

It all seemed too easy. Where was the reward in this? She

wanted him to challenge her. She wanted him to return combat and make her work for this victory!

Instead, she saw before her the image of a creature broken by his own decisions. He said he wouldn't fight her, and she believed him. Death would be a mercy he didn't deserve.

But I know what he does deserve. My gift to him could be a fate far worse than death.

Eyes closed, Anasofiya pulled small threads of her darkness back. Enough to let him speak, and fully appreciate the weight of her next words.

Agripin gasped, his breaths desperate and rasping as he fell back against the wall, sliding to the floor in a heap. "Murder me. Get on with your vengeance, Anasofiya," he rasped. "You'll meet no defense from me. I've earned this."

"Death would be a kind end to your long list of crimes," Anasofiya answered, casting a long shadow over him. "I've dreamt of the moment I'd have my hands at your throat while I took back control and demonstrated to you what *real* fear was like. Knowing you could do nothing to stop me as I extinguished the light out of your thousands of years. But then what? You go to your god? Your Emyr? You find peace in eternal life?" She shook her head, wrapping him in a new kind of darkness, easing him of the pain but securing him in a cocoon of her own self, a prison he could never escape as long as she drew breath.

"That is not why you let me live," Agripin accused. His voice rang heavy with a cloying tenderness that made her physically ill. "We both know why I'm still breathing."

"Please, share more of your delusions. It isn't as if I've heard enough of them while you rambled on into my sleep."

Agripin's eyes locked on hers, exhausted but not without passion still. "You love me. You hate me and love me at once, and it eats at you. It makes you question your own soul. I know the feeling."

Anasofiya crossed her arms over her chest, suddenly aware of herself in the thin shift he'd given her for cover. "In Farjhem, I tolerated you. I learned to work with you, because what we had was a *business* arrangement. Nothing more. I learned from my father how to deal with men I would never share a meal with if we weren't brokering a deal. You were a means to an end, a pawn for us as much as we were a pawn for you, and you have been for the Brotherhood. You betrayed us, and my indifference became loathing. You're only alive now because I have a way to use you again, and you're more useful breathing."

Agripin smiled through his agony. To see the once-great prince reduced to this should have given Anasofiya pleasure, but instead, it left her hollow. "You convince yourself of what you need to live with your passions. You could have broken free the moment Leif bound you. You did not. Why do you think that is?"

Anasofiya rolled her eyes. "I don't have to explain myself to you. I never have to do anything at your command again."

"You have always been more Empyrean than Child of Man," Agripin pressed on, grimacing as he pressed against his invisible constrictions. "Your desires run deeper than any Man I've known. I have no judgment on a creature who spreads her affections. But look at how you torture yourself. Even as you shared a bed with Finn and Aidrik, you delivered yourself internal floggings, living in denial of who you *really* are." He spat blood, but behind the barrier of Anasofiya's darkness it only dribbled down his lip. "Aidrik was too pragmatic for my liking, and Finn filled with too much bravado. But I'd have joined your triumvirate."

"I know what you would have done to me."

"I'd have fallen on my knees to serve you every evening."

"You've been waiting a lifetime for that."

Agripin shook his head. "I don't think so. Had my hand not been forced where Aidrik was concerned—"

Anasofiya struck him with the back of her hand, a force filled with the heaviness of anchored grief and hatred. "You have spent your entire life deflecting blame. You *will* own your responsibility in what happened to Aidrik!"

"The Senetat uncovered our plans—"

This time, she hit him with a fist. "Everything fell apart, and you had a choice. It always, always comes down to a choice. You chose yourself."

Agripin hung his head. "Aye. I chose myself. It does no good, I suppose, reasoning with a woman bent on vengeance, but had I not given them a sacrifice, all of our heads would have been on pikes."

"You're right, Agripin. It makes no fucking difference." Anasofiya delivered one final kick to his temple, knocking him unconscious. She focused her darkness on binding him tighter until he appeared a moth awaiting metamorphosis.

He isn't going anywhere. Well done.

Thank you, Wraith.

I confess, I did not know where your mind was until I burrowed deeper. Your plan is brilliant. I see it.

Is it safe to sleep for a bit, do you think?

You've been sleeping for weeks, Anasofiya.

I haven't really *slept since before Aleksei was born. I could sleep for days, I think, without waking.*

Aye, you are safe to relax. You've bound Agripin with a force even he is not capable of sundering. You rest. I'll keep watch.

Where's Aidrik?

Not to worry, Anasofiya. He is resting, and growing stronger. For you.

With a weary smile, Anasofiya pulled the wool blanket

from the bed she'd been bound to, and dragged it to the living room.

The room was Agripin's prison now, not hers. Never again hers.

Lying down on the couch, she was asleep before the blanket settled over her.

27
ALEKSANDR

Aleksandr lifted himself on his elbow so he could see all of her stretched out on his cloak, her soft, supple skin gleaming against the sheet of moonlight peeking through the canopy of trees.

He could watch her sleep forever, tracing his hand along the soft down of her arm, observing the way it responded to his touch. In these moments, the reality of their situation didn't matter, and fantasy could live unhindered.

"I wish this was our forever," he whispered.

With a languid smile, Fiona revealed she'd been awake all along. "Do you always talk to yourself?"

"I was talking to you," he answered with a fierce blush. "Well, sleeping you."

Fiona rolled on her back, revealing herself without a shred of self-conscious. "So you don't mean it if I'm awake?"

"Of course, I mean it, silly girl," he said. With his own smile, he realized he'd just used his father's words for his mother. *Silly girl.*

Fiona laced her hand through his. Her hair spread through

the leaves in a halo above her head, except a series of strands which had fallen over her left nipple.

He wanted her all over again.

"What if this could be our forever?" she asked, turning his hand over in hers, observing how their fingers twined and fit together like the pieces of a perfectly made puzzle.

Aleksandr resisted the powerful urge to cry. No simple tears, but the gut-bursting variety he'd cried when Aidrik had died. When his mora didn't come home. "Ona, you know how I feel, but I couldn't live with myself if I let my family suffer."

"Well," she mused, bringing his hand to her lips, where she let it rest a moment while she gathered her thoughts, "you only have to have a child with this heir, right?"

"You know a lot more about the prophecy than I do."

"There's nothing in any of Morrigan's words saying you have to keep having babies or stay together for the rest of your lives," Fiona said, rolling back over to face him.

Hope sparked within him, then fell as immediately as it had arrived. "I couldn't do that to you. I can't even imagine... being with another woman, but then to come back to you. How could you ever have me? Or want me?"

"Love doesn't work that way," Fiona said, curling her lip, a sign he recognized as her preparing to express her wisdom of experience. Aleksei loved that he already knew her tics and idiosyncrasies. He also hated it, for the loss he feared ahead.

"Enlighten me," he teased.

In punishment, she rolled atop him, pinning his hands above him before he could assault her. "I don't want you to be with anyone else, but don't you know I'd rather this than lose you forever?"

He frowned up at her. "I couldn't handle you with another man. Maybe that makes me selfish, or awful, but I don't care."

"You watched me love Declan," she reminded him. "You

even tried to help me secure a future with him. Did you forget?"

"Because I loved you," he answered, the words bringing the blood rushing to his head, as they did every time he said them. "And I wanted you to be happy."

"And I love you," she purred, landing her lips across the hollow of his neck, easing to his chin. He gulped, growing hard again. "I never thought I was capable of loving someone other than Declan, although, with some distance, I see now I was more attracted to the secrecy and being able to live in both worlds, without committing to either. I don't belong to both worlds, and though it was a hard lesson, it was one I needed. I never saw you coming, Aleksei. But now you're here, and I'm not letting you leave me so easily." She swallowed. "And you won't be happy if your family isn't safe. I can make this sacrifice if it means this is our forever."

Aleksandr's eyes burned with warm, stinging tears. Her lips moved there next, kissing away the evidence of his fears. "I know so little compared to you," he said.

"You know far more than you give yourself credit for. Have you ever wondered where your wisdom comes from? Empyreans grow to physical maturity fast, sure. And mentally they're usually on par. But they spend hundreds of years knowing the world and understanding it the way you do after your short time on earth. You have the wisdom of the ancients, Aleksei. If I had any doubt of who you were, I don't, after knowing you."

"And what about my immortality? We would get one lifetime, and then I would watch you... watch you fade away, and then I would go on."

"One lifetime with you, Aleksei, would be a priceless gift."

"I don't deserve your selflessness, Ona. You've been there

for me since the moment we arrived, without a clue where to go or what to do. I want to repay you, not take more."

Her hair tickled his chest. She pressed her forehead against his and whispered her next words. "Love me. Love me, and keep loving me, for as long as the goddess allows us time together. Do that, and you've already paid me back with interest."

Aleksandr's heart broke at her unselfish love. It was a gift he was not sure he deserved, but to turn it away would be to destroy them both.

"It won't be easy," he warned, accepting her shower of tender kisses. His hands ran the length of her back, committing every inch to memory. "When the heir is born, I mean."

"Of course not," she answered, reaching down, between his legs. He gasped, coming alive under her touch. "But that's why we make the most of every single moment before then, so nothing can break us when the time comes. Not now, not ever."

"Not ever," he said as she pulled him inside of her, where the world was theirs still, and safe.

28

NICOLAS

Dr. MacKinnon Memorial Hospital in Broadford was the nearest facility equipped to handle trauma, but even that was questionable by the standards Nicolas had come to expect living in the bayou, miles from a reputable hospital. As the ambulance moseyed into the lot of what appeared to host a series of quaint office buildings or even homes, he was already texting Oz to find a bigger hospital back on the mainland United Kingdom.

I thought you weren't bringing your phone, Oz texted.

I lied. Do you really think I'm dumb enough to leave the country without it?

Blind luck had brought the old man to Glen Brittle that day. He wasn't in the mood for a walk, but something told him he'd better get one in. Thought he was feeling a shift in the weather, and when that happened each year, his walks would stop for a spell, and he had no other means of exercise. His own cottage was a mile shy of the entrance to the Fairy Pools, and he considered it might be next season before he saw that crystal blue water again, so he ventured up the hill instead of down.

And there, as he stepped to cross the first pass of the river, was Mercy.

The water only ran parallel with the trail halfway, and then cut south, away not only from the path but also the road. Had fortune not intervened, she would have been swept downriver, away from the trail, away from help. No telling how far she would have traveled, or where she'd have ended up. The old man informed him the river terminated several miles out in Loch Brittle; a sea loch.

She wouldn't have been the first to be carried to sea, the man said. Especially this time of year, when the water levels were higher and the current more violent.

Oz texted to let him know he was coordinating with the hospital staff to have her transferred by chopper to a bigger hospital in Glasgow once they'd assessed her travel feasibility. Then the doors to the back of the ambulance flew open, and Mercy was ushered away against the backdrop of nervous, hurried doctors and nurses. Nicolas had the sinking feeling they saw very little action, and that a serious injury was similar to an early Christmas.

One, a young woman, approached him with a kind smile. "I'll show you where you can wait for her. We'll share news as we have it."

"I want to go in with her."

"I'm sorry, but that's not possible."

"Because she's not my wife?"

"Because the doctors can't have any distractions while they do everything in their power to save her life. Family or no, you'll have to wait here." The nurse laid a hand on his back and guided him through the double doors. The hospital smell, of linens and iodine and all manner of sickness hit him, and he suddenly wished he was anywhere else.

"There there, lad. We see our fair share of slips and falls on the isle. Your lass is in good hands."

Nicolas: *What's going on with the transport? She's been inside for hours.*

Oz: *They said they'd ring when they had a status. I've called back seven times. Think they're about to block me. Not giving up.*

Nicolas: *Have your dad call. Your uncles. I don't care. The fuckers won't talk to me.*

Oz: *I know you don't want to hear this, but maybe they're focused on her care. That's what they should be doing. They'll come tell you when they have news.*

Nicolas: *You're right. I don't want to hear it.*

A shadow fell over Nicolas. He looked up, bathed in white.

The doctor and his white coat came into focus. "Mr. Deschanel."

Nicolas jumped to his feet. "How is she?"

"Let's speak in private."

Nicolas followed the physician in an anxious daze down a small corridor and into an office. The man gestured for Nicolas to have a seat.

"I'll stand."

"Very well." The doctor lifted his coat and settled into a leather chair. "Allow me to start by saying Mercy is doing very well, all things considered."

Nicolas breathed out. He slowly lowered onto the chair. "She's okay. She'll live?"

"She was fortunate given the circumstances. A strong

concussion that we are going to continue to monitor, but the MRI revealed no brain bleeds or other injuries we're concerned with in these situations. She might have a fuzzy memory for a few days. It is also possible her memory of the ordeal might be unclear or missing altogether. The young lady also suffered several broken ribs and has bruising on over thirty percent of her body. It could have been far worse."

Nicolas nodded, trying to listen but all he could hear was *Mercy is doing very well.* "When can I take her home?"

The doctor shot him a look. "You're not still trying to get her transferred?"

Nicolas didn't have the patience to apologize. "If she's fine, there's no need. So, when?"

"We'd like to monitor her at least overnight, and do another MRI before we release her," the doctor replied, reclining back with his hands folded across his broad belly. "I believe it's in her best interest. I don't think a transfer is necessary."

"I'll allow it," Nicolas said. His eyes were drawn toward the door. Mercy was down the hall somewhere, alone. Probably wondering where the hell he was, and why he wasn't at her side. "Is there a chair in her room? I'll sleep here."

The doctor shifted uncomfortably. "There's one more thing."

Nicolas waved him to get on with it.

"Are you aware if Mercy has any history of mental illness?"

Nicolas bristled. "She's fine."

The doctor nodded with palpable skepticism. "Were you aware, then, that she believed she was pregnant?" When Nicolas sat in silence, he continued. "We performed an ultrasound before we did the MRI, and found no evidence of conception. Her uterus—"

Nicolas choked back the rising moan. "Stop, I already know."

The doctor's face caved in understanding sympathy. "This must be very difficult for you. But I want you to know, you have options—"

"I said she's fine!"

The doctor nodded in defeat. "I'm going to leave you with some literature that you can read at your leisure."

Fuck your literature. Fuck your ultrasounds and fuck you for shattering her illusion.

Nicolas rose, tripping over the chair as he struggled toward the door. The agony he'd suppressed for weeks and weeks bubbled to the surface and escaped in broken gasps as he stumbled into the hallway.

29
FINNEGAN

"You can do this, Far," Aleksandr said, eyes wide and hopeful, reminding Finn of the boy he'd been only months ago. He appeared so seldom now and even less since his infatuation with the lovely Fiona.

"Not if you keep looking at me like that," Finn said with a raised brow. "All full of expectations. Makes a man nervous."

"It's not as if you're trying to do something impossible or anything. Like time travel."

"Nah. Not like we're trying to save the world here."

Padraig cleared his throat. "Perhaps Aleksei should leave."

"He stays," Finn asserted. He focused his gaze on the thatched ceiling, gripping the sides of the cot. "It was his idea. If it succeeds, he should be here for it."

Padraig shrugged and began his usual pacing.

"Remember, think of Amelia and Jacob. I know you don't know Jacob so maybe just Amelia," Aleksandr said, in what Finn thought sounded like his own voice attempting a pep talk. "That long, snow white hair."

"You've never seen snow, kid."

"I read books, Far."

"Right. Hair like snow. Any other wisdom before I go in?"

Aleksandr's grin spread to the left, winding up for something clever; then it fell again. "Even if you don't find them, you're still the bravest man I know. I hope I grow up to be as brave as you."

Finn wasn't prepared for the sentiment and found himself at a loss for words when he went to respond. Before he could, one of the young Quinlan gals burst in, flustered. He hadn't learned this one's name, but Finn recognized her as Padraig's wife, who had been in and out with meals, but never more than that.

She aimed a nervous look at Finn, then snapped her head toward Padraig. "Nora needs you to come quick. We have a visitor."

Padraig regarded her with undisguised annoyance. "We're busy here, dearest. Please tell your aunt to find Flynn. He can help."

The young woman pivoted her eyes between both men, choosing her approach. "She asked for *you*."

"Regan," Padraig said, offering her a gentle head shake. "It's not your fault." He turned to Finn. "I'll clear this up and be back shortly."

Padraig's wife scuttled out first. "Hey," Finn called. "What has her looking so nervous?"

"I can't guess," Padraig answered, stepping under the door frame too short for his tall figure. "But don't let it be a distraction for you. Relax and find your focus. I'll be back before you know it."

"To hell with that," Finn muttered, sitting up. "How much you wanna bet he won't share a damn thing with us?"

"If I had the experience to appreciate the value of money, I'd bet all of it," Aleksandr responded.

"Thought so." Finn jumped off the tall cot, springing to his feet. "Let's go."

A VERY FAMILIAR AND EQUALLY UNWELCOME FACE STOOD OPPOSITE Flynn, Nora, and Padraig in the center of the forest clearing, the latter three employing defensive stances in the presence of a known traitor.

Padraig was the first to turn and see Finn as he stormed in their direction. "Oh, dear."

"Cyler! What the hell are you doing here?" he cried, pushing past Padraig. He reached for the turncoat's shirt, but Cyler drew his sword.

"Back off me, halfling. I didn't come here to harm you, but I won't lose sleep over having done it."

"Finnegan, Cyler has news of your wife," Flynn stepped in front of the sword. Cyler dropped it to his side but did not sheath it. "We were in the process of sussing out the legitimacy of his claims when you arrived."

Aleksandr rushed to his side as Finn strained for comprehension. "Ana? What do you know about her? Where is she? What have you and your bastard commander done?"

Nora pressed her hand to his arm. "Please stay calm. If you harm him, he's unlikely to share anything."

"He couldn't harm me with his best efforts," Cyler replied with a sneer while pointing the business end of his sword at Finn. Finally, he slid it back in the scabbard. "Come at me again, I'll take your head off in front of your boy."

"Threaten my far again, I'll change your entire reality," Aleksandr warned, growling.

"Enough!" Padraig cried. "Cyler, your welcome in this protected wood is contingent upon proof of your alliance to The Brotherhood, and by extension, us. Present it, and stay, or refuse to, and we will escort you out. You'll not find the entrance again on your own, and we won't present a second chance."

"I claim alliance to no one," Cyler spat. "Except the emperor, and that's why I'm here. Am I your ally? In a tangential sense, our aims are the same. I want Agripin free of his empress. You want her free of him. By elimination, we are aligned."

"The enemy of my enemy is my friend," Aleksandr muttered. "Sun Tsu."

"Not quite," Cyler snapped.

"Does that son-of-a-bitch know you're here?" Finn asked.

Cyler shook his head. "He'd have my head if he did, and I'd prefer to keep it for when he's restored to his former self."

Finn narrowed his eyes. "But he let you leave."

The response was a sardonic laugh. "*Let* me? Agripin cares for nothing anymore if it does not involve your worthless mate. I doubt he noticed my absence, and he might even be glad of it. If I'd have done as your mate asked, and brought her with me, though, he'd have been on my tail before the door closed."

"Mora wanted you to bring her to us?" Aleksandr asked. His budding hopefulness pained Finn, who favored caution above all else in this tenuous moment. "That means she thinks of us."

Cyler leveled his gaze on Aleksandr. "Who's to say what she does or does not think of? She has time to do nothing else, bound against her will at the mercy of the emperor."

Finn clapped a hand on Aleksandr's shoulder when he felt the young man start. "If you didn't want to bring her, why, then are you here?"

"Can't you guess?" Cyler's eyes twinkled with mischief.

"You'll take us to her," Aleksandr cried, sagging. "Won't you?"

"You're already improving your bloodline," Cyler replied. "Give this young man a tart."

"Where?" Finn asked. "We'll leave immediately."

"I'll take you as far as the town nearest their location," Cyler answered. "And that's where I leave you until you've retrieved your mate. You won't mention my involvement, and I won't be seen to have anything to do with this. Once you've been gone a reasonable time, I'll return to Agripin and attempt to correct the damage done."

Finn gaped at him. "Damage done? To Agripin? Are you as crazy as him?"

"He murdered my far!" Aleksandr cried.

"I can't deign to understand your plight, so let's not pretend you understand his," Cyler replied. "I'm not here to bicker. Time isn't on our side, as Ana's bindings could come free at any time, and if that happens, our intervention won't matter. Are you or are you not coming?"

"Let's go," Finn said, starting off without thought of a bag or a plan other than what lay at the end of the journey.

"What about our training?" Padraig urged, emphasizing the words to indicate secrecy in the presence of an outsider. "We're nearly there!"

"When I came to you, we had a deal. But now, everything has changed," Finn said. The blood in his veins scorched his flesh, too much for his body. He could burst with the anticipation if he stood still any longer. "I'll still help you, but she needs me now. First."

"We'll send reinforcements," Flynn said, stepping forward. "You have been true to your word, Finnegan. You've exercised patience, and good faith. We want Anasofiya's safety as well, and once you return, we can finish where you left off."

Finn nodded. "Once she's safe with us again, I'll try until

I'm blue in the face, or the world ends, whichever comes first. You have my word."

Padraig threw up his hands in surrender but ceased to appear as annoyed as before.

"Give us until dawn," Nora added. "We are not many, here, but I can rally strong and able Quinlans to your side. You don't know what awaits you."

Finn considered objecting, but Aleksandr's pleading eyes changed his mind. "We've waited this long. We'll do this right."

Aleksandr nodded, smiling. "I'm coming. You can't stop me."

"I wouldn't think of it," Finn replied.

Sleep evaded Finn that night. Or perhaps he evaded sleep, for his mind needed the quiet to wrap around what lay ahead.

About midnight, when he heard a knock on the window near his bed, Aleksandr peeked out and tiptoed toward the door, exiting with his best attempt to be noiseless.

"I'm coming with you!" Fiona exclaimed from outside. The thin walls carried her excited voice so efficiently she could have been standing at the foot of the bed.

"Ona, no. I'm already scared for my parents. I can't be scared for you, too."

"But it's okay for me to be scared for you?"

"I don't know if I can protect you."

"This is everyone's battle, not just yours," she countered. "Everyone, Quinlan and Empyrean, is on your side. I'm fair with a bow, and could handle a sword if needed."

"You know weapons would do no good there."

"And you don't know they wouldn't. Besides, you've seen what I can do with a little fire, too."

"You're safe here, and I need you to be safe. I can't take something happening to you."

"Aleksei, you can't protect me from everything! You tried to shield me from heartbreak with Declan, and you would turn me away to prevent my pain when your heir is born, but *I love you*. Don't you see that? I would do anything for you. I would die for you if it came down to it!"

"And I would die if you did," Aleksandr cried. "Don't *you* see *that*?"

"I won't let you fight alone. I'm either with you, or we have no business pretending to be anything more than a passing fancy. I can't be anything less than your equal, Aleksei. My mother instilled that in me, and that's just how it is."

"You are more than my equal," Aleksandr answered, softening to mask his pain. "But I can't let you come. I'm sorry, Fiona."

Finn heard his own voice on his son's lips, a battle he'd fought with Ana more than once before realizing to keep her close to his heart meant recognizing her equality in everything, even the worst dangers.

The exchange continued, but Finn forced himself to block it out. This was their moment, their lover's goodbye.

And if it broke his heart to hear it, he couldn't imagine what it was doing to his son's.

30
CYLER

Stian and Astrid showed up first. Nerys was next, looking as refreshed as someone who'd been on a long retreat.

Thorvald and Trygve appeared at the last minute, as Stian commenced the intense focus needed to create the portail.

Hey, it's the Fellowship of the Mora, Aleksandr teased, a joke Finn enjoyed, but Cyler found completely inane, even with an understanding of the reference.

A gathering of company he'd never asked for. Further, he searched for ways he could avoid it, even prevailing to the halfling in private that they should keep the party small. Leave under the cover of night.

"Agripin will sense the larger group. Who knows what he might do with that kind of threat incoming."

"Are you kidding? If I could bring an entire army with me, I would. We get one chance to save Ana. One. I won't blow it."

He should have known a Child of Man wouldn't see the logic. Their history was one without reason and filled with violence against their own. When faced with diplomacy or war, they saw no choice. Illogical bloodlust would be their end.

"If he slits her throat and then his own, do not avail to me for sympathy," Cyler snapped back, resigning himself to the increasing group.

And even larger it grew. Good on their word, the Quinlans offered up more of their own, draoi from across Ireland, though they refused to disclose the exact locations. Even though he'd risked everything coming to them, they still did not trust Cyler.

Well, he didn't *like them*. Their disingenuous take on peace and tranquility, the outward pacifism couched in the eagerness to send others to battle. It was no wonder to Cyler the Empyreans had left them to their own fates, all those years ago. If Cyler had been at the helm, he'd never have made a pact with them in the first place.

Because of their easy travel by portail, they assembled very few resources for the journey, only the essentials. Some food, in case Agripin had ignored the need for it. Medical assistance would come in the form of the army of draoi if injuries required mending. No physical weapons were needed, and they brought no additional items, only the ones they had each carried for centuries, or longer.

Cyler watched Finn standing off on his own, Aidrik's famed Ulfberht stretched across his hands. The halfling's biceps strained at the weight as he regarded the Empyrean steel.

Then, he slid the blade from its deep scabbard and lifted it toward the rising sun. The steel took the light and reflected it, casting a blinding swatch over the forest floor.

"I'm ready, brother," Finn whispered. He returned the blade to its home and then wrapped the sword belt around his waist. The tip of the leather holding Ulfberht tickled the ground. Finn cinched the strap tighter, standing tall. Just right.

Cyler turned away, confused by his conflicting thoughts of what he'd witnessed.

CYLER HAD NO ONE REQUIRING HIS GOODBYES, OR PROMISES TO return, and so he was forced to wait patiently while others performed theirs.

Of particular annoyance to him was the parting words between the halfling and his Child of Man brother, named Jonathan.

Cyler couldn't recall where he'd learned this, and did not particularly care, but the sole piece of knowledge he had about this Jonathan was that he'd wronged his brother, and hurt Anasofiya in a malicious manner. And though Cyler couldn't be concerned less with any wrongdoing against those two, Finn's capacity for forgiveness was not only foolish; it was obnoxious.

"I would still go, Finn. I told you when I came along on this journey. I would do anything to help you."

Finn shook his head. "It's too dangerous. Stay here with Anne. She needs you more."

"That's debatable." Jonathan smiled. "I'm not worried about any personal danger to me. You're my brother, and although she may never see it this way, Ana is... she's my sister. I'd lay my life down for either of you."

"I don't need you to," Finn answered, hand falling naturally against Aidrik's sword, a place it would likely rest for many years to come. "In fact, I'd prefer you didn't."

Not Aidrik's sword any longer, Cyler thought. *He's assumed rightful ownership, and the possession fits him.*

"And I'd prefer you didn't, either, but here we are." Jonathan, tentatively, stretched his hand toward his brother's shoulder. "What can I do? Sitting here doesn't help you."

"Knowing you and Anne are safe takes a weight off me,"

Finn answered. He then tilted his head in thought, considering. "There is one thing. Keep the Quinlans focused on reconciliation with the Empyreans. Something tells me this alliance is going to matter, in a life-or-death way, very soon. We can't repair thousands of years of damage, but we can do our part."

"Anne and I will help however we can. I'm not sure it will matter when Aleksei walks away from his supposed fate, and we help him."

Finn pressed his lips together. "We'll cross that bridge later. I never promised Aleksei's loyalty to them, only mine. Hopefully, I can live up to it when I return."

"You can. You will."

"Take care, Jon. And if things don't turn out the way we hope—"

"Stop—"

"—if Aleksei and I, or Ana, or any of us, don't make it back, I want you to know, I forgive you. I can't predict what our relationship looks like in the future, or if our lives can ever be the way they used to be, but you're my brother, and I love you. If this is the last time we see each other, you should know those things."

Cyler turned away at their embrace, eager to distance himself from the Quinlan encampment and these trite, tender goodbyes.

He believed his greatest failure as a soldier to be that he needed *any* of this to save the creature he loved. Cyler could no longer even *sense* Agripin as he once could. Whatever connection he'd felt to his master, his friend, his lover, had dulled, and he knew this to be through some fault of his own.

Should they succeed in their mission, Cyler decided he would need time alone, an uncertain amount, to consider where he fell so short of his path.

31
MERCY

The room didn't immediately come into focus.

Her first blurry sight was a sea of black spots. She blinked, and they only increased in number, but then edges appeared around the specks. Borders forming perfect squares, a seemingly endless number.

Dropping her head to the right, a brilliant strip of white, blinding even, nestled between two tan cliffs. Blinking again, she saw the cliffs were curtains.

Before she could regard the other side of the room, the myriad details swam back to her, congregating around the messy confusion and bringing all of it, every last bit, flooding to the surface in a tremendous rush.

She knew, before looking, what she would find on her left. Who.

Nicolas' head rested on his crossed arms, which lay on the side of her bed. He didn't snore, so she knew his sleep was light and guessed he hadn't found much of it.

"You're awake," he mumbled into his arm, raising his heavy head. "Thank God, Mercy."

"My head hurts," she croaked, not the most prominent thought on her mind, but the first that rose to her lips.

"I know, baby," Nicolas answered, coming to his senses almost immediately. He lifted her hand to his lips, then to his cheek. His tears moistened her fingers. "I know, darling.

"Emyr's child is no longer," she said next, again not the words she intended, but she wasn't sure anymore that she was in control of even the simplest aspects of her life. Not even her basic motor instincts, or her ability to make decisions.

Nicolas froze, lips parted. He wanted to object, she could see, but didn't have the heart to do it. Nic would let her go on forever in this delusion. His love for her ran that deep. A tremendous shock to her, as much as the one that had landed on her shoulders at the fairy pools.

"Nicolas, I know. I know there never was a baby," she said, this time, careful words she'd chosen. The cloudiness of her mind began to thin. "It's okay. I know."

His breath hitched. "You do?"

"I need to tell you something."

"You can tell me anything."

"Can I have some water?"

"That's what you wanted to tell me?"

"No, I need some water."

"Oh!" Nicolas jumped up and moved across the room, where a plastic pitcher and glasses sat on a wheeled table. He poured her a glass and returned, handing it to her.

Mercy drained the warm liquid in one long, satisfying gulp. The relief was more than satisfying; it was as if she'd been dehydrated for days. "More."

Nicolas went to refill her glass when she resumed her words before her courage failed her. "I have a confession. You won't like it, but I recall a time where I felt the same sorrow for you. So all I can ask is that you'll forgive me when I'm done."

"Mercy, whatever it is, I already forgive you," Nicolas answered with a short, fearful laugh as he handed her the glass. Even without the prior senses she'd possessed as an Empyrean, she could feel his apprehension. His words were more for himself. A pep talk for whatever lay ahead that might further yank the carpet out from under him.

The one kindness she could give him would be to make the confession quick, and relieve him of one tension for another. "I jumped. At the pools. I didn't slip."

"What? No, I saw you. You lost your footing."

"A voice called out to me, and I realized, finally, that it wasn't Emyr's. It never had been. It was mine." She swallowed more of the refreshing liquid, but the pained expression on Nicolas' face kept her from prolonging further. "Do you know... no, you can't know. You can't know what it is to believe in something bigger than you, in such a profound way. I surrendered everything to Emyr in my former life, only be abandoned by him in my final moments.

"And then. And then! Nicolas, he returned to me, slipping in between the words of my biography as I wrote them for the refugee children. First one or two words, then he took over entirely, whispering promises upon the page. Assuring me all my sacrifices, all my piety, had not been for nothing. I'd passed the final test, and I was to be rewarded."

Nicolas dropped his eyes, deliberating her words. He said nothing.

"We both know Emyr never did any of that. I know I should have been grateful for the new life given to me by your cousin, and I tried to be. Emyr knows I did. But how can anyone adjust from one reality to another so vastly different? Something fundamental snapped within me, and it brought us where we are now."

Nicolas stared at his hands and bent over his lap. "This all started when I couldn't keep my fucking hands off Eydis—"

"No," Mercy replied firmly. "It began way before that. It didn't help," she added, attempting to instill some gentle comfort to her tone, "But you're speaking of a single drop of water in an ocean of heartache for me. Please don't ever talk about the Eydis situation, not because it hurts any longer but because you'll never understand my thoughts on the matter. I knew who you were when I decided to stay. I also see the man you've become, and it's *that* man who brought me to Scotland, trying to save me from myself."

"Another thing I failed at," he said. No self-loathing in his words, only profound sadness. "You tried to end your life."

"I should have died under that oak tree at *Ophèlie*. What I am now is an abomination, against both our races."

"Would you stop? Just fucking stop!" Nicolas raised his head. His eyes were rimmed in bright red. Fresh agony. "We're both abominations, Mercy! I'm the black sheep of my family, and you're the black sheep of the Empyreans. Who the fuck cares? Tell me! Who do we answer to? Tell me!"

"If we can't stop from seeing our own selves through this lens, then the answer doesn't matter."

"Then try seeing yourself through *my* lens, as you see me through yours. Isn't that the damn point of love? To find someone who can see past the bullshit, beyond the darkness, farther than all the fucked-up corners of our lives in an effort to find something worth embracing?" He stood, and paced the room. "You view me for the man I should be."

"You're better than you think you are," Mercy said softly. "And it isn't only me who sees it."

"No, Mercy. Everyone else *wants* to believe it, and so they do. You do believe it. You actually fucking do, and that's what makes you different. And if you can see through to who I am deep down, why is it so hard to believe I can do the same for you?"

Mercy's shame began to blossom, and it left her speechless. But Nicolas wasn't done.

"I don't know if I'm the man you believe me to be. Not sure of much anymore, honestly. But the one thing I know, that I absolutely know beyond a shadow of a goddamn doubt, is that I love you, Mercy. I love you so much it feels like this hospital is dropping on my chest because I love you, and I'm losing you."

She watched him. His heaving chest, his eyes squinting tears away. His complete lack of both awareness or fear of the emotions overtaking him.

This creature was unlike any she'd ever met. He was arrogant, and at times thoughtless, passionate but imprudent. He was a lone wolf, a rogue, someone who had never needed anyone else, not his parents, not his sisters. Not love from another.

To receive love of that degree from someone like Nicolas Deschanel was a gift unlike any ever presented at her feet. Unlike, even, she could see now, the gift she'd believed Emyr ready to give her. For Nicolas had become who he was meant to be, in his love for her.

"I love you, as well," Mercy attempted, through her own tears, now blinding her. "I'm sorry for the hurt this caused you. I'm so unbelievably sorry, Nicolas."

He was at her side before she could end the sentence, kneeling at the bedside. "Can we agree we've both been wrong? Is that enough to put it behind us and try to figure out how to move forward?"

"It's not enough," she answered. Mercy wouldn't deceive him, even if it meant easing his pain. Their entire courtship had been a series of deceptions, small and large. "But I do want to move forward... with you."

Nicolas pulled both her hands between his, gripping them. "Tell me what you need. Anything."

"I want what was taken from me. A child."

"But..." Nicolas' grip slackened. She presumed he was about to point out the fact of her dead womb, but he took a gentler approach to the subject. "You want to adopt?"

"No, Nicolas. I want a child of my own. A child of our blood, yours and mine."

Nicolas processed, throwing out ideas as her words permeated. "We could find a surrogate. A Deschanel, maybe. Your uterus might not be viable, but maybe you have some eggs? Pretty sure I'm a virile guy."

"Please don't. You're saying yes without even thinking. Until now, you never wanted children. You made Aleksei your heir and were so sure of it. Don't agree with me out of fear of losing me. And anyway, I don't want a surrogate, I want to carry the child myself."

"You're throwing a lot at me, Mercy. You can't hold it against me that I have no fucking clue how to process it all."

"Did you hear me? I want to carry the child."

Nicolas looked as if he might slam his head into the wall, to jar the confusion. "Baby, forgive me for this, but we both know—"

"We came here for a reason, Nicolas."

"Yeah, because I was worried about you and hoped the change of scenery might make you better."

"You chose Scotland for a reason, even if you didn't realize it at the time."

He couldn't hide his growing frustration. "Because you said before it was a place you had good memories, and I wanted to take you somewhere that didn't have bad ones."

"There's a healer here. One who can do what your Aunt Colleen could not. One who can restore me," Mercy said.

"Here? Where?"

"Not on Skye, but near. In the Highlands. She can lay her hands on my womb, and give me back what was taken," she replied. Nicolas began to pull his hands away, but she clasped them. "Will you go with me?"

Nicolas looked away. His mouth hung open in shock, apparently trying to decide whether she was still out of her mind.

"I want a child, Nicolas. I'll go to this healer, with or without you, but, by Emyr, it is you I want at my side. More than anything, I want this child to share both our blood and genetics. And I desire to spend what life I have left on this planet finding some normalcy. With you."

Nicolas dropped his head on the bed but did not attempt to extricate his hands again.

"Will you share this journey with me?"

"I'll try," Nicolas whispered against the sheets, words heavy with emotions she could not yet decipher.

32
ANASOFIYA

Anasofiya slept for the first twenty-four hours following her dominance over Agripin. Knowing he could no longer hurt her, bound by a magic he could never penetrate on his own, eased her spirit enough to surrender to a rest months overdue.

On the second day, she observed him in silence, considering the steps needed to put her plan in motion.

She knew the following to be true:

Agripin must be punished.

Agripin must live.

To live was part of the necessary punishment.

His survival was only the first step of the penalty.

Agripin was to blame for Aidrik's physical death.

Agripin was responsible for her loss of control and the resulting deaths of those both innocent and not.

Agripin was not the only one to blame for Aidrik's death.

She must remember who the real enemy was. The bigger enemy.

Agripin could be used as a tool to fight this bigger foe.

Agripin's punishment could come in the form of using him toward this cause.

The Brotherhood must be reassembled.

The Senetat must be destroyed.

Agripin could assist in both these tasks.

Agripin would not do so willingly.

Anasofiya would have to force him.

Anasofiya would need to do this alone.

Not entirely alone.

Wraith whispered in her ear, reminding her of all the things, wonderful and terrible, of which she was capable.

Aidrik slept, growing stronger.

While she sat on the narrow stretch of floor in quiet contemplation, Agripin watched her in return. His face was a blank canvas, his thoughts guarded. Had he tried to share them, she'd have silenced him.

Likely, though, he wondered why she chose to sit before him, for hours on end, rather than in the other room. Anywhere but near him, really.

And, should he ask her, she would lie. She couldn't ever tell him that watching him strengthened her resolve. Away from him, she softened and questioned whether her revenge would solve anything. She asked herself whether it would make her feel better or worse. She even remembered moments with him that had bordered on tenderness and considering his actions very well may have been grounded in love for her.

So she sat before him.

Studying him.

Breathing him in.

Remembering every last terrible thing he'd done to her and those she loved.

Recalling the things he would still do to her if she'd not taken back control of her own destiny.

On the third day, Anasofiya resolved it was time to leave. She had no viable means of delivering Agripin to his judge and jury, so she determined there was only one way to do it.

One step at a time.

One breath at a time.

If she had to drag him through Siberia, she would.

If it took her years to get there, the time would not be wasted.

Only one question remained for Anasofiya.

Who would she be by the time she arrived?

33
FINNEGAN

Stian's portail opened on the outskirts of a town whose name Finn didn't bother to learn. Its only remarkable quality, aside from the proximity to his wife, was the piercing cold that shattered any keener sense of observation.

"The army stays here," Cyler commanded, nodding his head at the dozen or so Quinlans huddled together in the rear. "As I said, Agripin will sense the intrusion the closer we get."

"If something goes wrong, they're twenty miles from responding," Finn argued. His hand dropped to his sword, not casually this time. "Twenty miles, on foot, in the snow and ice."

"Stian can remain with them."

Stian grunted at the suggestion he be separated from the action.

"In fact, everyone but me should remain with Stian. Agripin won't see my presence as anything more than a return with my tail between my legs," Cyler added, contrary to his direction back in Ireland about hanging back. He was all over the place, and this worried Finn. "The rest of you are an immediate threat."

"You'll do nothing unless we are in accord," Thorvald boomed. Though his voice was not loud in timbre, his words had always carried the power of weight.

"You lost a right to a voice in this matter when you abandoned your emperor!" Cyler cried in response, approaching the ancient in a fighting stance Finn guessed he might later come to regret.

"A crime you're no less guilty of," Astrid answered. "We are all here for the same end: to free Ana, and thereby free Agripin. Do not forget, Cyler, all of us have also witnessed your master's obsession. He may call down the thunder, but he'll not harm Anasofiya."

Finn cringed at the continued mention of Agripin's "obsession" with his wife. What that preoccupation may have manifested into, all these weeks.

"Astrid is right," Nerys said. "My brother isn't the same being he once was. He's lost his self control and any reason he may have possessed."

"Fools," Cyler spat. "I see now why Agripin avoided your company all these years. Do what you wish. But if harm comes to the emperor, it is not the thunder you'll have cause to fear."

"We won't harm him unless he forces our hand," Birger said. A voice of reason.

"If he's hurt my mora, I'll kill him myself," sweet Aleksei hollered, standing tall. "You may think I'm only a child, but you have no idea of my capabilities."

Finn didn't silence his son's passion. It wasn't his place to do so. And besides, they were of the same mind, where Agripin was concerned, except that Finn wouldn't allow his son to live with the blood on his hands. Finn would handle the matter himself.

"Then I'll kill you, and your far will kill me, and this will all be one massive assassination ritual," Cyler cajoled. "Sounds much better than the plan to storm in and lose the element of surprise."

"Then go on ahead," Finn said. "Your arrival should be enough distraction for Stian to open one last portail."

Cyler had a defense loaded, but his expression faded first from annoyance to confusion and then to subtle assent. "Fine. Rent me a vehicle, then, because the walk will take all day, and none of us have the patience to wait that long to see this finished."

FINN USED HIS IDENTIFICATION TO SECURE THE CAR FOR CYLER, AND within the hour, he was off. Before he left, he gave the exact coordinates to Stian. All they could do was hope this was not misdirection or a trap.

"Wait one hour. The roads are not easy, and I'll need time to settle in with Agripin, to lower his guard. He may not have cared that I left, but he'll be suspicious of my return," Cyler requested. "Emyr only knows what you'll find when you arrive."

"If you even consider betraying us—" Finn charged.

"Far, he won't," Aleksandr whispered, as he had several other times with equal confidence. "I know he won't."

And how do you know? How do you always know?

"Go, then," he said.

NO HOUR HAD EVER PASSED SO SLOWLY.

Not a single word was exchanged within the rescue party. None was adequate for what lay ahead, which was more mystery than finality. Cyler had no way to communicate with them, and thus, no means of delivering a warning.

Aleksandr leaned against Finn, the weight of his frame and of his worries causing them both to sag. All Finn could do was wrap his arm around his son, and pull him closer. Nothing he could say would allay either of their fears, and he would not again, not ever, deceive his son, even in the name of protective love.

"It is time," Trygve declared, at last, his first words since re-joining them at the Quinlan camp with Thorvald.

Stian nodded and rose, closing his eyes.

A portail appeared.

Finn discovered his newfound patience had limits. As the dim circle in the center of the entrance broadened, Finn found himself leaping through and then plunging into knee-deep fresh snow.

His entire 360 degree view was a blanket of white, as far as his vision stretched.

All save the cabin.

Finn entered first, throwing the door open so wide it snapped back and nearly hit him in the face.

The rest of the party crowded in behind him, but he hardly noticed them, all except Aleksei, who slipped his hand through Finn's briefly, for strength, then nodded toward the interior.

Few furnishings decorated the front room. No personal effects were strewn about, and no evidence of its occupation, except the fire burning in the hearth.

A dim light spread out across the floor ahead. Light creaking sounds came from beyond. Then footsteps.

Finn's hand traveled to Ulfberht. Beside him, Aleksandr stopped breathing.

Cyler appeared, the color drained from his face. "We came too late."

Finn repeated his words, frozen in place. His son's sway brought him back.

He sprang forth, knocking a dazed Cyler into the front doorframe. Rounding the corner, he found the source of the light and followed it, landing in the doorway of a bedroom barely larger than a closet.

Finn was not the least bit prepared for what he saw.

Ana leaned against the wall, arms crossed over her chest while Agripin huddled on the floor, broken and defeated. His limited wriggling made it evident he was bound by something invisible, and all at once, Finn also understood who had done it.

That same person remained transfixed on her victim, frozen in time or thought or both. She hadn't noticed the intrusion.

Finn's first vision of his wife in months offered him a view of her through the many lenses of his love.

FINN SEES THE MILKY CURVE OF HER BALLERINA'S NECK AGAINST THE silk straps of her mother's royal blue dress, a thousand times more vibrant than the Atlantic they'd sailed with Portland's elite as a thank you for her support of Summer Island.

Finn sees her drowsy, languid expression as her head falls back against the cliff's edge, lost in the rhythm of their lovemaking. Not their first time together, but the first time she seemed aware of how deep her love ran.

Finn sees, for the first time, love staring back at him.

Finn sees the doe-eyed expression that belongs more to a young girl than the woman he adores, at the moment, she realizes he had, after all, come for her. When she realizes he'd come across the world, searching castle after castle, until he found her, she's in awe of him.

Finn sees her holding a swaddled Aleksei against her breast, the sweat matting her hair to her forehead and cheeks, and even over her eyes, and yet she's oblivious as she watches her son and slips a hand to her husband.

Finn sees her for the last time, the morning of the coronation. Her fear. Her need. Love blanketing both, and trust in him carrying her out of the bed and into her future.

Finn finds his voice.

"Ana?"

"I told you to leave, Cyler. This is between your master and me."

"Ana," Finn re-stated, more firmly the second time. He forced his voice to rise higher, crisp and clear. "Ana."

She went stiff. "You are the lowest form of creature, that you would use the voice of my own husband to get to me. Leave!"

"Turn around, sweetie."

"If you don't leave, I'll kill you, Cyler. I don't want to, but so help me—"

"Turn around, silly girl. I'm really here. Aleksei is here. We're here, and we love you. Put aside your anger for a moment and listen to what your heart is telling you. You're safe now, Ana. Just as you've been my safe place, I'm yours."

Aleksei paused behind him, trembling. Finn dropped a hand behind his back, offering it to his son who accepted it in a flash. He stretched the other out before him, past Ana, into her line of sight.

"I'm a part of you, Ana, and you're a part of me. Aidrik saw to that at our wedding and, because of it, you only need to search your heart to know what's right behind you."

Ana's knees were the first to give. She coughed out a choked gasp. "My Poseidon."

"Take my hand, silly girl."

Instead of complying, she lifted her own in the air, fluttering it in crisp turns in front of her face as if assessing its tangibility. Then, with less precision, she dropped it back to her side and out, resting her palm above Finn's.

He helped her the rest of the way and locked their hands together.

At the connection, the first genuine union with someone out of love and not bondage, Ana sagged. Finn was right there to pull her up, lacing his arms around her waist from behind. Aleksei's appeared next, twining through the arms of both his parents.

Ana's breath caught, beginning in slow, wheezing rasps. They increased in duration. Within seconds, she was hyperventilating.

"Shh, you're safe. You're safe. We're here," Finn whispered against her ear, wrapping his arms tighter. Aleksei erupted in sobs, pressing his face into his mother's back.

"How..." she moaned swaying. Finn knelt then and lifted her into his arms. She fell against him, and he physically felt the strength drain from her, passing through her limbs and into the nether.

"You've been strong far too long," Finn told her. Her ribs pressed through the thin shirt she wore, and her legs had lost some of their muscle, but she was alive. She was *alive*! "Let me be strong for you now."

"And me," Aleksei sniffled.

"Let us carry it for you," Finn whispered.

He knew he should take her out of that room, away from

the coward huddled in the corner, away from all of them. But he found, now that he had her, he was rooted in place. Afraid even one step might steal this moment he'd dreamed of for so long.

Ana nodded. Her erratic breaths had turned to tremors. Finn envisioned this as a physical entity leaving her, the grip of evil draining away. Her rescue would need to be so much more than bodily removing her from danger.

A long road lay ahead.

He didn't care, just then.

His wife was back in his arms, and their son stood at their side.

At this moment, nothing could touch them.

Not the darkness of the past, or fluid uncertainty of the future.

Not Agripin.

Not ever again.

They were three, and they were whole.

And that was enough.

34
CYLER

Astrid insisted they all give Finn, Ana, and Aleksandr a moment.

Cyler reminded them he had brought them there to save his master, and they had yet to do so. Who knew what damage the bitch had done?

Everyone else sided with Astrid, so Cyler was forced to wait while the halflings enjoyed their reunion. This left him feeling as impotent as the Quinlan army waiting in the kitchen, never to see the action they sought.

Not that it mattered so much, now. He'd had time to think. Two sets of ideas occupied Cyler, really, and always had: those on the surface, which were always immediately apparent, and those brewing barely beneath, working diligently toward a conclusion in collusion with his subconscious.

The obvious answer had bubbled to the surface. A realization that made him numb, but somehow, did not come as a surprise.

Cyler could have sat with his master. No one else wished to deal with Agripin; they were far more concerned with

Anasofiya's well-being, and, caught up in that, they'd not have noticed if he slipped away to comfort Agripin.

He found he no longer had comfort to spare.

So he waited, with these new thoughts, forming new plans.

Anasofiya's emotions cycled across the spectrum, beginning with confusion and disorientation, sliding briefly into anger, and then landing squarely into a resolved relief.

Cyler was quietly amazed at how quickly she was able to get to that point, but he had no strong desire to share any compliments with the creature at the centerpiece of his own pain.

Trygve disappeared to evaluate the magic binding Agripin and returned with his assessment around the time Anasofiya grew lucid. "Astounding. We must find cause to study the empress further when timing is more appropriate."

Finn and Aleksandr shot him a tandem look that said, *over my dead body,* and Cyler nearly laughed.

Astrid leaned forward on the vinyl chair where she perched, lifting one of Ana's hands into her own, preparing to demonstrate the bedside manner for which she was renowned. "You do not have to explain yourself, now or in the future," she assured Ana, with a gentle smile. "Your magic, and your darkness, is your own to ponder, or employ, as the need arises. I do have one question for you if you'll permit me to ask?"

Anasofiya made no movement for several seconds before slowly nodding.

"You could have killed him," Astrid continued. "You did not. Why?"

Finn squeezed his wife's shoulder as she stabilized herself with a long, exhaled breath. "He's no use to us dead."

"And what use is he to us alive?" Thorvald asked with a subtle grunt.

"His sister sits on the throne of Farjhem," Anasofiya explained evenly. Her posture straightened, and the confidence Cyler first saw in her, months ago, returned. "We can all agree that she isn't very good at it." Subdued, wearied laughter from around the room answered her. "But her ineptitude as a leader is the least of her crimes. What she is doing... what she continues to do... to our people is beyond the pale. We have to stop her, and we know this, but without raising an army that's already skeptical after Agripin's betrayal, I can think of only one way to her."

"You're going to let Oriana take his life, in exchange for stopping the slaughter," Birger concluded, but Anasofiya shook her head.

"She won't kill him," she said. "If she does, it will be a mercy, and she is not known for that virtue... or any virtue I'm aware of. She'll use him, to her own ends, and revel in him bending the knee to her. I'm no politician, and neither is she, it's clear, but I strongly suspect she's eager to get back to The Menagerie. She may even put him on the throne to rule in her name, with her own hand-picked advisors. Whichever she chooses, he'll have no ally to boost him up over her, so he will be at her disposal. I can't think of a greater punishment for a coward. And it puts him as much at our mercy as hers because we are his only way out of the hell he's earned. He'll find no allies in her court. We're the closest he has to any."

"You have given this considerable thought," Astrid said in wonder.

Anasofiya pursed her lips. "I had plenty of time to think. More than enough." Something else existed behind her words, a secret. Cyler wondered if and when she would choose to share it.

"Don't forget, the very last thing Oriana would want is me on the throne," Nerys added. "Positioning our brother as a figurehead ruling under her wishes is not only a reasonable idea, if you're Oriana, but likely the best."

"And what if we are not in accord? If we choose to deliver him to a more immediate justice he deserves for his betrayal?" Thorvald asked.

"You won't," Anasofiya answered with a thin, poised smile. "Because I did what none of you were capable of doing."

THE DIALOG CONTINUED FOR ANOTHER HOUR, THE BROTHERHOOD debating logistics and considering all potential obstacles to their success.

They could kill him, but that solved nothing other than the exacting of revenge. Not a bad reason, all things considered, but his demise would not stop the deaths of their compatriots.

They could keep him imprisoned in Ana's magic, and store him somewhere safe to let him suffer in solitude. The downside to this option was the same as outright killing him.

The group continued returning to Ana's demand to turn Agripin over to his sister. An enormous gamble, they said, but one that guaranteed the most reward. Until an army could be raised, they had no other means of defeating Oriana except through strategy, and in the absence of a better tactic, this was it.

Even Cyler had to concede, though privately, the plan came with more benefit than loss.

The final question, then, became the largest to solve: Who would deliver Agripin to Oriana, in turn exposing themselves to her mercy as well?

Cyler could have let them all present their case as to who

was better, or worse, for the task, but he was weary of getting it done.

"I will deliver him."

Stian offered to open a portail to Norway. Birger, a strong tracker, would go along because Cyler was still not to be fully trusted. He would hang back far enough to escape detection by Oriana's scouts, and leave only certain the task had been completed.

Cyler didn't fault them for their lack of confidence. He couldn't trust his own heart or mind anymore. Why should they?

In the end, all he asked for was a moment alone with his master before they departed.

No one denied him.

Agripin had only one word for him, as he stared up at Cyler in defeat from his prison on the floor.

"Why?"

"Aggie—"

"You owe me nothing except this answer, Cyler. And you *will* give it to me," Agripin commanded, in no position to make requests but nevertheless exhibiting the same arrogant confidence that had drawn Cyler to his side in those early days.

Cyler shifted his stance, avoiding Agripin's eyes. "I followed you for many years. I did whatever you asked, without question." He grinned. "Without question, for the *most* part. I killed for you and plotted and planned in your name. I loved you, Agripin."

"And so, why?"

"I no longer understand who that fledgling warrior was,

but I know it is no longer me. I have to think, now, of the world bigger than the one immediately around me. I lived, for years, in fear of losing my life to the activation of a mark, a power you held over me. I could ask you why, but I already know."

"Then no use in my explanation. You're so sure of yourself."

Cyler knelt before his master, summoning his courage. "I still love you. But you no longer hold sway over me. The power is mine. I choose to do this not to punish you, Agripin, but as one final kindness. The last eyes you see before being subjected to Oriana's illicit rule should be those of the one who has loved you most in all the world."

Agripin's head sagged. He whispered only one word, in the form of a whispered sigh.

"Cyler."

35
ALEKSANDR

Home, for Aleksandr's young body and old soul, was wherever his loved ones rested.

Now, for the first time in his life, they were not only together again, but safe. Aidrik's absence loomed over them like a wilted flower, but his mora, for reasons she had yet to disclose, no longer mourned him.

The Quinlans had wanted to move straight to celebration at their return, but Finn understood his wife needed something else a whole lot more: rest and time with her two greatest loves.

On that first evening, she'd lain atop the fur coverlet on the bed, eyes heavy with a broad range of emotions playing out like a movie across her flushed face. She insisted on listening to their stories, rather than sharing her own. Finn whispered to Aleksei that his mora may never want to share, and that would have to be okay for them.

Aleksei supposed it was all right. If he ever learned the details, he couldn't prevent himself from acting on them.

On the other hand, if he and his far did not, who would?

I would tear Agripin limb from limb with my own bare hands, Finn had said. By the look on his face, he meant it and then some. *But that isn't what your mora wants. And this, all of this, is for her. We brought her home, Aleksei. That has to be more than enough, for now.*

Where is home, Far?

He hadn't considered that his far wouldn't know the answer, either. Puzzlement rested on Finn's face, and then he broke into a smile.

Wherever we are. That's where home is.

ALTHOUGH HIS MORA WAS NOT YET READY TO SHARE HER OWN TALES, they had their own to share with her. He and his far started by catching her up on some of the surface-level stories of their adventures, slowly leading toward the purpose they were there. The reason the Quinlans were so eager to help.

"I never believed in the Deschanel Curse. I can't say I hold much stock in the idea of a prophecy." Ana shook her head against the pillow. "I grew up with superstitious kooks. Didn't realize I married one."

Far feigned offense at her lighthearted jab. "You didn't. Which is why you should pay attention, silly girl. I'm not making this up. These folks, they have assumed it for centuries, and the Empyreans believe it, too. The Brotherhood exists solely toward protecting all of us. They always have. If you don't buy into it, you're in the minority."

"So you're a lemming," Ana replied, but she was smiling. "Tell me why you really believe it. It isn't because the Quinlans or the Empyreans do. Tell me truthfully, because I know it's more than that."

Finn shifted in the chair he sat backward in, folding his arms across the top rung. He sighed, then drew the breath back in, sighing once more. "Before Aidrik died, he told me something. I never had the chance to tell you."

Ana watched him from the bed, her relaxed posture giving silent approval.

"He said I was a draoi. The word meant nothing to me at the time, but he told me that one day it would. When Aleksei and I arrived here, I was frustrated and angry, and aching to find you, but everyone forced me to slow down and learn about who I was. I had no other choice because I needed their help, and I trusted Nerys."

"She's one of the good ones," Ana concurred. "I sensed it in her the night we met in the cave."

"Not like her evil brother," Aleksei snarled but said no more. He was as eager to hear what his far would say as his mora was.

"No, not like Agripin," Finn agreed, patting his son's leg. "And so I stayed, on the promise what they could show me would help me get to you. They also pledged to come with me because we didn't know what we'd find when we arrived."

"So, what did they show you?"

"Most of it can wait until another time," Finn answered, looking down at his calloused hands. "But Padraig, that frustrating son-of-a-bitch, taught me that to use what's within me, I needed to find calm. I've never in my life had calm or patience. I can't remember ever having a need for it. That lack of tolerance and tranquility is what chased you across the world."

Ana grinned, pulling the cardigan over her.

"In that state of mind, I was able to do the things Padraig said I could. I traveled through time—yes, ask Aleksei! We have some badass stories to tell you, someday, don't we kid?"

Finn winked at Aleksei. He returned the gesture.

"The other thing I found in that sense of serenity was a

voice. I'd never heard any voice like it before. It sounded like softness traveling down a never-ending hallway, or a feather floating against the wind. Soft, inviting, and both unreal and absolutely real at once." Finn flashed him an apologetic look. "Even Aleksei hasn't heard this because I didn't know how to tell him. He was already so conflicted about his role in all this. I heard the goddess, Ana. Don't ask me how I know she was real. I did. I do."

"I believe you."

"I won't ask Aleksei to do anything his heart doesn't honor," Far went on, rapping his knuckle against the soft wood, "but I made a promise to the Quinlans that I would find your cousin, Amelia, and Jacob. I can't go back on that promise."

"Of course, you can't," she agreed. "Even if their help wasn't needed in the end, they sacrificed for us. It's our turn."

"I can't leave you again."

"I know."

"Not for a second."

"I know, sweetheart."

"You're going to get tired of me, and we'll become that couple who fights all the time because we can't stand one another, but I still won't leave you."

Ana chuckled. The sound warmed Aleksei more than any fire in the hearth. "Doubtful. And I agree."

"So, you see my conundrum."

"Not really," she replied. "Did I hear you right earlier, that you've taken Aleksei on your time travel adventures? And Amelia is no draoi, and yet she's off somewhere with Jacob."

Aleksandr nodded. "I can't wait to tell you about it!"

"It was an accident," Finn said, misinterpreting her question. His hands went up in defense. "I never would have dragged our son along to God-knows-where intentionally.

Anyway, Padraig thinks he did it on his own because he's a draoi too."

"Well, you're about to do it intentionally," she said. "Because you're going to go find my cousins and we're coming with you."

"You want... to come with?"

"That's what I said."

"Do you know how dangerous it is? I never know where I'm going to end up. We could drop into the middle of a terrorist cell. I can't control it."

"Don't forget what you were going to try before Cyler arrived," Aleksandr reminded him. "Focusing on Amelia and Jacob. Everyone thinks it will work."

"You say that because it was your idea," Finn teased with a sideways grin. "Okay, yeah, I think it might work. But what if it doesn't?"

"Then we face whatever happens together," Ana said gently.

"Do you really think Nerys will let us leave without her?" Aleksandr asked.

Finn grinned. "There's not much she can do if we don't tell her."

Ana watched them both for a moment, and then went on. "We can't protect each other any better than sticking together. I can see how much Aleksei has grown up in my absence, and it hurts, as a mother who wants her baby to stay that way forever, but I can also tell he's stronger because of it. We can't keep experiences from one another any more than we can keep secrets. That may be the way of others, but isn't ours."

Finn considered her words, wearing a thoughtful expression Aleksei recognized as the one that appeared when he didn't like what he was hearing, but couldn't deny it was the right answer. "And what if we succeed? We find your cousins and bring them back. What if Amelia is pregnant, as the prophecy predicts? What then?"

"As you said, only Aleksei can decide his path," she answered. She patted her hand on the bed beside her, beckoning him over. "Come lie next to me, both of you. I want to fall asleep next to all my pretty boys."

They didn't correct her. To have *all* her pretty boys would mean Aidrik remained with them too.

Instead, he answered her request in an instant, eager to be near her once again and breathe in the scent of her, feel her heartbeat through her skin. Amazing as it seemed, she was right here, right now, okay.

"I mean it, Aleksei," she whispered against his forehead, lips pressed into the center of his brow. "You won't carry this weight on your heart. Whatever you decide, your far and I will stand by you. We love you until the end of time."

"I know, Mora," Aleksandr cried, not wanting her to see his tears. He wished for her to view the man he'd grown into, not the terrified boy still living inside.

"And you," she said, turning toward Finn, whose head lay pressed to her breast. "Are my hero. Always, always. My Poseidon."

"My silly girl," Finn said in return, voice choked. "My safe place."

"No more talking for tonight," she decided, arms folded over them both, eyes already closing. "Tonight, I want to enjoy the absolute bliss of holding you both close."

His parents were both asleep within minutes, lost to their exhaustion and relief, safe in the knowledge that no matter what tomorrow delivered, they could face it together.

Aleksandr wished he could share the same relief. He did, in

a way. Having his mora back was the greatest gift he'd ever received, but he still felt a piece of him missing.

The answer wasn't hard to find. Fiona.

As the tribe welcomed them back with exaltations and open arms, Fiona had stood off to the side, watching, waiting for others to finish their greetings so she could offer her own.

Delaying, Aleksandr supposed, for a sign he would welcome one from her.

His heart called out to her, summoning her forth. It burned for the thrill of her touch, and the comfort that, until now, he could only find from his mora. Fiona's arms had replaced his mora's in many ways, and yet now he had one and not the other.

While his heart sought her out, his mind knew better. It protected both, from the inevitable hurt awaiting each of them. He wasn't worried about himself. He had already been through a lifetime of tough events and could weather many more. But Fiona was a precious gem, sheltered in the hinterland veil for all her life. He would keep her this way, forever. For his sake. For her own.

The pain of missing her rocketed to the forefront every few moments, causing him to doubt his own resolve. It made him forget about everyone else and see only her. Potential agony of missing her made him willing to put aside his responsibility and spend the world hiding... wrapped in their love, forsaking everything else.

But Mora had said it: He was a man now. And he had to face this future as a man, not a child.

The world rested on Aleksandr's shoulders, and he would not—not for anything—let it down.

EPILOGUE

They'd reached the intersection. The one where paths and fates diverged.

"His future does not need to be yours," Birger said. "There are other ways."

Cyler glared down at Agripin, hunched over on a sled they'd fashioned from rope and old siding. It would not do for a long voyage, but they didn't have far to go. "Aye. Only one way for me, though."

Birger attempted no further dissuasion. He clapped a hand on Cyler's shoulder, and they shared a brief nod. "I will remain nearby until the deed is done. Even should you send them after me, I won't be found."

"I have no reason to send them after you."

"Everyone has cause when the stakes are appropriate."

"I have no quarrel with the Brotherhood," Cyler returned, then said no more on the subject.

Or any other subject.

Their final departure was swift and wordless.

• • •

Cyler and his master passed through the secret clearing in the mountains of Farjhem. When last they'd taken this journey, Cyler had stayed several paces behind, in respectful deference. Now it was Agripin who lagged behind, unable to carry his own weight forward.

Most would welcome such a shift dynamic, but not Cyler. He was born to serve, and he'd only ever wanted to obey one creature.

The cover of night meant they drew very little attention. A few curious eyes peered from behind lace curtains, but no one assailed them or dared ask where they were going. Likely no one recognized the pile of flesh on the rotting wood as their fallen emperor. Their eyes couldn't see what brains could never conceive.

Cyler had only chanced a handful of glances at his master during the short journey. Each time, pain stared back, but it was his own, reflected in Agripin's eyes, that cut the sharpest.

Through the valley and up the mountain pass they journeyed, and only at the palace gates were they finally halted by guards.

None of them could believe what they were witnessing. One ran off, Oriana's name upon his lips. The others drew their swords.

"I assure you, this is no deception," Cyler replied, lips curling in derision.

"We shall see," one replied, hand gripped tightly on his hilt. "We shall see."

The other guard squinted, watching Cyler with a curious expression. Cyler was unruffled by the attention, but something about the creature struck him as familiar.

The Menagerie. One of Oriana's frequent patrons. Cyler didn't know what his birth name was, but underground he was known as Cicero.

Abject horror washed over this guard's face, as he alone realized the madness that had landed at their feet, on their watch.

The throne room had not changed under Oriana's rule. Whether it be that she hadn't yet gotten around to it, or that she was hoping she might not have to deal with politics much longer, was unclear. If Anasofiya's theory held water, it would be the latter. But Anasofiya had never been privy to Oriana's true nature. She'd not witnessed her senseless cruelty.

Oriana appeared as a snapshot in time, in her white brocade gown sweeping the floor, even as she sat upon the satin cushion. Unprepared for their midnight entrance, she'd not had time to bind her hair, and it lay in crimson waves down her shoulders.

Someone unfamiliar with her dark heart would say she was beautiful.

"Ahh, Vakkar," she sighed. Her eyes were heavy with fatigue, but also disbelief. Apparently, for all her posturing to get the attention of the Brotherhood, this was the one gift she had not anticipated.

"You asked for the surrender of the Brotherhood," Cyler recited. He dared not let his eyes drop toward Agripin, not now. "They've sent me with their leader."

Oriana diverted her gaze toward her brother, eyes twinkling in amusement. "And who did *this* to you?"

Cyler remembered Birger's words. *Anasofiya is dead, as far as Oriana knows. I can't force your loyalty on this, but if you truly mean to serve your kind, you will consider the impact of your words when you enter Farjhem.*

"Leif," Cyler answered. "He wouldn't come of his own accord, so we had no choice."

"I see." Oriana rose and approached her brother. She knelt before him, her dress falling around like a broken crown. "And what am I supposed to do with him?"

"Whatever you desire," Cyler replied. He tightened his jaw but was careful not to betray any emotion. She had always maintained the gift of detection, though, it would not be long before she saw through him, as she always had, since the very first.

Gaze still fixed on her brother, Oriana raised one hand in the air and snapped her fingers. Two guards in crimson robes rushed forward.

"Take him to his old chambers. I want ten guards attending him, day and night. No exceptions," she commanded.

Cyler didn't turn to watch his master dragged away by the guards he'd once commanded. He didn't stop to consider the impact of this swing in power, or what their futures might hold. How could he?

To think on any of this would be to accept the madness as fact.

Then it was only he and the creature who had started him on this path centuries ago.

"You are the only being I have ever allowed to defect more than once, Vakkar," she reminded him, the soothing voice of a caretaker couched in a life-threatening scold.

Cyler nodded, only now turning his head toward the door through which Agripin had been dragged, moments ago.

"Have you ever thought to ask why?"

"I have not."

"Better you don't," she answered, running a hand across his brow. A loving threat. "Beware of testing my limits. You may find them narrower than you believed."

"I volunteered to bring him."

"A noble and brave soldier, until the very last," she mocked.

"You know you can never leave. You'll serve him, even now, in this reduced form his machinations left him."

Cyler nodded.

"Most of all, you'll serve me. Me above all others. Above *any* others. You understand this?"

He understood, yes. That penance came in often unusual forms.

MERCY HAD LED THEM WITH THE PURPOSEFUL NAVIGATION OF ONE who had taken the steps a thousand times before.

She insisted, of course, that she'd never been where they were going, only that she'd heard tell of the shaman who occupied this enchanted stretch of Highland wilderness.

They parked the car when they ran out of road. A clear, trodden path carried them for a few miles but eventually the vines crossed over, the boundaries of where their feet should fall became less clear.

Mercy didn't slow when the trail ended. Her navigation held true. The fortitude she exhibited, as branches slapped her in the face and bushes stung her, was nothing short of bewildering.

Nicolas struggled to keep up, dodging the plants she shoved to the side, finding himself not nearly as graceful in his maneuvering. Never in his life had he enjoyed the outdoors, and he was paying for that disregard now.

As the last of the light disappeared behind the mountains, the path broke into a clearing. A blanket of emerald, as dazzling as staring into the sun, decorated everything from the ground all the way to the vines and ivy snaking up and over the lone structure in the center.

A house. One that, despite the earth attempting a reclaiming, had the spirit of a dwelling well-loved.

Smoke billowed from an old double chimney.

"At last," Mercy declared, finally slowing her pace now that her destination lay before her.

"Are you sure you know what you're doing?" Nicolas asked, glancing between her and the cottage in the middle of nowhere. He'd followed her this far, and now, at the moment of truth, his doubts crept forward.

"No, but I know what I want." She started toward the house, and all he could do was follow behind.

The door had opened before they landed on the stoop. A young woman, fresh-faced with the serenity of youth, greeted them.

"Fiona St. Andrews. Been expecin' ye."

"St. Andrews?" Nicolas' eyes widened.

"Aye. Finn's grandparents," Mercy answered, without looking at him. Fiona had Mercy's hands in hers with all the warmth of greeting a long-lost relative.

Both his brows went up. He pointed at their host. "That woman is younger than Finn."

"The magic that sustains her is the same I believe can strengthen me," Mercy explained. Fiona entered, beckoning them forward. "Are you coming?"

Nicolas began to say yes, but an invisible hand stayed his tongue.

Love had brought him from New Orleans to Scotland, and now miles into the hinterland. He'd followed her blindly, his fear of losing her so acute, and so physically painful he hadn't stopped to think.

Say it, you asshole. Say yes. Open your fucking mouth and say it.

Sorrow tinged Mercy's eyes as her lips curled into a sad smile. "You brought me this far. For that I'm grateful."

"So that's it?"

"Only you can answer that, Nicolas." Mercy stepped over the threshold, focused inside, not back. "This is my path. It may or may not be yours."

Nicolas watched the door close behind her.

The splintered oak whispered its secrets, but Nicolas was not ready to hear them.

Anasofiya's heart was a series of dark tunnels, despair painting the walls in haphazard patterns. Finn would meander those halls for the rest of his days, scrub clean the pain, warming her from the inside out.

As she stood before him, hand laced with her son's, ready for their next adventure, Finn no longer feared the road ahead or the forks in it. The past may haunt her, but he would be her light in the yawning darkness.

"Are we ready?" Finn asked his son and wife, linking his hands in theirs to complete the circle.

"We are," Ana replied.

"Affirmative," Aleksandr chimed in.

Finn smiled. The two halves of his heart, the only true purpose he'd ever known other than navigating the endless sea. Before him, they stood, and would always stand. "I have no guarantee this will work, but this is Aleksei's idea, and so it has to be a good one, right?" He winked at his son.

Aleksandr blushed and looked down.

"We'll keep trying until it does," Anasofiya said with confidence. "However long that may be. A vow is a vow. And Amelia is my cousin."

Forbia barked and circled their feet. For the first time since his reunion with Ana, Finn felt the knot in his heart re-form. "I'm so sorry, girl. Wolves don't really blend in. We'll be back soon, I promise. Jon will watch over you."

At the mention of Jon, Ana flinched but said nothing. Whatever she was thinking—whatever Finn, too, was considering about that matter—would need to wait until their return.

For now, they had a more pressing matter.

Finn's eyes closed.

He couldn't remember meeting Jacob more than briefly, but Amelia's was a face he could not ever forget, proof of the strength in the Deschanel genetics; it was Ana's face, painted with less pain and framed with a halo of white gold.

All right, Goddess. You brought us here, and these are your guiding words. So show me the way. Wherever Amelia and Jacob are, we need to be as well.

THE WORLD LAUNCHED INTO A DOZEN SOMERSAULTS.

PERPETUAL MOTION CARRIED ALEKSANDR FORWARD, KNOCKING BOTH his parents over onto their backs. They landed in grass. Overhead, the sky was edged in purple, welcoming the first whispers of dusk.

"Sorry," Aleksandr said with a shy grin, rolling off to the ground. "That happened faster than last time."

Finn sat up to gather his bearings. Anasofiya was a step ahead of him, both in maneuvering off the grass and in her recognition of the surroundings.

"It can't be..."

Aleksandr's eyes brightened, and he sprang to his feet. "No *way*!"

Finn's vision cleared and he examined his surroundings. The looming Big House came into view. All around them the familiar live oaks stood sentry, though they appeared smaller, or perhaps trimmed.

"*Ophélie*," he mused, pushing himself off the ground. "I'll be damned. We came home."

"Not exactly," Ana replied in wonder, wandering off ahead. "This is *Ophélie*, yes, but look at the height of the levee. You can see the river at ground level. Usually, we can only see it from the third floor. And the oaks, Finn, look how much smaller they are. They've only recently been planted. The grass hasn't even grown around the roots yet."

"Look at the size of those boats!" Aleksandr pointed toward the Mississippi, where two steamships passed in transit.

"*When* is this, do you think?" Finn asked, gaping wide-mouthed at the fresh white paint on the plantation home. And that *garçonierre*... it still bore the shine of new construction.

"Before the war, maybe," Ana replied, lost in thought. "I guess it depends on who opens the door when we knock, right?"

"You really think that's a good idea?"

"I don't think we came here to be spectators," she answered.

Aleksandr studied his clothes and grimaced. "We're really not dressed for this. Like, at all."

"We'll say we're cousins from the Low Countries," Ana said. "Or descendants of the Habsburgs. They had their hands in every house of Europe. It would take years to disprove us."

"You're enjoying this when you should be crapping your pants," Finn accused.

"If the alternative to enjoyment is shitting myself, I'll choose a good time any day, thank you," she teased.

God, how he wanted to take her in his arms and crush her in a hug that never ended. To see her smile, her lips tilted at the corners on the verge of a laugh... he could admit it now, when she was back and safe, that he half expected never to see either again.

"Earth to Poseidon," she said. "We doing this?"

"I love you," Finn said, unable to help himself. "Both of you. So damn much."

Ana regarded him from the short distance, and she was, for a moment, the beautiful mystery girl living next door on the island in Maine with the shy, unsure smile as she ran toward him down the coastline, book clutched to her chest.

And then she was in his arms, Aleksandr right behind her. All was right. All was okay. The world had stitched the broken seams, and the fabric had its stretch back.

"This is love," she whispered, pressing her lips against his neck.

"This, right here," Finn replied, planting his feet firmly in the soil.

THE SECRETS AMONGST THE CYPRESS EXCERPT

Amelia and Jacob followed Ophélie Deschanel across the freshly seeded, sprawling grassland of the property bearing her name, in a century not their own, toward a future they could not predict.

Jacob hadn't had the luxury of time to think through the consequences or results of time dancing, any more than he'd had when he joined form with the bear, recognizing the creature's own beastly vigor roar and rip through him as he quite certainly saved his wife's life. Jacob still didn't even know how he'd done it. He didn't quite remember the exact moment he'd been stripped of his own mortal skin and thrust into the warm, vital flesh of the bear, becoming one. Could he replicate it? He didn't know that, either. This gift of warging emerged only in times of great need, which was true of all his gifts, according to Padraig.

He may have saved Amelia, but the world remaining for her offered a fate perhaps worse than death. What happened in Ireland had changed them both, but no one more so than his wife, who had endured horrors neither of them could even speak of. This was the rule that hadn't been voiced but was true regardless.

Then they had made it even riskier by entering Farjhem in turmoil. This trek was more than a gamble in Jacob's estimation, and it left them with few choices and even fewer minutes to make them. Always quick on his feet when his back was up against the wall, he searched for the answer, and it appeared. Once he decided, there was no un-deciding: The couple had to do more than leave the *where.* They had to leave their *when.*

He couldn't say why that, of all solutions, had popped into his head, only that he couldn't bear his broken wife's wide eyes surveying the landscape like a cornered animal.

Are you sure? Amelia had asked, putting all her faith, all her hope, in him, despite her obvious doubt. *How can you be so sure? How do you know this* when *is any better than the last one?*

"I'm not," he mumbled, under his breath at a volume neither his wife nor the historical figure ahead of them could hear. "Not sure of anything anymore."

"You've brought your appetite with you, I hope?" the young woman called over her shoulder as they meandered toward the dusty drive leading to the front door. She lifted her skirt and bustle as she prepared to ascend the stairs. A few men in dusters and frock coats leaned against a nearby column, a cloud of smoke swirling the air around them as they engaged in animated discourse.

Several young black men worked to calm and corral a handful of horses with a carriage attached. Jacob's stomach tightened. He was witnessing slavery in action. Amelia offered him a cheerless smile from his peripheral. They would see more before their time here was at an end, he knew, and it would take tremendous willpower not to act on it. Only the two of them possessed the hindsight of a past never lived through.

"Famished," Amelia answered when Jacob did not.

A cacophony of deep voices followed a strong wind carrying cigar smoke, pouring from inside the Big House of the plantation. He grimaced. *More people. Lots more.* Later, he might find himself in the mental shape to appreciate that they stood on the lower gallery of one of the finest homes in Louisiana, at the height of its prime. For now, much of him existed in suspended animation, a place where he wasn't quite convinced they weren't still stuck outside of Farjhem almost two centuries later.

"The men retired to the parlor early," Ophélie explained with a light cluck of disapproval. "They never can wait!" She paused at the door, lowering her skirts, leveling her gaze at Jacob. "Would you like me to introduce you to Papa, so you may join them?"

Jacob shook his head a little too emphatically. In his peripheral he saw Amelia look away, biting back amusement.

"No, I suppose you brought manners with you across the sea," Ophélie decided, then blushed at her own forwardness.

As if answering an unspoken command, the double doors yawned open, revealing a bustling hall filled with a half-dozen brightly colored hooped skirts swishing across gleaming cypress boards. The high lilt of excited young debutantes competed for volume against the men congregated in the nearby parlor. A young butler offered mint juleps from a silver tray.

Jacob's breath caught. He blinked hard to bring himself into the moment. Surely, he'd stumbled into the ballroom scene at Twelve Oaks. Ashley Wilkes would descend the staircase any moment.

A cluster of ladies ceased their animated chatter, running

their eyes over he and Amelia, not disguising their appraising looks. Where Ophélie had latched on to them being from England to explain their strangeness, these ladies didn't know what to make of the sight before them. The gossip later would be interesting, to say the least.

Jacob caught some of the excited whispers. They seemed especially scandalized by Amelia wearing pants.

"I will see you to your quarters so you can dress for dinner. I expect us to be called shortly and do hope Clara hasn't assigned all the guest rooms yet," Ophélie commented to herself, boldly separating the gathered girls in two with outstretched arms. They parted, and as they did, their judgmental curiosity faded to silent reverence as the beautiful young mistress of the house ascended the staircase.

She paused at the top, whirling. "Why, forgive me, but I'm not sure if you two are..." her gaze fell to the diamond on Amelia's left hand and her eyes expanded to saucers. "Well! You know how to treat a lady in England," she exclaimed in a breathy whisper, her earlier question apparently answered.

Jacob glanced between both women, flushing. Diamond rings were a more recent trend. The women in this period would be wearing plain bands.

If they weren't careful, it would be the small details that did them in. "Aye," he answered. "I'll not have my wife in anything but the best."

Amelia hid an eye roll, but Ophélie blushed, clearly smitten. "I daresay we neglected to bring along some of the finer traditions when we created this great nation," she declared in a fluster, then turned to continue up the stairs. "I've never heard accents quite like yours. Of course, I've never been across the ocean. My brother, Jean, has been on his Grand Tours of Europe, as I said, and my youngest brother will be along on his soon, but it isn't proper for the women."

"Colonists," Jacob muttered with a shrug, falling into character. Amelia elbowed him.

"How rude of me. I haven't asked your names!"

Amelia went rigid, paling. She wasn't in the frame of mind for these rapid fire, on-the-spot answers, so the bulk of creativity fell upon him. He saw no reason to lie. "My name is Lord Jacob Donnelly, and this is my wife, Lady Donnelly."

Amelia released a slight, disapproving sigh, as if in acknowledgment. *Now you've done it.*

Okay. Maybe a small lie.

"You're of the peerage, then!" Ophélie declared. Her hands crossed over her décolletage. She appeared positively star struck. "Papa never mentioned we had such distinguished cousins. He'll be so pleased to have you at our table this evening."

"You must be Charles' daughter, Ophélie," Jacob replied in his most charming tone. "We weren't aware we'd be arriving to help you celebrate. How old are you now?"

"Sixteen." She beamed. "Tonight, I'm to meet my betrothed."

"How lovely," Amelia said, her hand still latched tightly to Jacob's. She barely held it together. "Happy Birthday."

They stopped in front of a set of French doors leading to, in the future anyway, Lucienne's bedroom. Jacob didn't know who stayed there anymore. After Lucienne had died, he believed the room had remained empty until Nicolas turned the house into a refuge for Empyreans. "I do hope this will be suitable. I know it's not what you're used to in London, but—"

Jacob's smile stopped her in midsentence. "It's perfectly fine."

Ophélie sagged in relief. "Oh, wonderful. I do want you to be comfortable here. Where did you leave your trunks? I'll have Edwin bring them up straight away."

Amelia glanced away, her stiffness fading to slack. Jacob realized she was moments from a breakdown. “I’m afraid that’s a long story. They didn’t make it with us off the ship.” He held his breath; he’d almost said *plane*.

Ophélie appeared genuinely mortified. “You poor dears. My brother, Jean, lost an entire trunk on his Grand Tour and never saw it again.” Her hands wrung over her corseted waist. “Not to worry. Ruth can fit you for a new wardrobe later. There are sleeping garments already in the room. Though that doesn’t help us for this evening’s events, and what you’re wearing won’t do...”

Jacob reached out and laid his hand on Ophélie’s delicate upper arm. She looked mildly scandalized. “If it isn’t terribly rude, my wife and I could use some rest after the long journey. She doesn’t fare well on the sea.”

Ophélie skimmed Amelia’s peaked countenance and shook her head. “Poor dear. Since you don’t have a gown... why, perhaps it *is* best for you to retire for a short while. After the ball, we’ll serve a late evening course. The young women and their chaperones will have departed by then so it will be the local gentry and their wives. Ruth can bring up something suitable for you to wear, and tomorrow we can see about a wardrobe. I won’t be permitted to attend into the later hours, as a maiden, but perhaps Papa will allow me to do so as a hostess. Shall I retrieve you then?”

Jacob nodded, feeling Amelia sway to his left.

“Very well. There’s fresh water from the well on the serving table, and should you need anything, the servant’s bell is on the left wall, near the windows.”

“Thank you, Mademoiselle Deschanel. And happy birthday.”

Don't miss a minute. Download ***The Secrets Amongst the Cypress*** today.

ALSO BY SARAH M. CRADIT

KINGDOM OF THE WHITE SEA

Kingdom of the White Sea Trilogy

The Kingless Crown

The Broken Realm

The Hidden Kingdom

The Book of All Things

The Raven and the Rush

The Sylvan and the Sand

The Altruist and the Assassin

The Melody and the Master

The Claw and the Crowned

THE SAGA OF CRIMSON & CLOVER

The House of Crimson and Clover Series

The Storm and the Darkness

Shattered

The Illusions of Eventide

Bound

Midnight Dynasty

Asunder

Empire of Shadows

Myths of Midwinter

The Hinterland Veil

The Secrets Amongst the Cypress

Within the Garden of Twilight

House of Dusk, House of Dawn

Midnight Dynasty Series

A Tempest of Discovery

A Storm of Revelations

A Torrent of Deceit

The Seven Series

1970

1972

1973

1974

1975

1976

1980

Vampires of the Merovingi Series

The Island

and more

The Dusk Trilogy

St. Charles at Dusk: The Story of Oz and Adrienne

Flourish: The Story of Anne Fontaine

Banshee: The Story of Giselle Deschanel

Crimson & Clover Stories

Surrender: The Story of Oz and Ana

Shame: The Story of Jonathan St. Andrews

Fire & Ice: The Story of Remy & Fleur

Dark Blessing: The Landry Triplets

Pandora's Box: The Story of Jasper & Pandora

The Menagerie: Oriana's Den of Iniquities

A Band of Heather: The Story of Colleen and Noah

The Ephemeral: The Story of Autumn & Gabriel

Bayou's Edge: The Landry Triplets

For more information, and exciting bonus material, visit www.sarahmcradit.com

EMPYREAN & QUINLAN
ENCYCLOPEDIA

Aanya: A kind and beautiful Empyrean Agripin once loved, but was forbidden from claiming as his duchess her due to her lack of lineage.

Aidrik (Also: Aidrik the Wise): Once a well-respected member of the Eldre Senetat. After Aidrik discovered their true nature, he sliced the Mark of Emyr from his face, freeing him from the Senetat's tethers. He met and saved Anasofiya from death, becoming her evigbond. Lived in a triad with Anasofiya, and her husband Finn, until his death, at the hands of the Senetat.

Aleksandr: Empyrean son of Anasofiya, Finn, and Aidrik. Shy, introspective. Named heir of the Deschanels by Nicolas. A mystic, and time shaper, whose abilities are still surfacing.

Anders: An Empyrean Mercy co-habitated with for a short period of time. She believed him Ascended, but he was, actually, a scout for the Brotherhood, under the direction of Thorvald. His most recent assignment brought him to *Ophélie*, where he is tasked with training and protecting the Brotherhood children.

Arborkinetic: A form of telekinesis involving flora. A strong arborkinetic can command plant life to do their bidding, and some can communicate with plants. Anne Fontaine Deschanel and Duchess Nerys are both arborkinetics.

Ascension (Also: Grand Ascension): The ultimate death and rebirth all Empyreans are promised. It is tied to Emyr's Mark, which is said to come alive when their time is near. Once active, the mark is then supposed to usher them through death and rebirth, into the arms of Emyr. The truth is the mark is simply an infusion of dark magic administered by the Eldre Senetat, from which they control the activation and subsequent death of Empyreans.

Astrid: Brotherhood leader of Ireland and the British Isles, alongside her evigbond, Birger. Birger and Astrid are in the minority in their decision to make peace with Quinlans. They also co-exist peacefully with humans in the nearby villages where they live in a tribe of other similar-minded Empyreans. Many look to them as the moral compass of the Brotherhood. They have one child, Eydis.

Baldur: A sadistic scout for the Senetat who captures Amelia and Jacob, torturing them for information. Is killed by Jacob.

Bestiakinetic: One who can commune with animals. Finnegan becomes a bestiakinetic after being given the Sveising. Yiva and Jorun are also bestiakinetics.

Birger: Brotherhood leader of Ireland and the British Isles, alongside his evigbond, Astrid. Birger and Astrid are in the minority in their decision to make peace with Quinlans. They also co-exist peacefully with humans in the nearby villages where they live in a tribe of other like-minded Empyreans. Many look to them as the moral compass of the Brotherhood. They have one child, Eydis.

Blacksmith: Forger of Ulfberht, and creator of Empyrean Steel.

Bodhran: Goatskin drum used in Quinlan ceremonies.

Brotherhood: See "Dragon Brotherhood, The."

Brother of Emyr (Also: Sister of Emyr): Another way to reference a halfling (or, someone who has both human and Empyrean blood).

Brynja: One of the oldest, original Empyreans. Together with her partner, Einar, they are Brotherhood leaders, residing in Russia. Part of Runa's rebels who escaped after her execution, they are often called, by Runeans, "Adam and Eve."

Child of Man/Men: What Empyreans call humans.

Christiane de Laurent: Aidrik's original evigbond. Human. Lived at the end of the 16th century, as a courtesan of the French court. Wife of Marquise Deschanel, and mother of Claude.

Cianán (Also: Jacob Donnelly): One fourth of the prophecy, descended from the Tuathan tribe of Gorias. He has been reincarnated over thousands of years, with his lover, Cerridwen. Their journey evolves in each lifetime, with the ultimate test being their love bringing them together in their final lifetime, when they have no memory of former lives, thus fulfilling the prophecy. Their child is meant to join with the descendant of Falias and Murias. Jacob is the reincarnated soul of Cianán.

Cerridwen (Also: Amelia Donnelly): One fourth of the prophecy, descended from the Tuathan tribe of Findias. She has been reincarnated over thousands of years, with her lover, Cianán. Their journey evolves in each lifetime, with the ultimate test being their love bringing them together in their final lifetime, thus fulfilling the prophecy. Their child is meant to join with the descendant of Falias and Murias. Amelia is the reincarnated soul of Cerridwen.

Claude Deschanel (Also: Viscount Deschanel): The first halfling Deschanel, being both human and Empyrean. Child of Christiane and Aidrik.

***Crann bethadh*:** Also known as the "Tree of Life," and the center of the Quinlan tribe. It gives life to the tribe, by providing everything they need, from food to shelter. Also a portal between worlds, and the spiritual link to the goddesses.

Crimson Guard: The official guard of the Farjhem, under command of the Senetat. Their uniform consists of blood-red robes.

Cumdach: A lavishly ornamented shrine used in Quinlan ceremonies.

Cyler: Agripin's young, brash second-in-command, and lover. Often shirks orders and goes his own route, though he is known for being excellent with strategy. Is a frequent visitor to Oriana's Menagerie.

Dagr: 7,000 years old. Born without Senetat knowledge, and is one of the Brotherhood leaders, residing in Morocco.

Daughter of Emyr (Also: Son of Emyr): Referencing pure-blooded Empyrean women.

Deschanel Magi Collective: A secret, ancient society, created with the intention of cataloguing all the family's abilities, as well as protecting and preserving the family. Each generation has a Magistrate, the current one being Colleen Deschanel.

Dragon Brotherhood, The: Secret organization of Empyrean rebels. There is no central leader, but instead regional leaders across the world. Some leaders are ready for battle, others content to live in peace.

Dragon Empire, The (Also: Dragon Brotherhood, The): Another name for the wider Dragon Brotherhood.

Draoi: Male Quinlan. It is said these males are sacred, as their occurrence usually portends something important, and prophetic. Draoi are often quite powerful, able to spin wards and time dance. To birth a draoi is to be considered blessed. Male druids often come into their powers when they reach sexual maturity. Attempting to draw from them earlier can sometimes lead to disastrous results. Jacob, Finnegan, Padraig, and Father O'Connor are all draoi.

Drekar: A term of familiarity amongst the Brotherhood. Translates roughly to "dragon."

Duchess Nerys: Nomadic daughter of Grand Emperor Aeron, and sister to Agripin and Oriana. Known for her love of all creatures, and her call to traveling. A bestiakinetic, with loyalties to no one and nothing except peace. Joins forces with the Brotherhood, as she believes they are most likely to achieve that.

Duchess Oriana: Beautiful, wayward daughter of Grand Emperor Aeron, sister to Agripin and Nerys. Known for having a menagerie of human pets, and for her cruelty toward defectors. Is loyal to the Senetat.

Einar: One of the oldest, original Empyreans. Together with his partner, Brynja, they are Brotherhood leaders, residing in Russia. Part of Runa's rebels who escaped after her execution, they are often called, by Runeans, "Adam and Eve."

Eldre Aeslius: One of the nine members of the Eldre Senetat. Following the events at Aidrik's execution, his fate is currently unknown.

Eldre Brutus: Was originally a member of Emperor Elof's privy council, but when he discovered Elof was plotting with rebels, Brutus betrayed and exposed him. The Senetat "Ascended" Elof, giving the crown to his son Aeron. Following the events at Aidrik's execution, his fate is currently unknown.

Eldre Cassian: One of the nine members of the Eldre Senetat. Following the events at Aidrik's execution, his fate is currently unknown.

Eldre Felix: One of the nine members of the Eldre Senetat. Following the events at Aidrik's execution, his fate is currently unknown.

Eldre Lucrecia: One of the nine members of the Eldre Senetat. Following the events at Aidrik's execution, her fate is currently unknown.

Eldre Maxima: One of the nine members of the Eldre Senetat. Has been a secret sympathizer of the Brotherhood for many years, and officially joined their cause following the events at Aidrik's execution.

Eldre Tacita: One of the nine members of the Eldre Senetat. Following the events at Aidrik's execution, her fate is currently unknown.

Eldre Valerius: One of the nine members of the Eldre Senetat. Right hand of Grand Eldre Servius. Following the events at Aidrik's execution, his fate is currently unknown.

Eldre Senetat, The: The ruling government over the Empyrean race. Established many millennia ago, they claim to be blessed by Emyr, and charged with doing His will through enacting and protecting laws. The Senetat grew corrupt with this power, and unknown to most Empyreans, are controlling the fates of all citizens. The creation and installation of Emyr's Mark is the vehicle by which they exact their control.

Empath: The ability to sense feelings, emotions, or sensations in others. There are varying degrees of empaths. Amelia Deschanel is considered the strongest empath in the family. Lucia and Livia are also empaths.

Empyrean (Also: Farværdig): Also known as the Farværdig ("Father's Chosen"), Empyreans are as old as man, and similar genetically, but with several key differences. Where some DNA is dormant in humans, the entire strand is active in Empyreans, giving them special, paranormal abilities, including greater strength and speed, and immortality via perfect cell replication. Their home is Farjhem, in the northern expanses of Norway, but most Empyreans live scattered throughout the world, blending in with men. All Empyreans are born with red hair (which fades to a chromatic silver as they age), and are exceptionally tall. They are also primarily solitary, not subscribing to traditions such as a nuclear family, marriage, or commitment. The exception to this is evigbond. In their early days, they enjoyed a strategic alliance with Quinlans, but, once broken, both races were thrust into strife.

Empyrean Laws: Mandates set by the Eldre Senetat. include regulations around childbirth, mating with humans, and other fundamental freedoms.

Empyrean Steel (Also: Crucible Steel): A rare steel with high carbon content, smelted in a small furnace, and cooled slowly. In swords, it was both strong, and flexible. The technology was not used anywhere else in the world, and was considered better than Damascus Steel, which is the closest point of comparison.

Empyrean traits: Born of fire. Elevated body temperature. Red hair (the redder the strands, the more pure the blood) that takes on silver chromatic hues as they age. When emotions are heightened, they are said to emit an orange glow. Most have pale, smooth skin, and are very tall. All have special telepathic/telekinetic abilities, with some stronger than others. Average lifespan is two thousand years, though it is believed without the mark, an Empyrean could be functionally immortal.

Emyr (Also: Our Father): God, to Empyreans. He is represented by a phoenix, rising from the ashes.

Erikr: Brotherhood resistance leader who led one of the only semi-successful rebel revolutions after Runa's. Was executed in a block of ice. Leader of the Second Runean War, and considered the father of the Dragon Brotherhood, which was formed with the help of Ptolemy I.

Etheric Summoning (Also: Etheric Summoner): More rare than a mystic, an etheric summoner can draw from their greatest weakness and manifest it into a physical strength. Also known as a wraith. Anasofiya is an etheric summoner.

Evigbond: The physical and chemical bonding process that occurs when an Empyrean meets their permanent mate. It is irreversible, and only severed by death. An evigbond between Empyrean and humans is especially potent. Aidrik's first evigbond was Christiane, and his current is Anasofiya. Mercy experienced evigbond with Nicolas, until her "death." Evigbond can occur in two different ways. The first is an uncontrolled, chemical reaction. The second is through consummation.

Eydis: Fifty-year-old daughter of Brotherhood leaders Birger and Astrid. She is halfway to maturity, and emotionally equivalent to a young girl of around nineteen. Wide-eyed, rebellious, but kind-hearted. She sees how in love her parents are because of their evigbond, and is determined to find hers. Her birth accompanied a year of great prosperity for crops in Ireland. Is an illusionist with a specialty in influencing.

Falias: One of the four tribes of the Tuatha Dé Danann. All Quinlans descend from one of these four tribes. The tribe of Falias is mentioned in The Prophecy as such: *A male Quinlan, pure of heart, and a special affinity for animals.* It is not yet known who the subject of this reference is.

Far: Empyrean word for father. Can be used by a child speaking to a parent, or in reference to Our Father, Emyr.

Fardag (Also: Father's Day): Annual Farjhem celebration held in homage to Emyr.

Farjhem: The homeland of the Empyreans. Translated to "Father's Home." Located between two glaciers in northern

Norway, it is not accessible by anyone except Empyreans, or those with Empyrean blood.

Farsengel: The place of law and order in Farjhem, where suspected criminals are sentenced and detained awaiting further punishment. Many stories high, the outside edges contain hundreds of cells, and the inside of the arena has a large stage.

Farskilt: Deep in the bowels of Farjhem, beneath a volcano. "Separated from father." Empyreans are sentenced here for "rehabilitation" when they commit spiritual offenses. Citizens are told that offenders are "reunited with Emyr" and the end of their rehabilitation results in guaranteed Ascension. The reality is they are labor mines, and Empyreans work there until their inevitable starvation and death. The Empyrean equivalent of a prison camp.

Farvann River: (Also: River Farvann): The river flowing through the fjord and glaciers of Farjhem.

Farværdig (Also: Empyrean): See "Empyrean."

Father O'Connor: A draoi descended from the tribe of Gorias, and the man who saved Jacob from tragedy as a youth, sending him to New Orleans. Brother to the tribe elder, Seara. Great-uncle of Amelia.

Feast of Officium Maximus: Once every hundred years, the Scholars graduate their group of fledgling Empyreans into the world. This ceremony, for which many return home, is accompanied by a great celebration.

Findias: One of the four tribes of the Tuatha Dé Danann. All Quinlans descend from one of these four tribes. The tribe of Findias is mentioned in The Prophecy as such: *A female Quinlan, and halfling Empyrean, reincarnated over two-thousand years, originally Cerridwen. Lover of Cianán.* Amelia Jameson Donnelly is the subject of this reference.

First Father: When an Empyrean child has multiple

fathers (via Sveising), the initial father, at conception, is referred to as First Father.

First Runean War: Resistance to the creation of the Eldre Senetat, led by Runa, a warrior who represented the opinions of many Empyreans. Despite her strong supporters, the rebels were destroyed, and Runa publicly executed. Their stunning defeat weakened the resolve of many Empyreans who believed in her cause (henceforth dubbed Runeans by the Senetat), and most went into hiding.

Fledglings: What the Empyrean youth are referred to when they reach the age of spiritual maturity and are released into the wider world.

Forbia: An abandoned Hudson Bay wolf pup discovered and adopted by Finnegan. She becomes his familiar, and he names her Forbia, after his beloved ship he left in Maine.

Galon: A kinsman of Aidrik who was forced into Ascension by the Senetat after he angered them.

Goddess Danu: The goddess and leader of the Tuatha Dé Danann.

Goddess Morrigan: The goddess of divination, and one of the surviving Tuatha, foretold one day that four individuals—one descendant from each original clan—would unite the Empyreans and Quinlans once again. This prophecy was delivered to both a Quinlan and an Empyrean, and said that they would go through nearly two millennia of war and strife before finding peace.

Gorias: One of the four tribes of the Tuatha Dé Danann. All Quinlans descend from one of these four tribes. The tribe of Gorias is mentioned in The Prophecy as such: *A male Quinlan, known as Cianán (little ancient one), reincarnated with Cerridwen.* Jacob Donnelly is the subject of this reference.

Grand Eldre Servius: The ruling grand eldre of the Senetat for several millennia. Was lesser-ranked at the time of Aidrik's service. Was known for his "scorched earth" policy and for taking the restrictive laws of the Empyrean race to the far extreme. Killed by Anasofiya at the execution of Aidrik.

Grand Emperor Aeron: The last ruling Grand Emperor of Farjhem, and the Empyrean race. Had a reputation for being kind, and benign, but showed no interest in meaningful involvement with his people. Was activated when Agripin spread false rumor of his treason. Agripin then succeeded him as grand emperor.

Grand Emperor Agripin: The current ruling Grand Emperor of Farjhem, and the Empyrean race. Previously Grand Duke Agripin. The only son and oldest child of Aeron and Theda, both deceased. Fought in the Second Runean War, where his distaste for the Senetat was born. Over the years, his love of easy living kept him from taking action, but his partnership with the Brotherhood grew over time. He used Aidrik and Anasofiya as part of his campaign, which results in the burning of Farjhem. Is currently in Trondheim with the rest of the Brotherhood, plotting their next move.

Grand Emperor Elof: Father of Aeron, who succeeded him when he was "activated" for suspected trafficking with the rebels. Betrayed by Eldre Brutus, who was his closest confidante.

Grand Emperor Seti: Ruling emperor of Farjhem at the time the Senetat was created. Supported the Senetat's inception, as he was not interested in being the upholder of laws.

Grand Empress Anasofiya: Born a halfling of the Deschanel clan in New Orleans. Aidrik gave her the Sveising to save her life, which gifted her with more potent versions of her existing abilities, as well as suspected immortality. Married to Finnegan, but evigbond to Aidrik, which created an unorthodox polyamorous triad between them. Mother to Aleksandr, who is the son of both men. Her skill as a resurrection shaman pales in comparison to her most potent ability of all, etheric summoning. She is currently magic-bound by Agripin following the execution of Aidrik, where she destroyed hundreds of Empyreans.

Grand Empress Theda: Mate of Aeron and mother of Agripin. Deceased.

Great Cleansing: Following the creation of the Senetat, Empyreans who refused the mark were sought out and executed. Those who survived were branded Runeans.

Great Commitment (Also: Officium Maximus): The graduation ceremony, once every hundred years, when Empyreans reach their age of maturity and are released from the Scholars' tutelage, out into the world. This ceremony includes the installation of Emyr's Mark, a magical brand in the shape of a phoenix that is said to include a part of Emyr Himself. In reality, it is a device of the Eldre Senetat, as a means to control the Empyreans once they leave Farjhem.

Hakon: Still a fledgling, son of Emperor Aeron through a tryst he had with Hakon's mother. The mother escaped from Farjhem, and she died after birthing Hakon. Trygve took him in, under his wing, in Mongolia. Is a bestiakinetic.

Halfling: Humans with some amount of Empyrean blood/ancestry. A human is considered a halfling even if their Empyrean blood is many generations back.

Holger: Kind and helpful scout of Birger and Astrid, sent to look after Jacob and Amelia.

Illusionist: One who can manipulate the reality of others. Some do this by changing the physical interpretation. Others do this through influence. Markus is an illusionist who can change his appearance. Eydis can influence people to do her bidding.

Inner Voice: Empyreans believe in the concept of an "Inner Voice" guiding them toward their destiny. For Mercy, the Inner

Voice was an illusion crafted by Aidrik, who was guiding her toward safety.

Isabella Deschanel: Daughter of Margarethe and the necromancer. Was the first starlight awakener in the family, raised in secrecy due to her rapid growth. Her life, and eventual burning at the stake for witchcraft, was chronicled in the propaganda pamphlet, *La Sorcière de Villeneuve*. The current Deschanel line descends through her.

Jorun: The Brotherhood leader over South America. Quiet and reclusive, she relates better to creatures on four feet, as a bestiakinetic. Lives apart from the other Empyreans of the region, but looks after them from afar.

Killianshire: A small village in southern Ireland, where Jacob was born and raised. Father O'Connor presides over the cathedral here. The village is Quinlan-friendly.

Kjære: Aidrik's term of endearment for Ana. Translates roughly to "my dear" or "my dearest" in Empyrean.

Leif: The Brotherhood leader over the Caribbean region. Was once a member of the Senetat, but over time grew weary of their hypocrisy. He escaped and became a critical leader amongst the Brotherhood. Can bind the magic of others.

Livia: Born in Spain to an Empyrean mother and human father. Her father had dark olive skin, and her darker skin tone puts her in danger, as no purebred Empyrean has these tones. Is closely guarded under the wing of Thorvald, and has a special bond with Lucia. Empath.

Lucia: Escaped the Scholars when she was still a student, leaving Farjhem without a plan other than the idea of her freedom. Thorvald found her and took her under his wing in Spain, dubbing her *mi belleza*, and fostering her great loyalty. He makes her a scout, and pairs her with Anders. Her most recent assignment took her to *Ophélie* to help train and protect the children of the Brotherhood. Is an empath who can absorb the pain of others without impact to herself.

Margarethe Deschanel: Granddaughter of Claude Deschanel and, therefore, a great-granddaughter of Aidrik. Refused to accept death was the end, and married a famed necromancer, learning his secrets. Upon her death, she was determined to come back, immortal, through a starlight awakener. She pushed her daughter, Isabella, to instruct the family in maintaining pure bloodlines, to increase the chances of a starlight awakener being born into the family. Her attempts to come through non-necromancers and necromancers alike led to many Deschanel deaths over the centuries, which was falsely attributed to the Deschanel Curse. When at last starlight awakeners are born, in the form of Stella and Sebastian, she is prevented from coming through. It is believed she has not given up.

Mark of Emyr (Also: mark, Emyr's Mark): A magical infusion, in the shape of a phoenix, given to all Empyreans at their Great Commitment. The mark is about two inches in diameter, and can be placed anywhere on the body, a choice made by the Empyrean receiving the mark. Empyreans are told the mark includes a part of Emyr Himself, and that when it is time for their Grand Ascension, the mark will call them home to Emyr. In reality, the mark is a sinister plot by the Eldre Senetat, created as a means to control the Empyreans and destroy them.

Marquise Deschanel: Husband of Christiane de Laurent (Aidrik's first human evigbond). He was the First Father of Claude Deschanel, the first Deschanel born with Empyrean blood.

Mercy (Also: Clementyn): Lived three thousand years as an Empyrean who believed in the illusion of Grand Ascension. Piety drove all of her life decisions, often to the point of folly. In her youth, she spent many years with Aidrik, and they did not part on good terms. She found herself crossing paths with Nicolas Deschanel, and when her mark activated, she died but was resurrected by Anasofiya, then becoming human. She currently resides with Nicolas at *Ophélie*.

Mora: Empyrean word for mother.

Murias: One of the four tribes of the Tuatha Dé Danann. All Quinlans descend from one of these four tribes. The tribe of Murias is mentioned in The Prophecy as such: *A female Quinlan, born halfling Empyrean but given far more at maturity.* It is not yet known who the subject of this reference is.

Mystic: Most powerful of all magi, among Empyreans and halflings. Mystics manifest their abilities in different ways. Some are strong healers, others can engage in nested visions, dream suggestion, wards, and other unique traits. All are strong telepaths. Aidrik, Nicolas, Agripin, and Aleksandr are mystics.

Necromancers: Can speak with the dead, though limited to those who have not "crossed over." Quillan is a necromancer.

Nested Vision: A nested vision is an ability only accessible by mystics, wherein the mystic can travel into the mind of another and observe the world through their eyes. The most powerful mystics not only observe, but also control the host. Nicolas Deschanel has newly discovered he is a mystic who can engage in nested visions.

Old Aita: Believed to be the oldest living Empyrean, she is shamed for not having experienced her Grand Ascension. Scholars use her as an example of how not to end up, and as a means of driving fear amongst the fledglings. She is said to have pure white hair.

Ophélie: A plantation on the west bank of the River Road in Louisiana, about an hour from New Orleans. *Ophélie* has been the family seat of the Deschanels for over 200 years, and is passed down through the oldest male in each generation. Nicolas Deschanel, the current heir, has lived there his whole life.

Our Father (Also: Emyr, Our Father of Light, Our Father of Fire): Additional names for Emyr.

Portail: A portal created by a terrakinetic that can send travelers to any point in space.

Quinlans: An ancient line of druidic women, descendants of the Tuatha Dé Danann, and more recently, the Goddess Morrigan. All Quinlans descend from one of the four Tuatha tribes: Findias, Gorias, Falias, and Murias. They believe nature is unconditionally sacred, and that everything is interconnected, and balanced. Their powers are all drawn from nature. They live in secrecy, in protected groves and simplistic structures, all centering around their *crann bethadh*. In their early days, they had a strong alliance with the Empyreans, but that alliance was broken and both races have suffered the consequences. While the Quinlan genetics are passed through the females, in rare cases the male will also manifest. These males are known as draoi, and are more power than the females of the tribe. Most Quinlans keep the Quinlan surname.

Quinlan, Deirdre: Daughter of Seara. Mother of Noah, Nora, Nevina, and Niamh. Grandmother of Amelia. Is the youngest, and so has never taken a strong position of leadership. More of a free spirit, even for a druid. Married Kellan Jameson, a human. Kellan did not know what she was, until after Noah (her youngest) was born. When he threatened to leave, she secreted her daughters away to the tribe. Upon return to fetch her son, she learned Kellan had taken him to New Orleans.

Quinlan, Fiona: Only daughter of Nora. Is young—25—as Nora did not have her until later in life.

Quinlan, Meara: Middle child of Seara, sister of Deirdre and Philomena. Always happy, joyous, but simple-minded. The rest of the tribe closely protects her. Childless, she is not capable of a mutual relationship.

Quinlan, Nevina: Middle daughter of Deirdre, sibling to Nora, Niamh, and Noah. Does not travel outside the tribe. Is worried Jacob and Amelia are too "modern" for the job, and that the goddess waited too long to manifest the prophecy,

Quinlan, Niamh: Youngest daughter of Deirdre, sibling to Nora, Nevina, and Noah. Kind-hearted, and powerful, but often quiet, and whimsical.

Quinlan, Nora: Oldest daughter of Deirdre, sibling to Nevina, Niamh, and Noah. Tapped to take over as leader when the current one passes. Her practical nature makes her a competent leader.

Quinlan, Padraig: A draoi, and husband to Regan. He descends from another tribe of Falias. Trains Jacob, who has newly come into his draoi nature.

Quinlan, Philomena: Oldest child of Seara, sibling to Meara and Deirdre. Bitter to not be her mother's choice as successor. Strong-willed and often quick-tempered, especially now in her old age, which is why Seara did not choose her. Had one son in her youth, and gave him away when he was not a draoi.

Quinlan, Regan: Daughter of Nevina, sister to Kieran. Married to Padraig.

Quinlan, Rosemary: Mother of Enid, and grandmother of Jacob. A member of a tribe of Gorias, she has traveled to Seara's tribe to help with the prophecy.

Quinlan, Seara: Current leader of her tribe. Mother to Philomena, Meara, and Deirdre. Great-grandmother to Amelia. Sister to Flynn. All three of her children were intentionally conceived by men she picked herself, and planned a one-night stand. Has the essence of an oracle, who sees all (the prophecy was passed to her by the last leader). Knows her time is near, and is training her granddaughter, Nora, to take over.

Resurrection Shaman: A healer who is able to resurrect the recently deceased. Resurrection shamans are incredibly rare, and the ability is often volatile. Rarely do subjects come back exactly as they were before death. Anasofiya Deschanel discovers she is a resurrection shaman after Aidrik infuses her with Sveising.

Royal Palace of Farjhem: Residence of the royal family of Farjhem.

Runa: Leader of the minority opposition who rose up when the Senetat was created. Her execution is a symbol of strength for her followers, Runeans. She is often deified amongst her most devout followers. Her uprising is known as the First Runean War.

Runeans: Rebels. Those who oppose the Eldre Senetat are generally lumped together as Runeans (followers of Runa). Secretly, they have organized as the Dragon Brotherhood. Some in the Brotherhood are bloodthirsty and feel a call to action. Others are content to live quietly, off the grid of Empyrean society.

Scholar Saxon: The philosophy Scholar who carried out the execution of Mercy's parents after they were accused of heresy.

Scholars: A group of instructors selected by the Eldre Senetat to oversee the education of all Empyrean children. Their teachings often include propaganda-style support of the Senetat, and a fear-based deterrence of breaking rules. The Scholars spend a hundred years with Empyrean children.

Scholars' Temple: Place of instruction in Farjhem.

Second Runean War: Led by Erikr, the Runeans came together once more, in the spirit of Runa's beliefs, to overthrow the Senetat. As with the first uprising, they were squelched, and Erikr encased in a block of ice. This was the last large uprising of the rebels, who are now scattered and in hiding.

Senetat Sanctuary: Meeting place of the Senetat in Farjhem. Known for being sterile and devoid of any color excepting the crimson of their robes.

Shaman (Also: Healer): Another word for healer. There are varying degrees of shaman in the Deschanel family. Colleen Deschanel is said to be the strongest.

Sindre: Hails from the same Irish village as Birger, Astrid, and Eydis. A young elementalist who can conjure both fire and water, and often employs this skill to the hazard of others.

Skadi (Also: Skadi the Ruthless): The Brotherhood leader of Eastern Europe, residing in Bulgaria. She is known to be ruthless, cutthroat, and volatile to approach. She is remiss in her duties as a leader, in comparison to her peers, but is fiercely protective of her region.

St. Andrews, Finnegan: Husband of Anasofiya, father of Aleksandr. Born and raised in Maine to a normal, magic-free life. At his wedding, he accepted Aidrik's gift of Sveising, to grant him longer life and keener abilities. Recently learned he is descended from the Quinlans, and is a draoi, through this mother's side. Through his father, he is also descended from strong magic. Is a bestiakinetic.

St. Andrews, Ennis: Grandfather of Finnegan, father of Andrew, husband of Fiona. Lives in a protected, secluded clearing in the Scottish Highlands with his wife, who he keeps alive and young through potent magic.

St. Andrews, Fiona: Grandmother of Finnegan, mother of Andrew, wife of Ennis. Lives in a protected, secluded clearing in the Scottish Highlands with Ennis and is kept alive and young through his magic.

Starlight Awakener: An exceptionally rare form of necromancers said to "awaken the starlight," and employ the power of the heavens to occupy the living, and achieve immortality. Margarethe bred the family for centuries in search of a starlight awakener to come back through. Stella and Sebastian are starlight awakeners. Before them, the only known starlight awakener was Isabella.

Stian: A Brotherhood leader who chose Africa as his region because of the strife. He never stays anywhere for long, and is always moving around, helping where he can. As a terrakinetic, he can create a rift in the Earth, allowing a man to leave one place and appear in another, called a portail.

Sveising: DNA fusion unique to Empyreans. It is the process that allows multiple fathers for offspring, as well as the means by which Aidrik is able to save Anasofiya. Sveising can occur through sexual consummation (in the case of creating multiple fathers), but a mystic can also do it without consummation.

Telepath: One who can read the thoughts of others. Rare telepaths can read thoughts over long distances. Very few telepaths can also break a telepathic block. Tristan is a telepath who can reach across long distances and breach blocks.

Telepathic Block: A block employed my magic users to keep telepaths out of their head.

Terrakinetic: The ability to manipulate the spatial elements of Earth to your advantage. Example: a portail. Stian is a terrakinetic.

Thorvald: Brotherhood leader of Spain. He resides in the *Costa del Sol*, where he trains warriors and scouts in preparation for the inevitable war against the Senetat. Also one of the ancients, or earliest Empyreans.

Time Dancing (Also: Time Dancer): A skill unique to draoi. The time dancer can "dance" through time, a form of time traveling, but cannot change the past. Jacob is a time dancer.

Time Shaping (Also Time Shaper): An Empyrean skill that allows the individual to stop time and "reshape" it. The effect can be catastrophic if the caster is untrained, or if time stops for too long. Aleksandr is a time shaper.

Tribe: A group of Quinlans, usually descended from the same Tuatha tribe. All tribes have an elder, and a scribe.

Trygve: A Brotherhood leader, over Mongolia. One of the oldest Empyreans, having also been from the time of Runa, Brynja, and Einar, and has the markings of the ancients: exceptional height, dark red hair. Has one of the larger followings of the leaders. Known to be fair and loyal, but also quick to action and swift to justice.

Tuatha Dé Danann: Descended from Goddess Danu, early deities in Gaelic history, originating in Norway and later settling in Erin (Ireland). Ruled Ireland from 1897-1700 B.C. Many of the tales of faeries stem from their legends. There are four major tribes of Tuatha, each with a unique talisman of power. They hid in *Tir Non Og*, the otherworld, after Milesians drove them out of their lands. They believe strongly in reincarnation. Tuatha were the original druids, though modern day druidism became its own unique thing. The Quinlans descend from the four tribes of the Tuatha.

Ulfberht: A Viking sword produced between 800 and 1000 AD, made from Empyrean Steel (known to Man as Crucible Steel), known for its unusual combination of strength and flexibility. Though man believes this sword was crafted for Vikings, it was, in fact, created by Blacksmith, an ancient Empyrean metallurgist. The technology used to make Ulfberht baffles scientists to this day. Aidrik wielded one of the last of the originals, but gave it to Finnegan prior to his death.

Ward: A magical protection with unclear barriers, most

potent at its center. The ability to create wards came as a result of the alliance between Empyrean and Quinlan, and it was set forth that only an Empyrean (mystic) may create a ward, and only a Quinlan (draoi) can adhere it. Aidrik's ward is one such example, the center of it cast over *Ophélie* where it is most potent, with effects radiating out to protect other relatives. The protection diminishes the further out you go.

Yiva: Brotherhood leader of Southeast Asia, specifically residing in Thailand. Yields a body-length spear and is a powerful bestiakinetic. Known as the "she wolf."

ABOUT THE AUTHOR

Sarah is the USA Today and International Bestselling Author of over forty contemporary and epic fantasy stories, and the creator of the Kingdom of the White Sea and Saga of Crimson & Clover universes.

Born a geek, Sarah spends her time crafting rich and multi-layered worlds, obsessing over history, playing her retribution paladin (and sometimes destruction warlock), and settling provocative Tolkien debates, such as why the Great Eagles are not Gandalf's personal taxi service. Passionate about travel, she's been to over twenty countries collecting sparks of inspiration, and is always planning her next adventure.

Sarah and her husband live in a beautiful corner of SE Pennsylvania with their three tiny benevolent pug dictators.

www.sarahmcradit.com

www.ingramcontent.com/pod-product-compliance
Lightning Source LLC
Chambersburg PA
CBHW020338310726
48979CB00015B/2419/J

* 9 7 8 1 9 5 8 7 4 4 0 8 6 *